HOW TO ROMANCE A RAKE

"With her trademark wit and charm, Manda Collins has penned a deeply romantic and emotionally satisfying story in *How to Romance a Rake*. Her heroine is plucky and tremendously appealing, and I cheered for her well-earned happily ever after."

—Vanessa Kelly, award-winning author of *Sex and the Single Earl*

"Collins's second installment of the Ugly Duckling trilogy is both a lovely, sensitive romance and a taut thriller. Collins brings a dashing hero and a wounded wallflower together in the type of love story readers take to heart. With compassion and perception, she delves into the issues faced by those who survive physical and emotional trauma. Brava to Collins!" —*RT Book Reviews*, 4 stars

"Absolutely delightful, *How to Romance a Rake*, the second book in talented author Manda Collins's Ugly Duckling series, is an emotion-packed, passionate historical romance."

—*Romance Junkies*, 5 stars, Blue Ribbon Review

"*How to Romance a Rake* is a wonderfully moving story about two damaged people coming together to form a unique bond. Manda Collins is now on my auto-buy list, and I can't wait for the final book in this series."

—*Rakehell, Where Regency Lives*

Also by Manda Collins

How to Dance with a Duke
How to Romance a Rake
How to Entice an Earl
Why Dukes Say I Do
Why Earls Fall in Love

Novella

The Perks of Being a Beauty

Praise for Manda Collins's delicious Regency novels

WHY EARLS FALL IN LOVE

"With its shades of *I Know What You Did Last Summer* and strong gothic overtones, Collins's latest is a chill-seeker's delight. Along with the surprising climax, readers will thoroughly enjoy the well-crafted characters, the charming setting, and the romance that adds spice to the drama."

—*RT Book Reviews*

"Sparkling romance amid mystery."

—*Publishers Weekly*

"Combining love, wit, warmth, suspense, intrigue, emotion, sensuality, interesting characters, romance, and plenty of danger, Ms. Collins has created another enthralling story."

—*Romance Junkies*

"Award-winning author Manda Collins brings sensual historical romance to a new level with wit, heart, and beautifully written detail, finely drawn characters, and a flair for fun."   —*Examiner.com*

WHY DUKES SAY I DO

"Witty and smart, Collins's prose flows smoothly as she merges a charming, compassionate love story with gothic suspense . . . Add strong pacing and depth of emotion, and there's no doubt this is a winner."

—*RT Book Reviews* (Top Pick, 4½ stars)

"Collins has a deft touch with characterization, and she expertly weaves a thrilling thread of danger throughout the story. *Why Dukes Say I Do* is highly recommended for readers who enjoy their historical romances with a generous soupçon of suspense."　　　*—Reader to Reader Reviews*

"Manda Collins pens a charming, romantic tale with *Why Dukes Say I Do*."　　　*—Single Titles*

"Totally engrossing, witty, and suspenseful."
　　　　　　　　　　　　　　—Tulsa Book Review

HOW TO ENTICE AN EARL

"The last of the wallflowers moves into the spotlight as Collins spices up a charming love story with a liberal dose of suspense . . . The passion sizzles and the mystery holds reader attention enough to satisfy."　　　　　　*—RT Book Reviews*

"Another very pleasant read by Manda Collins. She writes Regency with a light, enjoyable touch. Nicely sensual, and very steeped in the period. Good romance."　　　　　　*—Affaire de Coeur*

"There were enough twists and turns in the murder mystery to keep me guessing [and] the love scenes were deliciously sensual. This was an entertaining ending to the trilogy and I'm looking forward to reading more of Manda Collins's books in the future."　　　　　　*—Rakes and Rascals*

Why Lords Lose Their Hearts

Manda Collins

St. Martin's Paperbacks

This is a work of fiction. All of the characters, organizations, and events
portrayed in this novel are either products of the author's imagination or
are used fictitiously.

WHY LORDS LOSE THEIR HEARTS

Copyright © 2014 by Manda Collins.

All rights reserved.

For information address St. Martin's Press, 175 Fifth Avenue, New York,
NY 10010.

ISBN: 978-1-250-02386-5

Printed in the United States of America

St. Martin's Paperbacks edition / August 2014

St. Martin's Paperbacks are published by St. Martin's Press, 175 Fifth
Avenue, New York, NY 10010.

10 9 8 7 6 5 4 3 2 1

For Mamaw, who taught me to love books.

Acknowledgments

As with any publishing endeavor, I could not have made this book happen without a great deal of assistance from a great number of people. Thanks as always to my wonderful editor, Holly Ingraham, who gets what I'm saying even when I sometimes do not! To my savvy agent, Holly Root, who even when I'm at my most neurotic, always finds a way to make me feel like a rock star. To everyone at St. Martin's Press who works on getting my books out to the readers, especially my publicist, Amy Goppert, the sales team, the art department, the folks at Heroes & Heartbreakers, and my lovely copy editor who has saved me from making egregious errors more times than I can count. Any errors are mine and mine alone. Thanks also to my dear Kiss and Thrill blogmates: Amy, Rachel, Diana, Sarah, Sharon, Krista, Gwen and Lena; my sister, Jessie; the entire Moody clan; Julianne, Janga, Santa, Terri, and Lindsey; and my furry writing companions, Charlie, Stephen, and Tiny.

Prologue

"Put the knife down, Your Grace," Perdita heard her friend Mrs. Georgina Mowbray say to Gervase as he held the penknife closer to her own throat.

She wasn't sure how long they'd stood thus, her husband's sour breath panting across her cheek as he held her in a death grip against his powerful body. A while, at least. Time seemed to get away from her when Gervase was in one of his moods. And Perdita had found long ago that ignoring such things would make it easier to pretend later that it had never happened.

Only this time, she wasn't sure she'd need to pretend. If he killed her, she'd forget everything. Which for one blissful moment sounded as close to heaven as she'd ever come.

She'd known for a good while that things would come to this point. Gervase's moods had risen and fallen with much greater speed than they had when she'd first married him five years before. Then he'd seemed—in retrospect—almost normal. And she thought she was the luckiest woman in the world.

But like everything else in life, there was a before and an after. A point at which one was able to judge things had changed irrevocably. For Perdita, it had been the first time he hit her. And everything after that had been hastily reshuffled into the "after" pile.

If she hadn't had the courage to confess her predicament to her sister and their friend Georgie, who had both endured their own bruises at the hands of abusive husbands, she would still be in constant reaction mode. Never making things happen herself, but only responding to what others did. And, as Gervase's wife, that meant that she reacted to each blow, every threat, every insinuation that he held all the power while she held none.

Now, however, she'd learned to stand up to him. And finally, she and her sister and friend had judged it to be time for her to leave him. Perdita had known the discussion would not be an easy one, of course. She'd known he would lash out or worse, try to keep her from leaving. But even after years of his abuse she was still capable of being surprised. Which is what happened when he pulled the knife out and held it to her throat.

"Killing your wife will not make you feel any better." Georgie's voice was calmer than Perdita's would have been had their situations been reversed. But then Georgie had grown up following the drum, so was used to sounding authoritative.

They'd only wanted this to be the first step, Perdita reflected as his arms tightened around her. She would leave Ormond House and set up her own establishment. Since Gervase spent much of his time away anyway, it shouldn't be too taxing for him. It wasn't as if Perdita would be in the Antipodes. If he needed her, she'd be in Mayfair a few streets over.

But, they'd miscalculated. Not only had Gervase been unhappy about the plan, he translated his unhappiness into physical retribution against his wife. Which concluded in his pressing the blade of a knife to the vulnerable skin of her neck. He was not going to let her go without a fight.

His next words only confirmed it. "She wouldn't be able to leave me," the duke slurred. His lips twisted with resentment. "She was fine before the two of you got hold of her with your lies about me."

Afraid that he would turn his anger on her sister and friend, Perdita glanced over to see them exchanging a speaking look. To save them from being harmed by him, she considered telling him the truth, that she had chosen to make this appeal based on her own initiative. After so many years of enduring Ormond's cruelties, this week Perdita had reached the point at which she no longer cared what her husband would do to retaliate against her for leaving. She only knew, she'd told her sister and Georgie, that if she did not leave now, she was unlikely to live for much longer.

If this was how Ormond behaved when he suspected Perdita's friends of luring her away, though, his response to learning it had been Perdita's own idea would send him over the edge.

Deciding that she had to appease him somehow, Perdita said, "I would never leave you, darling." Trying desperately to remain calm even as she felt the press of his blade against her skin, she continued, "You know I love you."

While she waited for him to reply—the alcohol

had made him a bit slow today—she dared a look at Isabella and Georgina again. This time she saw Georgie silently make a figure with her thumb and forefinger. To anyone who knew her and her penchant for carrying a small pistol in her reticule for safety, it was obvious. Perdita felt her heart speed up as Isabella gave a quick nod to let Georgie know she understood.

Perdita and Isabella had been slightly appalled when Georgina first informed them of her habit of carrying the small pistol in her reticule, but Georgie explained that she'd done so for her own protection in the peninsula, and it had simply become habit. And the two other women had reluctantly agreed that there were some occasions when having a pistol might be beneficial for a lady traveling alone in London.

Perdita was unsure whether she felt relief at knowing her friend was armed, or terrified that somehow Gervase would learn of it and punish her friend for it. Or worse, use it on all three of them. Georgie had often accused her of being too pessimistic, but in this case, she knew whereof she spoke. No one knew her husband's capacity for violence better than Perdita. And the Gervase she knew would not hesitate to shoot them if he decided it was what he wished.

Perhaps to distract him from Georgie and her pistol, Isabella began to speak. "Ormond," she heard her sister say with the self-assurance that only Isabella could muster. Then, perhaps thinking better of it, she softened her tone. "Gervase," Isabella said, switching to the duke's Christian name, "we aren't here to take Perdita away from you. We simply wish for you to perhaps be a bit gentler with her."

Perdita felt his arms tighten around her. "Why?" he demanded petulantly. "She's not gentle with me. She scratched my face earlier. Damn her." He shook her as he said those last words, and Perdita heard herself whimper.

Perdita's mind raced, wondering if there was any possible way for her to get the knife out of his hand.

Isabella spoke up again, her tone imperious now as she spoke to her brother-in-law. "You should be gentle with her because she might be carrying the next Duke of Ormond." Perdita bit back a gasp at the suggestion. She wasn't enceinte, but he had no way of knowing that. And if it infused his heart with kindness and joy, so be it.

Unfortunately, her sister's words only served to make him angrier. With a sound like a bull about to charge, he twisted Perdita's arm up behind her back.

Moving as one, Georgina and Isabella stepped forward. Closing her eyes, Perdita sent up a swift prayer that they'd survive.

"There, now," Isabella said, her voice placating, as if she were trying to soothe a skittish horse, "you don't wish to harm your heir, do you?"

But they'd no sooner stepped forward than it became clear Isabella's words had been woefully miscalculated. Rather than being transported with joy, Ormond instead became even angrier. "What? Is this true?" he asked, turning Perdita in his arms so that he could look her in the face. She tried with some difficulty not to cringe back from him. "You lied to me?" he demanded. In his haste to get his hands on her, he brought the knife down where it became trapped between Perdita's arm and his own fist as he began to shake her. "You lying bitch! You told me it wasn't possible!" he cried.

"No!" Isabella shouted, rushing forward to pull him away from her sister. "Stop it! Stop it!"

"Your Grace," Georgina said in a hard voice, stepping forward as she jerked the pistol upward. "I warn you to stop that at once."

In a blur, Perdita watched Isabella grasp the duke by the shoulders and attempt to forcibly pry him away from her. When her sister finally managed to hook her arm around his neck, cutting off his airway, the duke gave a muffled growl and shoved his body backward as if trying to dislodge his attacker.

Finally, as they spun away from her, Perdita saw Georgie lift her pistol, take aim and fire.

At almost the same time, the knife, which had been held between Perdita's body and Ormond's hand, fell to the floor, and must have been in the right position at the right time, because when the duke fell mere seconds later it was upon the same blade with which he'd threatened his wife.

Sliding to the floor in a heap, Perdita wept. Though she wasn't sure why.

One

"A pair of prime goers, Lord Archer. The best I've ever seen at Tattersall's."

Lord Archer Lisle nodded and tried to look somewhat interested as the overeager Earl of Wrotham waxed rhapsodic over his new pair of matched bays. He was as fond of horseflesh as the next man, but tonight his mind was on another sort of flesh altogether.

He'd accepted the invitation to Lady Sumrall's annual ball knowing that Perdita, Duchess of Ormond, would also be in attendance. In fact, Perdita's presence was the sole reason he'd chosen to come at all. Since both her sister, the former Lady Isabella Wharton and now Duchess of Ormond, and her friend the Countess of Coniston had had their lives threatened by an as yet unknown assailant earlier in the year, the widowed duchess had become the sole focus of their attacks. So far the threats had come in the form of anonymous notes taunting the widowed duchess with the knowledge that he—Archer assumed this person was a he—knew what she'd done last season, when her deceased husband, the brutish sixth Duke of Ormond, had been killed. Never mind that the dead nobleman had been killed while attempting to cut his wife's throat. Whoever this mastermind was, he'd appointed himself judge and jury and had found all three women guilty of the crime of killing Ormond. Never mind that there had been no suspicions, as far as Archer knew, from the authorities.

Thus far, the threats against her had not persuaded the headstrong Perdita to curb any of her normal activities, a resistance for which she was inordinately proud. But Archer, who had been there for the aftermath of the attempts on the lives of both the Duchess of Ormond and Lady Coniston, was not so happy about her resistance to any kind of curtailment of her behavior. Yes, he wished to see the coward who threatened her thwarted, and Perdita going about as if nothing were amiss did so, but knowing that her defiance put her life in jeopardy frightened him and he wasn't afraid to admit it. And since Perdita refused to listen to reason—especially when it came from the mouth of Lord Archer Lisle—he'd decided to see to it that she remained safe whether she chose to listen to him or not.

At present Perdita was waltzing with Lord Dunthorp, a viscount of middling years who had spent the last few weeks dancing attendance on her. Her luxuriant strawberry-blond hair was dressed in a simple chignon that put the fussier styles of the other ladies to shame. And her gown, a cerise-colored silk that was simply cut but hugged her slim figure in all the right places, also put the others to shame. He'd seen Dunthorp's eyes wander from her pretty face down to her impressive décolletage more than once since they'd taken to the floor—a circumstance that made Archer long to gut the other man, though it would be dashed bad manners toward his hosts.

He'd been half in love with her ever since they'd met. And it hadn't taken long for that half to expand into a whole.

It wasn't just because she was beautiful—though she was. No, though he appreciated her fine-boned loveliness, it was her spirit that solidified his affection for her. Perdita wasn't an angel. What woman was? But she had a way about her. A sweetness in the way she dealt with people—he'd heard the servants at Ormond House speak of it—that set them at ease. Even her bad moods—which were rare—were short-lived and often ended with a self-deprecating remark.

But the thing that most endeared her to Archer was something she likely didn't even recall. It had been a moment some three years earlier when one of the housemaids had fallen pregnant. There were few secrets in a household as large as Ormond House, and Archer had a strong suspicion that it had been the duke or one of his cronies who forced himself upon the girl. But when the housekeeper had informed Perdita, she'd handled the matter with kindness and compassion, giving the maid enough money to return home to the country and with the offer of a reference should she need one in the future. Perdita hadn't considered the matter in terms of its reflection on herself. She'd only considered the little maid's feelings. And it had been that bit of selflessness that did him in. From that moment on he'd been a goner. And in spite of himself he'd fallen all the way in love with his employer's wife.

From the corner of his eye, he could see her red gown as they made the circuit of the Sumrall ballroom. He wasn't jealous. How could he be when his position as private secretary to the Duke of Ormond made her virtually his employer?

No, Perdita was not for the likes of him. No matter how he might, in his heart of hearts, wish to declare himself to her.

"I say, Lord Archer," Wrotham interrupted his thoughts. "I think Mrs. Fitzroy is attempting to get your attention."

Pulling himself together, Archer glanced across the room to see that indeed the comely widow was casting a speaking glance his way. And if he were any interpreter of glances, hers was saying something that was not appropriate in mixed company. The lady had been trying to lure him into her bed for weeks now, but though Archer could appreciate the joys of the bedchamber as much as the next man, he was too busy protecting Perdita from herself to succumb. Then there was the whole unrequited business.

He snagged a glass of champagne from a passing footman and took a drink before he spoke. "I believe you're correct, Wrotham," he said, nodding to the other man. "But I'm afraid I have other plans this evening. Lovely though Mrs. Fitzroy may be."

The other man touched his index finger to the side of his nose. "Say no more, old fellow," he said with a knowing look. "Just between us, I've heard Mrs. Fitzroy is a bit possessive, so it's probably just as well that you not try to juggle her with another woman, if you catch my meaning."

Since it was impossible not to catch Wrotham's meaning, Archer just nodded.

"I hope you won't mind if I have a bit of a try at her," the other man continued, straightening his cuffs as he placed his own empty champagne glass on an obliging side table. "It's just that I'm in search of a new mistress and I like the look of your Mrs. Fitzroy."

Archer would have told the other man to be his guest, but that would have implied that he did indeed have some sort of connection with her, so he simply nodded again and the two men parted ways.

The waltz having just ended, Archer threaded his way toward the side of the ballroom where Dunthorp had just left Perdita—presumably in search of champagne for her. But before he'd made it halfway there, their hostess clapped her hands from a position near where the musicians were set up. "Lords and ladies," she said once the chatter in the ballroom had descended to a low murmur, "if I could have your attention, please!"

Not wishing to do her the discourtesy of walking while she spoke, Archer paused.

"I am delighted to tell you that I've arranged a wonderful bit of theater for you this evening, thanks to the gracious proprietors of the Theater Royale," Lady Sumrall said. "For your enjoyment, we have not just one, but three superb actresses: leading lady of the stage Mrs. Alicia Lloyd; her charming understudy, Mrs. Pfeiffer; and the soon-to-be-famous ingénue, Miss Desdemona Wright. And playing opposite all three is the incomparable Mr. Charles Keating. All starring in a pantomime that is sure to bring everyone to rapturous applause!" As she introduced each of the actors, they stepped forward. Archer could see more than one gentleman eyeing the actresses, and Lord Carston, who was rumored to be Mrs. Lloyd's current paramour, beamed, despite the fact that his wife was also present in the room.

"Let the play entitled *The Secret* begin," Lady Sumrall said, before stepping aside while the actors took their places before the musicians' dais.

Intrigued despite himself, Archer folded his arms across his chest as the performance got under way.

Mrs. Pfeiffer and Miss Wright stood to one side while Mrs. Lloyd and Mr. Keating took center stage. As both of them remained silent, Mrs. Lloyd stood before an imaginary table arranging flowers, moving them this way and that as she assessed them. Behind her, Keating stormed forward, his face thunderous as he roughly touched her on the shoulder. As she turned in surprise, he brandished an invisible letter as if to admonish her with whatever was written there. Her eyes wide, Mrs. Lloyd clasped her hands before her, pleading with him as he glared at her, his grip on her arm tight and painful-looking. The actress exaggerated her actions, throwing her head and making as if to escape his grip. Then Keating grabbed her by the shoulders and shook her.

Though it was obvious that the two were acting, Archer shifted his weight from one foot to the other, the scene making him uncomfortable.

From stage left, Mrs. Pfeiffer entered, and stomped her foot. Keating and Lloyd turned, feigning shock. From stage right, Miss Wright entered and gasped loudly. Seeing the other woman, Keating pulled Mrs. Lloyd against him and placed an invisible knife to her throat. Archer watched in dawning horror as Mrs. Pfeiffer clasped an invisible pistol between her hands and pulled the trigger. At the same time, Mrs. Lloyd twisted out of his grasp. Then Miss Wright and Mrs. Pfeiffer rushed toward Keating as he fell senseless to the floor. All three women embraced and stilled, the performance over as the ballroom erupted in thunderous applause.

His mouth agape, Archer stood motionless as the three actors took their bows and Lady Sumrall's guests continued to rain praise upon them. Then, he pushed his way through the crowd, desperate to get to where he'd last seen Perdita. Because he knew without doubt that she would have been as disturbed as he was by the performance.

Not because the subject matter was so shocking. One can and did see more melodrama at the theater every evening of the week.

No, she'd be shocked by this show for another reason altogether.

Because the actors from the Theater Royale hadn't simply been performing a play written for the entertainment of Lady Sumrall's guests. It had been written to instill fear in the heart of one person and one alone. Perdita.

The scene hadn't depicted a scene from the imagination of the playwright. It had been the retelling of a scene that was all too familiar to the widowed duchess. Because she'd not only witnessed it, but lived it.

On the day her husband died.

Perdita, Duchess of Ormond, stood chatting with Lady Entwhistle on the side of the Sumrall ballroom, slightly out of breath from her waltz with Lord Dunthorp. He'd gone in search of champagne for them both, and if she were completely honest with herself, Perdita was slightly relieved to be out from beneath his watchful eye.

Dunthorp was a nice enough man, but his unrelenting pursuit of her had become a bit of a discomfort to her in the past few weeks. It wasn't that she disliked him. If that were so she'd have sent the man packing when he'd first begun to show interest. No, it was just that Perdita, having only last year emerged from beneath her husband's controlling thumb, was not quite ready to call someone else her lord and master. She liked being able to make her own decisions and come and go as she pleased. She enjoyed choosing her own gowns and not having to worry that the bruises Gervase had left on her the night before would show no matter how she tugged down the sleeves.

One would think that since her severed engagement to Lord Coniston, she'd have learned her lesson about attaching herself to single gentlemen before she was quite sure of her feelings for them. Fortunately for her, her friend Georgina had married Coniston shortly thereafter, so he was none the worse for wear. Not that he would have been at any rate, since theirs had been a betrothal of convenience more than anything else. But Dunthorp was not as indifferent as Coniston had been, and Perdita had no more friends waiting in the wings to sweep him off his feet. And if her intuition was right, he was working up to offer for her sometime in the next few weeks. An offer she had no intention of accepting. And rejection would put an end to their friendship.

"Are you aware that Lord Archer Lisle is staring at you as if he wished to carry you off and ravish you, darling?" Lady Entwhistle asked, jerking Perdita from her reverie. "If I had a man of his looks desperate for me," she went on, "I'd not be wasting time here in Lady Sumrall's crowded ballroom, darling, that's certain."

"Don't be absurd, Letitia," Perdita said with a laugh, "Lord Archer is simply playing the duenna. He has taken it upon himself to look after me and he's worse than an old mother hen." That she found Lord Archer, with his golden good looks and tall, impressively strong physique, to be devilishly handsome was neither here nor there. She and Archer were friends. That was all, and as she'd just been telling herself, she had no wish for another husband.

"If you say so, my dear duchess," Lady Entwhistle, who was known for her affairs as much as she was for her impeccable taste, said with a shake of her head. "It's a shame, though, if you don't take advantage of all that deliciousness while you still can. Dunthorp is a nice enough man, but look at Lord Archer's shoulders!"

Perdita was saved from replying by their hostess, who announced a particular entertainment had been arranged for them this evening. It had been thus since the beginning of the season. Each hostess of the ton had made it her business to outdo the ones preceding her. Thus, Lady Glenlivet had imported a real Venetian gondola to give rides in the pond behind her house in Hampstead, though that had come to grief when Lord Glenlivet had attempted to get a bit too close to his mistress in the boat and overturned it and them in the waist-high water. Then Lady Moulton had hired a pair of acrobats from Astley's to perform in the garden of her Grosvenor Square town house, complete with flaming hoops through which they leaped most impressively . . . until one of the hoops caught a lemon tree aflame and the fire brigade had to be summoned. Now, it would seem, Lady Sumrall had found yet another means to entertain her guests. Though having mere actors perform in her ballroom was a bit of a letdown, if Perdita were to be honest with herself.

When the players had finished their little tableau, however, Perdita was gasping for breath and trying desperately to make her way through the crowded ballroom to one—any—of the doors leading into the rest of the house. She was on the point of shouting to make herself heard above the din of applause when she felt a strong arm guiding her.

"Easy," she heard Archer say before she could wrest herself from his hold. "I'll get you out of here," he told her, the reverberation of his voice at her ear strangely reassuring.

Silently, they pushed their way past what for Perdita was a blur of colorful gowns, black coats, and white cravats toward the French doors at the back of the Sumrall ballroom. As soon as they stepped outside she was able to breathe again, and she gripped his arm tighter than was strictly necessary as he led her toward a picturesque little bower just out of range of the torchlight coming from the terrace.

"Sit," he said brusquely, and she knew that if she were in a different mood she'd have chided him for talking to her as if she were one of his spaniels. But she was so relieved to be out of the ballroom, she lowered herself to the little bench beneath the rose arbor and hugged her arms. It was then that she realized her teeth were chattering, and with a curse, he sat down beside her and pulled her against him, warming her with the heat from his body.

"I'd give you my coat but I don't think I can get the damned thing off without help," he muttered, rubbing her bare arms with his gloved hands. To her astonishment, she began to cry, with gulping, hideous little sobs that even as she heard them mortified her. But she was unable to stop herself, and Archer, being Archer, seemed prepared for it, and pulled her against his chest and let her sob into his beautifully tied cravat before giving her his handkerchief and instructing her to blow her nose.

When she had recovered herself and dried her eyes, Perdita pulled away from the comfort of his arms and moved cautiously over a bit so that they were no longer plastered against one another like peas in a pod.

"I'm sorry for that," she said stiffly. "I don't know what came over me."

He laughed bitterly. "I'd say you were overset by seeing the scene of Gervase's death reenacted before a ballroom full of London society," he said. "And I can't say I blame you."

She closed her eyes, the tableau blending with the actual scene in her mind as the horror of what had just happened revealed itself to her once more. Whoever it was that had been threatening her, had threatened Isabella and Georgina, was sending her a message. A very public and very terrifying message.

"He's raising the stakes," she said grimly. "He's no

longer content to threaten me in private. He's willing to bring his threats out into the open. To risk my reputation by accusing me in a ballroom full of witnesses."

"But he's too much of a dam . . . dashed coward to reveal his own identity," Archer agreed. "Do you think anyone noticed your reaction to the pantomime?" he asked, his jaw tight.

Perdita thought back to the scene around her as the players had acted out their drama. But all she could remember was her own response to the show. The sick feeling in her stomach, and the dawning horror as she realized just what it was they were performing. Aloud she said, "I don't know. I was too intent upon my own reaction."

He nodded, and Perdita watched his profile as he stared out at the garden beyond them. They were silent for a few minutes, both lost in their own thoughts. Perdita wondered what would happen if someone had noticed her fleeing the ballroom with Archer at her side. Belatedly she remembered Lord Dunthorp and suspected that she might not need to worry about rejecting him now. Though she didn't want to marry him, she did feel bad for disappointing him. He was a nice man, and deserved better than that.

"You have to leave town," Archer said, turning to her, his expression determined in the torchlight. "It's the only way to keep this madman from ruining your reputation before the ton."

She stiffened. She'd lived with the fear that this person's threats had induced in her for months now. And though tonight's had been his most public attack upon her to date, she wasn't about to let him scare her from leaving the field altogether. "I disagree," she said firmly.

"We don't even know if the others in the ballroom were even aware of the meaning of that little show. Why on earth should I allow him to make me leave town and let him think his threats are working?"

"They are working," he said hotly. "You were shaking a few minutes ago, and weeping. Or don't you remember that?"

She sat up straighter. "I don't like your tone, Lord Archer," Perdita said calmly.

"Well," he said, standing up to loom over her, "I don't like the way you're ignoring the very real danger this person poses." He ran a hand through his hair, leaving it sticking up on one side. "Perdita, he's already sent proxies to make attempts on both Isabella's and Georgina's lives. Everything he's done thus far has indicated that he means to make you pay the most for what happened to Gervase. Do you honestly wish to remain here while he escalates his campaign against you?"

"I am more than aware of what this person did, or tried to do to my sister and my friend," she retorted. "But that doesn't mean that I will simply walk away. Besides, how long should I remain in hiding? One year, two, ten? I'm not going to let someone with a vendetta against me dictate the terms of my life to me. If I do that he wins."

"But you'd be safe," he argued. "And Ormond and Coniston and I could find him while you're away. When the coast is clear you could return."

She shook her head. "You don't understand. I spent years letting Gervase dictate my every move. I refuse to let someone I don't even know do the same. I'm sorry, Archer, but I can't do it. I won't."

He stared at her. She watched as it dawned on him that nothing he could say would change her mind. His lips tight, he said, "Then it would appear there's nothing left to be said." With a short bow, he left her.

He couldn't have gone very far before she heard him say, "She's there in the bower. I wish you joy of her."

With an inward sigh, she watched as Lord Dunthorp came around the corner.

"Your Grace," Dunthorp said, stopping before her. "I simply wished to assure myself that you were well."

Clenching her fist, Perdita realized that she still had Archer's handkerchief. Schooling her features into a smile, she greeted Dunthorp and tried to put Archer from her mind.

Two

Since she was the only member of the Ormond family in residence—the new duke and duchess having returned to their country house in Yorkshire, and the dowager duchess having long since removed to her own town house—Perdita breakfasted alone the next morning, while reading the gossip papers. It was perhaps not seemly for a duchess to pay such heed to the ramblings of the press, but she found the drama and scandals amusing, and when the news was salacious, she did what she could to stanch the flow of blood in her own way.

As she'd feared, today's papers were full of the tale of last night's drama at Lady Sumrall's ball. "Players Tell a Tale of Murder at Sumrall Ball!" cried the *Daily Mirror*. While the *Ladies' Speculator* suggested, "Could truth lie beneath the ballroom melodrama?" Though none of it suggested that there was any real evidence behind the speculation, Perdita allowed herself to indulge in a bit of worry over the situation as she sipped her tea. It wasn't that she hoped for trouble, but if someone should begin to take the talk seriously, she would need to be prepared to rebut the stories.

She was pouring herself the last cup of tea when the door to the breakfast parlor opened to reveal Archer. He looked none the worse for wear after last night's argument, and indeed he was turned out with a precision and elegance that made Perdita clench her fists to keep from touching his spotless coat.

Bowing, he said, "Your Grace, I apologize for interrupting your breakfast, but I had hoped that we might talk for a few moments about what is to be done with regard to your situation."

She'd been willing to listen to whatever it was he wished to tell her, but that was before he revealed that he wished to talk about her. She was in no mood to be handled by Archer's oh-so-charming diplomatic method. Especially after last night's disturbance. "I'm afraid I don't follow you," she said, pretending she didn't understand him. "I do not have a situation."

He stepped closer, and when he gave a questioning look toward the chair beside hers she nodded. Once he was seated, he brought his fingertips together to form a point. "Your Grace," he began again, "if I may speak plainly, what happened last night was that you received what was in essence a threat that was seen by every one of Lady Sumrall's guests. Not only did the person who orchestrated things know the circumstances surrounding the late duke's death, he felt bold enough to let you know that before your peers. These are not the actions of a circumspect person. The sort of person who will think twice before he risks calling a duchess a murderer. And I believe that since he was successful last night, he can only continue to attempt to catch your attention in bolder and louder ways."

It was not far from what he'd said last night, and in the cold light of day, Perdita was inclined to believe him. It had been bold to try such a scheme in Lady Sumrall's drawing room. Not to mention incredibly skillful. A mere amateur couldn't have pulled off such a feat. No, the person who'd planned last night's trick was in the habit of orchestrating big events, directing several people at a time.

"All of this is interesting," Perdita said calmly, "but I'm not sure why you are telling me about it. I can hardly keep to my bedchamber for the rest of my days in fear that this person will act again. That would have done my sister no good, considering that the person who was stalking her turned out to be her own maid!"

"You deliberately misunderstand me, Your Grace," Archer said with a frown that did nothing to diminish the handsomeness of his face. It was quite unfair, Perdita mused. One should look cross and unhappy when reading a scold. Archer only looked beautifully stern, dash him.

"And how is that?" she asked, knowing that by questioning him she was simply making him more annoyed. "It is true what I said about my sister, is it not?"

"Of course it's true," he said his lips tight. "And I didn't suggest that you remain in your bedchamber until we catch this person."

"Then what are you suggesting?" she asked, leaning back in her seat and offering him a bland look.

His mouth quirked a little, as if he were aware that

she was teasing him. Of course he'd have figured her out by now. He was always clever, was Archer.

"I think that you should reconsider my advice about leaving town," he said flatly.

She opened her mouth to object—why on earth did he wish to revisit this when she'd settled the matter last night? But he spoke first. "Now, do not protest until you've heard my full argument," he said. "I do not mean for you to leave town permanently. Not even for six months. I simply suggest that you remove yourself from this person's gaze while Ormond, Coniston, and I conduct our own investigation to determine who the devil he is." Belatedly realizing he'd sworn, he said, "Beg your pardon, Your Grace."

"And where is it that I am supposed to go while you three wander all over town pretending to be Bow Street runners?" she asked with a raised brow. "To the Ormond estate in Derbyshire? Living circumspectly in Bath? Pretending to be a sea captain's widow in Dover? Really, Lord Archer, there is nowhere that I can go that this person won't be able to find me. He has already shown himself to be adept at infiltrating my household, and since we were never able to find where the leak is, he presumably still can."

"All are perfectly valid arguments, Your Grace," Archer said in a placating tone. She hated being placated. "But we have to try something. Otherwise there will be another attempt to publicly shame you, and every time he makes his case before the ton, a few more people begin to doubt the truth of what you said about the late duke's death."

That was true enough, Perdita reflected with a sigh. Even so, she wasn't ready to give up the field just yet.

Which she said to Lord Archer, though not unkindly. "I do appreciate your attention to the matter," she said after she rejected the idea. "It's just that if I let this person frighten me from town, I'm letting him win. And besides that, in the country I'll be a sitting duck. Here in town, there are all sorts of crowds to blend into."

Archer ran an agitated hand through his hair. "Yes, but you're just as vulnerable, if not more so here in town. I cannot protect you against every random person who appears in Bond Street while you shop, or in the theater while you watch, or even the park while you ride. He could literally come from any direction."

Knowing she was being troublesome, Perdita shrugged. "Then you shall simply have to accompany me to all those places. It's not as if you have all that much to do these days what with Ormond away in the country. I doubt very much that one interesting political letter has crossed your desk in weeks."

"That's not the point," he said through clenched teeth. "What if I . . ." He stopped, closing his mouth with a snap.

That intrigued her. Archer was never at a loss for words, but it would appear something had got his tongue.

"What?" she prompted. "What if what?"

He shook his head. "It's nothing. Forget I mentioned it," he said firmly. "I suppose you're right that I'll have some time on my hands now, so I'll resign myself to becoming your companion. But this means I'll follow you everywhere. No matter how embarrassing."

"Oh, please." Perdita said, waving her had dismissively. "There is nowhere you could accompany me that would put me to the blush. Nowhere at all."

"I meant embarrassing to me," he said pointedly. "Not that it matters, of course."

"Excellent," she said, bringing her hands together with what felt suspiciously like glee. "This afternoon I am engaged to ride in the park with Lord Dunthorp. I hope you'll be able to accompany us."

For a flash, his eyes looked pained, but then the expression was gone again and in its place was resignation. He didn't like Dunthorp? Curious, she decided. Especially since Dunthorp was such a pleasant fellow that it was difficult to find anyone who didn't like him. With the exception of Archer. This day became more interesting by the minute.

With a brisk nod, Archer said, "Then I had best go change and ask for the horses to be saddled and brought around."

When he was gone, Perdita allowed herself a little grin. It might be frustrating to have one's comings and goings so closely monitored, but she was rather looking forward to digging beneath Archer's calm exterior a bit. If it weren't for the danger to herself and others, it might even be fun.

Hurrying upstairs to get changed, she hummed a waltz.

"Your Grace," said Dunthorp some minutes later as he helped her into the sidesaddle of her mare, "may I say what an honor it is to ride with you today."

When she was firmly seated with the reins in her hand, Perdita offered him a bright smile. "Do not speak of it, Lord Dunthorp," she said firmly. "It is I who am honored. And so is Lord Archer, aren't you, Lord Archer?"

Playing ladies' maid to the widowed duchess was turning out to be just as unhappy-making as Archer had expected it to be. Not only was he forced to listen to Dunthorp make verbal love to Perdita, but he was also expected to remain just behind the couple, like a baronet in a party of dukes and marquesses. Still, Perdita seemed impervious to Dunthorp's flirtation on some level, so that made his situation a bit less awkward than it might have been. If she'd responded to the other man in kind, he might have been forced to hang himself from the nearest tree.

"Indeed," he responded to the widowed duchess's question. "Quite honored." He wasn't sure, but Archer thought he heard Dunthorp mutter something unflattering beneath his breath. Look, old chap, Archer thought bitterly, I'm just as unhappy with this situation as you are.

"I was not aware just how skilled an equestrienne you are, Your Grace," Dunthorp said as he and Perdita followed the trail through the parklands. "I suppose you learned as a child?"

"Indeed," Perdita agreed, patting her mare on the neck. "My father's head groom taught both Isabella and me when we were quite small. Papa believed that a lady should consider riding second only to dancing."

"Something else that you do exceedingly well," Dunthorp said with a grin, his voice a caress. "Your father was just as intelligent as his daughter."

At the other man's fatuous compliment for Perdita's long-dead father, Archer nearly spoke out to correct him, but knowing it would embarrass her he said nothing. His silence was, however, difficult to maintain.

Perdita, however, had no such reticence. "I'm

afraid there you're dead wrong, Lord Dunthorp," she said grimly. "My father was hardly the pattern card of propriety everyone thinks him, and was an even worse parent, I'm afraid. If you don't mind, I'd be pleased not to speak of him again."

As Archer had expected, upon hearing her words, Lord Dunthorp apologized profusely, declaring himself to be everything that was sorry for bringing up such a painful topic.

"Don't be absurd," she responded, catching Archer's eye as he rode along behind them. "You had no way of knowing."

As they neared the Serpentine, Dunthorp said, "I thank you for taking me into your confidence. I simply hope that Lord Archer will be as discreet as I plan to be with the information."

That took Archer aback. And Perdita, too, if her expression was anything to go by. Bastard must be feeling annoyed at not being able to ride alone with her, he thought, sizing up the other man. Aloud he said, "Oh, I don't think I'll be telling anyone about Her Grace's secret. After all, I've known for some years now and haven't blurted it out before." Take that, you great looby, he thought, watching with satisfaction as the other man's eyes narrowed to hear he'd not been the first to learn of Perdita's difficult relationship with her father.

"I see," Dunthorp said thoughtfully. "I suppose as a family servant you would be privy to such things, wouldn't you?"

Perdita, whose fair skin and red hair made her prone to wearing her emotions on her skin, flushed an angry red. "Lord Archer is not a servant, sir," she said, her clipped tone making it very clear that she was not best pleased with her suitor's words. "He is a dear friend of the family, and indeed as the son of the Duke of Pemberton he is included among the top families in the ton. I suppose you were unaware of that since Lord Archer is so modest that he chooses not to bruit about his family connections like the veriest mushroom. I hope you'll keep that in mind in the future. I should hate for you to embarrass yourself, Lord Dunthorp, by showing Lord Archer any discourtesy."

It was an impressive speech, made more so because she did not raise her voice, or indeed allow any hint of dislike to enter her tone. She was civil and friendly as ever. But if one were to go by Lord Dunthorp's expression, she'd just shouted at the top of her lungs and made good use of her riding crop. Archer was aware only of how magnificent she looked, and when she glanced back to catch his eye, something passed between them that felt as alive as electricity.

"I b-beg your p-pardon, Your Grace," Dunthorp stuttered. "I didn't mean any disrespect to Lord Archer." He turned to Archer and though his face looked ashamed, the expression didn't reach his eyes. "Your pardon, old fellow," he said with a dip of his head. "No harm intended."

Not one to hold a grudge, Archer nodded his forgiveness, and as they turned their horses back around for the return trip to the Ormond town house, all three riders were silent as they kept their own counsel.

He couldn't have said what sparked his awareness, but the hair on the back of Archer's neck stood up as he heard the sound of hoofbeats and another rider coming up behind them. Before he could bring his mount up beside Perdita, the other rider was next to her, taking hold of her arm and pulling her hard, as if trying to unseat her.

A combination of fear and fury rushed through Archer as he tried to get to her, but Dunthorpe, oblivious to what was happening, blocked his way. "Get out of the way, man!"

Startled, Dunthorpe pulled up short, but it was too late. Archer watched helplessly as Perdita shrugged out of the assailant's grip, and tried in her turn to throw him off balance. But the man shook off her grasp and this time got his arm round Perdita's shoulders and jerked her. Hard.

Terrified, Archer watched as her foot came out of the left stirrup and she lost her balance, trying desperately to regain it without spooking her mount. Taking advantage of her instability, the masked man pulled her toward him, almost as if he wished to pull her onto his own mount. But as soon as she began listing sideways toward him, the man unhanded her altogether and, spurring his own mount, thundered off.

With nothing left to block her fall, Perdita tumbled onto the hard ground of the bridle path.

Cursing, both Archer and Lord Dunthorp were able to keep their own mounts from trampling her, but it took some moments to bring them to a halt. Finally, his gelding under his control again, Archer turned him around and walked back to where Perdita lay unmoving on the ground. His heart in his throat, he hopped down and threw his reins over an obliging tree branch. Kneeling beside Perdita, he was relieved to see that she still breathed, and turning her onto her back, he watched as her eyelids flickered.

Archer had never been a particularly religious man. He left that sort of thing up to his brother Benedick, the vicar, as a general rule. But as he looked down at Perdita's wan face, he could not help but pray silently that she would open her eyes again.

He was assessing her arms for broken bones when Dunthorp dropped to his knees on her other side. "Is she alive?" the other man asked, his face filthy with sweat and dust.

Wishing the other man anywhere but here, Archer bit back a curse and instead nodded. "She's breathing," he told Dunthorp.

Dunthorp's obvious relief made him feel a bit of a heel, but he couldn't help it. When he'd seen Perdita fly through the air, Archer had lost all sense of perspective. If Perdita had been killed, he wasn't sure what he'd have done, but it wouldn't have been pretty. Of that he was sure.

"I need for you to ride to Ormond House for a carriage," he told Dunthorp, his mind already planning how to get her home and in the care of a physician. "Tell the butler that there's been an accident and the widowed duchess needs to be brought home. Tell him to send to Harley Street for Dr. Johnson. He'll have the fellow's direction."

"Why can't you do it?" Dunthorp asked, his voice revealing just the hint of a whine. "I am hardly an errand boy."

"Because the widowed duchess is hurt and I asked you go," Archer said icily. "I hope you don't think that I won't tell her if you behave as less than a gentleman in her time of need. Because I will. I have no reservations about doing so."

Dunthorp's lips thinned. "You would, wouldn't you, conniving rogue?"

"I have no care what you think of me," Archer said, his eyes not leaving Perdita's wan face. "I only wish for Her Grace to be in the care of her physician immediately."

His face reflecting his anger, Dunthorp rose and retrieved his horse. Once he'd mounted he turned to Archer. "I'll send the carriage as soon as I get there. Then I'll ride to Harley Street myself. I have some familiarity with Dr. Johnson."

If he was hoping for effusive thanks, he was doomed to disappointment. Instead Archer gave him a sharp nod, and began chafing Perdita's hands

He heard Dunthorp leave and hoped that the man wouldn't allow his pique to get in the way of Perdita's health.

Three

The first sensation Perdita became aware of was pain. Her head hurt worse than the morning after she and Isabella had secretly drunk half a bottle of their father's best brandy while still in the schoolroom. It had been the first and the last time she'd overindulged like that, and some part of her brain couldn't make sense of the fact that she'd done it again after vowing so vociferously not to.

But when she opened her eyes, it wasn't to see Isabella—her eyes bloodshot from too much alcohol—leaning over her but a very worried Archer.

"Thank God," he said, closing his own blue eyes. "Thank God."

She opened her mouth to speak but all that came out was a dry croak. "What . . . happened?" she asked before he brought a glass of water to her lips. She drank greedily, appreciating the smooth slide of the water over her parched throat.

"What do you remember?" he asked, taking the glass from her hand and setting it aside. "The doctor wishes to know how much of your brain has been affected."

The mention of a doctor made Perdita mentally sit up. If a doctor had been called, she must have been very ill. "I don't know," she said, after thinking the matter over for a few moments. "The last thing I remember is going out for a ride with Dunthorp—and you, as well—but only leaving, not returning," she said, remembering the events as if they'd taken place years ago. "Did we go riding?"

His finely sculpted lips were tight. "Yes, that happened this morning. I insisted on accompanying you and Dunthorp because I was worried for your safety."

Her brow furrowed as she tried to remember. "You were worried," she said finally. "For my safety."

"Yes," he said, his voice clipped. "I accompanied you, and it's a good thing I did because we weren't in the park for more than a few minutes before a masked rider came racing toward us and tried to unseat you."

She tried to remember, but the images simply were not there. But the aches in her back and on her bottom, as well as her foot, which she supposed had gotten caught in the stirrup, all told her that the mysterious man had succeeded. "How long have I been unconscious?" she asked, closing her eyes against the tears that threatened. She knew it was the situation that brought her emotions to the surface, but even so the weakness was lowering. Especially in front of Archer.

"Only about a half hour," he responded, taking her hand in his and squeezing it, as if he knew instinctively that she needed comfort. "The physician said there were no broken bones and that as long as you awoke within an hour or so you'd likely be well."

"Thank heaven for small favors," she said, moving to shake her head, then stopping as she realized how much it would hurt. "What happened to the man who attacked me?"

She knew before he spoke that the blackguard had gotten away. "I'm sorry," he said simply. "I was too focused on seeing that you were all right, and Dunthorp could not leave while you were as yet unconscious."

Something in the way he said those last words told Perdita that there was a story buried in his words. But she was too tired suddenly to worry about what Dunthorp had or hadn't done. "So sleepy," she said, hearing the fatigue in her voice as she spoke, but unable to control it.

"Rest," Archer said, his hand caressing her cheek in such a tender way that if she'd been in her right mind she would have remarked upon it. As things were, however, she hadn't the strength of a newborn kitten and her eyes closed before she could complete her thought.

Archer's jaw was clenched so tightly that he feared some damage to his teeth. He looked down at Perdita, the shadows beneath her closed eyes giving her a pale and wan look that worried him. For as long as he'd known her, Perdita had been a fighter. Even during the worst of her marriage to Gervase, she'd tried desperately not to let her fear or hurt show. But seeing her thus, laid low by someone they didn't even know, terrified him in ways he could only begin to explain. When he'd seen that masked figure put his hands on her, Archer had wanted to kill the other man and damn the consequences. But when she'd fallen to the ground, in danger of being trampled by the horses, his priority had shifted to protecting Perdita. A few more inches and she'd have been facing an injury to her head that would not be so easy to come back from. The very notion was unthinkable. And he was more grateful than he could say that she'd escaped with only a bump on the head.

"She'll come around, my lord," said Simmons, the dowager Duchess of Ormond's personal maid. She'd been at the Ormond town house to visit the housekeeper—she now lived with her mistress at another house in town—and Archer was grateful for her help. Perdita's own maid had dissolved into a fit of tears and shrieks just as soon as she'd laid eyes on her mistress and had had to be sedated by the physician. Simmons, however, had been through every sort of family injury with her mistress and was really the best candidate for looking after the widowed duchess. "I'll just send a note round to my mistress and let her know where I am," she continued. "It's a good thing I came today, else you'd have been left high and dry, if you don't mind my saying so, your lordship."

Stretching his back, which had grown stiff from tension while sitting at Perdita's bedside, Archer couldn't help but agree. "I'm grateful, Simmons," he told the dour woman. "And I know the duchess would say so, too, if she were awake to do so."

Her harsh features softening for the barest moment, Simmons, ran a gentle hand over Perdita's brow. "She's a sweet lady, is Miss Perdita," she said, unconsciously referring to the young duchess by her name before marriage. "She takes enough care of the rest of us, I'm sure."

Archer couldn't help but smile, because her words were true. Perdita did take care of everyone. And perhaps it was time she allowed herself to be taken care of. Standing, he laid a companionable hand on the maid's shoulder. "I do thank you, ma'am," he reiterated. "And now, if you don't mind my leaving you here with her, I must go inform Lord Dunthorp of her condition and find someone to stand watch over the house."

"I don't understand, Lord Archer," she said, her gray brows furrowed. "I thought it was an accident."

Not wishing to let on more than he was ready to, Archer merely raised his brows. "I am just being extra cautious," he assured her. "Nothing more."

He left before she could ask him any further questions. The problem with old family retainers, he decided, was that they expected one to tell them the whole truth of the matter. And in this case, he wasn't prepared to tell even a fraction of the truth. Not only because it might endanger Perdita's life, but also because to say the words aloud would make Archer feel like an insane fool. Even so, the situation threatened to strain the bounds of credulity no matter whom he decided to tell. For Perdita hadn't simply been accosted for no reason. He was quite sure the man in the park today had intended to do something much worse.

To kill her.

And he could hardly admit such a thing to the dowager's maid without being prepared to talk the matter over with the dowager herself. Something he wasn't quite sure he'd ever be prepared to do.

Hurrying down the stairs, he went in search of Lord Dunthorp.

He found Dunthorp in the little drawing room, his fingers drumming repeatedly on the mantel over the enormous old-fashioned fireplace. "Is she well? Dammit, Lisle, you must tell me," the other man said as soon as he saw Archer.

"Easy," Archer said. "She is fine. She'll have a bump on her head for a few weeks, but other than that the doctor thinks she'll make a full recovery."

The degree to which Dunthorp's shoulders relaxed said a great deal about what he'd thought the duchess had been up against. "Thank God," he said finally. "I was so afraid there would be permanent damage and that she'd blame me . . ."

"Well, never fear," Archer retorted smoothly. "She is quite well and will doubtless be calling for tea soon."

To his surprise Dunthorp moved forward and took Archer's hand between his massive paws before he could stop him, and began pumping it up and down. "Thank you, Lord Archer," the other man said firmly. "If you'd not been there to take the matter in hand I have little doubt that the duchess would be facing a much more serious injury. Perdita and I will see to it that you are handsomely rewarded once we are wed."

Any pleasure he might have taken from Dunthorp's effusive praise was canceled out by the annoyance he felt at the way Dunthorp linked his own name with Perdita's. In a manner which Archer was quite sure Perdita had not and would not have sanctioned. It was opportunism at its worst and Archer wondered for a moment whether he should call the fellow to task now, or simply let Perdita cut him down to size later. At last he decided to go ahead and nip the other man's encroachment in the bud, especially considering that Perdita needed her rest.

"I'm sorry to say it, old fellow," he began, "but if you mean to convince the duchess of your serious intentions, then simply pronouncing your engagement as if it were a fait accompli is not the way to go about things. Especially when one considers that the widowed duchess has suffered a head injury. She may have forgotten some of her memory, but she hasn't lost her mind, you see."

As Archer continued to speak, the other man's face grew redder and redder until, finally, he seemed to burst like a bladder filled with air. "How dare you, sir?" Dunthorp clenched his fists at his sides in rage.

But Archer was not to be easily cowed. "I dare, sir, because I have known the lady for some five years now and do not believe she has ever expressed the intention of marrying you. Oh, she's considered it, of that I'm sure. But that is hardly the same thing as agreeing. Especially if one considers your exchange earlier this morning."

Dunthorp's jaw clenched and his fists shifted back and forth at his side, as if he were unable to decide whether to take a shot at Archer or not. Archer suspected not. Men like Dunthorp were never quite sanguine with the notion of being hit back, no matter how eager they might be to throw the first punch.

"You have overstepped your bounds, sir," he said, his teeth bared like a cur protecting a bone. "I will allow the lady to tell me whether she will or won't have me. Not some hanger-on, with delusions of his own importance."

His shoulders raised in a shrug, Archer said, "Suit yourself. Though I'm afraid that the duchess won't be able to see you today. She's had quite an upset this morning and I should like to see her rest before she gets involved in monetary matters again too soon."

At the mention of money, Dunthorp's mouth opened and shut like an angry fish. Finally, he said. "I won't stand here and be insulted."

"I perfectly understand, Lord Dunthorp," Archer said, flicking an infinitesimal speck of dust from the arm of his coat. "Pray, feel free to sample the insults somewhere—anywhere—but here. I feel sure once she hears your tender proposal to love, cherish, and protect her money for the rest of your days, the duchess will be beside herself with delight."

Dunthorp bit back a curse and stalked out. Archer could hear the other man's every step as he stormed down the stairs and out the front door.

Suddenly exhausted, Archer collapsed into the nearest chair and scraped his hands over his face.

"I never did like Dunthorp overly much," a voice rang out from the other side of the room. "The nerve of the fellow thinking to just assume an engagement because the duchess was unconscious."

Archer was on his feet as soon as the first words emerged from his visitor's mouth.

"Con!"

Seated in the shadows of the drawing room was

the Earl of Coniston, a glass of Ormond's best brandy in one hand and an unlit cigar in the other.

"It looks as if you need a bit of assistance, my dear fellow."

That, thought Archer, was a gross understatement.

Four

When Perdita awoke again, it was to see faint light through her bedroom window. It was difficult to determine whether it was very early morning or very late afternoon. While she was sleeping someone had removed her clothes and dressed her in a nightgown, and her hair was neatly braided in one long plait down her back. Remembering her maid's hysterics yesterday—or today, or whenever her accident had happened—she supposed that someone else had been called in to act as maid for her. For a flash she remembered Archer seated on the side of her bed, but though the thought sent a jolt of electricity to her belly, she dismissed it immediately. Not only would he not do something so unseemly, but she suddenly remembered Simmons, the dowager's maid, had been here. It had likely been she who undressed her.

Grateful that the only remnant of the horrific headache she'd sustained from her accident was a faint throb, she threw back the covers and padded over to the dressing room to use the chamber pot and wash her face and hands. Feeling much more the thing, she donned a robe and stepped back into her bedchamber and pulled the bell.

Instead of a maid or footman, however, the knock at her door revealed a remarkably disheveled Archer, his hair sticking up as if he'd been running his fingers through it, and his coat having been abandoned. Closing the door behind him, he stepped forward, and Perdita found herself stepping back until she stopped at the bed.

"I apologize for invading your bedchamber," he said, looking sheepish, "but Simmons had to go back to care for the dowager and your own maid is still sedated."

"Surely another of the maids could have been assigned to care for me," Perdita said, her heart beating far more quickly than it should. "Anyone will do."

Twin flags of color appeared on his cheeks. "That is true enough," he agreed, looking at the floor. "I just . . . that is to say . . . I wanted to see you."

Her legs suddenly giving out from beneath her, Perdita sat down on the edge of the bed. "Oh."

He thrust a hand through his hair. "I was just worried about you, and I didn't trust another one of the maids to look after you given what happened in the park this morning." His expression turned fierce then. "In fact, I don't know that I trust anyone to look after you at this point but myself. And Trevor, Con, or their wives."

Her heart was beating faster now, but for another reason. "Surely you don't think one of the servants would do something to harm me," she said quickly, thinking about the older members of the staff who had been with Ormond House since the dowager had married the old duke. "I mean, I know what happened to Isabella, but her maid was newly hired. These servants have been here for years."

"And might just as easily be convinced to harm you as a new servant, I'm afraid," Archer said, his blue eyes serious. "Or maybe someone who holds you responsible for Gervase's death. That has been the context of the threats against you, as well as Isabella and Georgina, hasn't it?"

Thinking back to the tableau at the Sumrall Ball, Perdita nodded silently. Though her sister's and Georgina's assailants had seemed to wish them harm for reasons specific to them that had nothing to do with Gervase's death, they had been recruited by someone else. Someone who linked all three of them to Gervase's death. With Perdita, however, the motive had been to threaten her because of her husband's death from the beginning. Not only had the notes said that they knew what she'd done last season, but they'd also asked why she would murder her husband. And of course there had been the little reenactment, for the members of the ton to see, of the night of her husband's death. Yes, whoever wished to make her suffer did so as punishment for what she'd done—or what they thought she'd done—to Gervase. And Archer was right. Any of the servants who had been with the household since Gervase was born could be behind the threats against her. A chill ran up her spine as she contemplated the fact that she was safe nowhere. Not in her home at least.

"What can I do?" she asked him, schooling her features not to show the utter panic she felt at what he'd just suggested. It was one thing to indulge in hysterics in the privacy of her own bedchamber where no one could see her, but to stand before Archer trembling with fear was something she could not do. She wasn't sure why, but every fiber of her being rebelled against the notion.

As if he sensed the way she held her emotions in check, Archer stepped closer. "You need not do a thing," he said softly. "I'll keep watch over you."

"But that's . . ." She tried to come up with a rational reason why she should object. But if the truth were known, she felt only an overwhelming sense of relief at knowing he'd protect her. More than any man she'd ever known, Archer had always felt to Perdita like a solid bet. Someone she could rely on no matter how he frustrated her or made her want to tear her hair out in vexation. He could be as stubborn as a mule, but he could also be warm and funny and caring. All of which was why she couldn't allow herself to fall under his spell if he was going to be spending more time in her company. It was all too tempting, but she could not allow herself to fall under any man's spell again. Ever. "That's unnecessary," she finished lamely.

"Not if you wish to stay safe," he returned. "In fact, I'd say it's quite necessary."

It was difficult to argue with him when she was so weak. It was quite unfair. But she would do it all the same.

"My safety is not your responsibility," she said as a sudden wave of weariness washed over her. "You know it's not." She heard the fatigue in her voice, and almost involuntarily lay down upon the bed. She should feel embarrassed, but she was past that. The pillow felt so good beneath her cheek, and she couldn't have risen if she'd tried.

"Not quite my responsibility," he agreed, but she no longer remembered what she'd said to prompt his words. "But I don't mind." He pulled the covers up to her shoulders and Perdita felt more protected than she had in years. "I'm your friend."

He stepped back from the bed. "And you'll be happy to know reinforcements have arrived."

She blinked against the heaviness of her eyelids. "What 'forcements'?" she muttered, wishing she could stay awake for what she was sure was a very important conversation.

"Lord and Lady Coniston are here," he said. "And Ormond and Isabella as well."

But why? she said, though his lack of a response told her that she'd not spoken the words aloud.

"Go to sleep, Perdita," she heard him say. "We will keep you safe."

And unable to fight sleep any longer, she let herself drift off.

Archer had just shut Perdita's door behind him, the housekeeper having agreed to sit with her for a bit while he went down to report on her progress to the others, when a commotion at the front entrance drew his attention.

"Why wasn't I informed of this at once?" the dowager demanded, on seeing him descend the staircase. "I am still the matriarch of this family even if my grandson and that wife of his wish to see me relegated to the dower house!"

He might have received these complaints with a

sharper tone if he hadn't seen how pale the dowager was beneath the powder she wore. "I apologize, Duchess," he said, stepping forward to bow over the hand she extended to him. "I hadn't any thought beyond seeing to it that Perdita was taken care of. Of course you were worried."

Inclining her head in acknowledgment of the apology, the dowager said in a more conciliatory tone, "When Simmons informed me that she had been attacked in the park like a commoner, I do not mind telling you that I was taken aback. It is simply unheard of. What can the world be coming to when a duchess cannot even ride on the row without being accosted like the veriest fishwife, I ask you?"

"I agree that the situation is most unacceptable, Duchess," Archer said, amused despite himself. He offered the old woman his arm. "Won't you allow me to escort you to the drawing room? I believe Ormond and his lady are there."

He had received word that they'd arrived while he was looking after Perdita.

She took his arm, even as she asked querulously, "What? Are they in town again? In my day ladies had the decency to remove themselves from the public gaze when expecting a happy event. But I daresay I shouldn't expect anything else from my goddaughter for all that I know she was raised to know better."

Archer forebore to mention that her own drawing room was hardly in the public gaze, but simply nodded and agreed with the old woman as they processed up the stairs and into the brightly lit drawing room.

"Godmama!" Isabella cried upon seeing the dowager in the doorway. "I hadn't expected to see you here. I was planning to come pay a call on you to-morrow."

As the duke, the duchess, and Lord and Lady Coniston greeted the dowager, Archer took a moment to cross to the sideboard and pour himself a brandy. If nothing else, the alcohol would settle his nerves, which were still on alert at the idea of just how close he'd come to losing Perdita.

When he turned back to the room at large it was to see that Ormond was watching him with something akin to sympathy. Which made sense since the other man knew full well what it was like to see the woman he loved in danger. For that matter so did Coniston.

"Since you are all here," the dowager said abruptly, interrupting Georgina who was in the middle of asking after a shared acquaintance, "I want to know what you mean to do to ensure Perdita's safety."

To his surprise, Archer suddenly felt the eyes of the room upon him.

"I'm hardly in a position to dictate to Perdita on the matter of her safety," he said, then drained his glass. "She is as stubborn as anyone I've ever met. And she'll hardly listen to the likes of me."

"Piffle," the dowager said with disgust. "Don't pretend we haven't eyes in our heads, Lord Archer. I know well enough that my granddaughter trusts your opinion. Didn't she listen to you on the matter of the butcher? If not for your counsel the household might still be patronizing that extortionist Hamilton. What can the man have been thinking to charge such a price for an inferior joint of beef, I ask you?"

Archer did not dare point out that the matter of a butcher who was overcharging the household was not the same as someone trying to cause Perdita bodily harm. It would do no good. Besides, he really did think Perdita was stubborn. That didn't mean he would abandon the field, however.

"You're right," he said, watching with amusement as the dowager preened at how quickly he'd agreed with her. "I will see to it that she's kept safe."

"But how?" the dowager demanded, her pleasure turning to annoyance.

"Yes, Archer," Con said with a suspiciously innocent expression. "How?"

"I cannot tell you," Archer said with asperity. "Otherwise whoever wishes her harm might learn the details. It is too delicate a situation for me to give all the details away."

He was precluded from saying anything more by a knock on the drawing room door and the appearance of the dowager's maid, Simmons.

"I beg your pardon, Your Graces, my lords, my lady," she said to the assembled company, "but, Duchess, we must return to the dower house before Dr. Johnson arrives."

The mulish set of the dowager's jaw told Archer that she was not pleased at the interruption, but after some silent communication passed between the two women, the older woman sagged a little. "I suppose I must be off," she said to the others. "But I expect you," she said, nodding toward Archer, "to keep me apprised of developments on the matter we discussed."

Archer bowed to acknowledge the order and the dowager seemed to relax a bit. Allowing Simmons to assist her to stand, she left the room, leaving nothing but silence in her wake.

"Well," Isabella said finally, "that was pleasant."

The laughter that followed burst the bubble of tension Archer hadn't even realized had enveloped them all.

But the light mood couldn't last. Almost apologetically, Isabella turned to Archer, her brows knitted with worry. "Now that Godmama is gone, you must tell us the truth about how my sister fares."

Five

I would have gone up first thing but I was told she was sleeping," Isabella continued. "And then God-mama arrived and there was no question of leaving you to her tender mercies."

Archer took the glass of brandy Ormond offered him and lowered his tall frame into the nearest chair. "She *is* sleeping. Not by choice, though. It just sort of overtook her while we were talking."

"Poor thing," Georgina said, taking her husband's hand. "Rest is probably the best for her, however much she might wish to resist it."

"Any news on the attacker?" Ormond had remained standing behind Isabella's chair. His normally pleasant expression had been replaced by one of determination. He'd gone through something similar with Isabella at his country house and knew how dangerous this person could be. "I stopped by the magistrate's office on our way here. The authorities need to be brought in on this as quickly as possible."

"Thank you." Archer rubbed his hands over his face. It was not quite six in the evening but he felt as if it should be midnight given all that had happened. "I doubt Perdita will appreciate it, but I think it's a good idea to have a proper investigation into this matter. I plan on doing my best to hunt down the bastard, too, but there is no harm in asking for help. Especially when the attack took place in the park. Though his focus seemed to be on Perdita, he might have harmed others in his determination to harm her."

"Well, she will simply have to accept it." Isabella's mouth pursed. "My sister is the most stubborn person I've ever known, but in this case, she is overruled. Anything that will keep her safe is perfectly acceptable to me."

"She won't like it one bit." Georgina, who had faced her own terror in Bath earlier in the year, looked worried on her friend's behalf. "Perdita might be stubborn but I think she'll see reason once we explain the situation to her. I certainly don't believe she will wish to put others in harm's way by continuing to move about freely in town without proper protection."

Archer sighed. "I thought that's what I was supposed to be this morning. But you see how well that worked out."

"You weren't expecting something like that," Ormond said. "How could you? The reenactment at the Sumralls' ball was sinister but it was meant to threaten her feelings, not her person. Thus far, that's all this fellow has done. It's as if he wishes to drive her mad. Which is the same tactic he used with Isabella to begin with. It just seems as if he's moving more quickly this go-round."

"Even so." Archer's jaw clenched with frustration.

"I should have guessed it. If she'd been seriously harmed I would never be able to forgive myself."

Isabella reached over and squeezed his shoulder. "You cannot think like that. You are the very reason she's still alive and resting in her bedchamber. You and no one else. Certainly not Dunthorp."

"What is the story on Dunthorp?" Coniston leaned forward, and for the first time Archer noticed that he no longer had the cigar and whisky from earlier. Clearly Georgina had exerted her authority there. The thought made him smile for what felt like the first time that day.

"He is also a fast mover." Archer tried not to let the very real dislike of the other man show in his face. He didn't trust Dunthorp, but it was as much because he had designs on Perdita, as his attempt to take advantage of her current weakness to stake his claim. "Though I suppose he cares for her in his own way."

"I've never liked the fellow," Con said firmly. "We were at Eton together and he was one of those boys who took advantage of his bulk to threaten those who were smaller. Once a bully, always a bully."

"Never met the man." Ormond had not moved about in the ton until this last year, and even then he preferred to keep his distance from them. "Though I'll take your word for it that he's not someone I'd wish to cultivate."

"I cannot help but feel a bit hopeful," Isabella said with an apologetic smile, "since he's the first man my sister has shown interest in since her engagement to Lord Coniston came to naught. But I cannot understand why it's him of all people. I've never been overly fond of him, either. He's so disgustingly condescending."

Archer knew that the diffidence Isabella had just shown before voicing her opinion was for his own benefit. Clearly he'd not been as clever at hiding his feelings for Perdita as he'd thought. He'd learned early on what it took to fool his elder brothers, of course. As the youngest of five boys, he'd needed to do so else risk merciless teasing at their hands. But fooling women was another thing altogether. He hoped that Isabella was able to see through to his true feelings only because after the day's events he was exhausted, and not because he was simply unable to mask his thoughts. The notion of going about town with his heart on his sleeve for all the world to see was unpleasant at best.

Still, he didn't really care if the Ormonds and the Conistons knew which way the wind blew. He trusted them, or he'd never have told them the truth about the day's events. And at this point all he cared about was keeping Perdita safe.

"She's chosen him because there's no possible way she can fall in love with him," Georgina said without hesitation, breaking into Archer's thoughts. "He's one of those men one likes, but only to a certain point. I don't know Perdita's taste fully, of course, but I can imagine that he seems safe enough to her. And I have little doubt that it's because she thinks she can make him dance to her own tune."

With an apologetic look at her husband, Georgina continued, "It's why she chose to become engaged to you, Con. Though I think it was more because neither of you really fancied one another than because she could manipulate you."

"Well, thank you for that, my dear," Con responded without any real heat. "And here I thought she chose me because of my excellent calves."

"They are quite good, aren't they?" Georgie returned with a speculative look at her husband's legs.

"Getting back to the matter at hand," Ormond interjected, drawing groans from the others at his awful pun. "I daresay you're correct about her reasons for choosing both Coniston and Dunthorp. It's because she fell hard for Gervase. Stands to reason she'd not trust her own judgment on the matter. And with Dunthorp there's the added bonus that he's likely to dance to *her* tune and not the other way around."

The others nodded, and Archer once again wished he'd realized what was going on between Gervase and Perdita before it was too late. He might have been able to stop things before Perdita's trust in herself was eroded to the degree that she'd contemplate marriage with someone like Dunthorp.

Then there was the fact that he really wished he'd been able to treat the bastard to a taste of his own medicine before he got himself killed.

Con broke into the silence that had fallen as they each thought of Gervase and his brutality. "Enough about Dunthorp. What are our plans for keeping the Duchess of Stubbornness safe while she remains in London?"

"I had planned to convince her to leave town as soon as possible." Archer knew it was a stretch, however. Perdita would not want to run away from a fight. "Perhaps she could be persuaded to go to stay with one of you in your country houses. If you're willing to go back so soon, that is."

"I would be more than happy to take her if she can be talked into it." A line of worry had appeared between Isabella's brows. "I don't, however, think that obtaining her agreement will be an easy undertaking."

"She might be convinced if we two suggested it to her," Georgina said thoughtfully. "No offense to you three, but we have been in her shoes and know what she's going through."

"That didn't work with you," Con argued. "If I remember correctly, you were dead set against 'running away' as you called it."

His wife shot him an exasperated look. "I would have been willing to leave, but I'd nowhere to go. And I didn't wish to endanger any of you who chose to go with me."

Before their discussion could turn into a true argument, Isabella broke in. "She has been due to visit us in Yorkshire for ages. And I'm not above using my condition"—she gestured to her pregnant belly—"to convince her."

"Remind me never to get myself in the position of being persuaded by you," Archer said with a shake of his head. "We are in the presence of ruthlessness, gentlemen."

"Oh, pooh," Georgie said with a wave of her hand. "It's not as if you all don't find equally terrifying ways of convincing us to do your bidding."

"Indeed," Isabella agreed. She lowered her voice in an approximation of a man's. "Isabella, of course you cannot accompany me to the races. Think of the child. Isabella, there is no reason why you should visit the tenant farms this week. Think of the child."

"Ouch," Con said to Ormond, whose face was red

enough to match the auburn in his hair. "I believe that's what's known as turnabout, old man."

"I don't sound like that," Ormond said, his voice clipped. "And I most certainly could not countenance her going to the races in her condition. The crowds get very rough sometimes."

"Oh, don't go all stiff upper lip, darling," Isabella said, taking her husband's hand. "I was only funning. Besides, I did agree not to go to the races or the tenant farms, so it's not as if I can blame you fully for it. I could have told you to go rot if I'd wished to."

"What a charmer you are, my dear," Ormond said, bringing her hand to his lips. "I look forward to the day when you whisper sweet nothings like 'go rot' into my ear instead of to the company at large."

Now it was Isabella's turn to blush.

Archer felt his chest burn as he watched the strong affection between Perdita's sister and her husband. He'd grown up with parents who were just as affectionate as Ormond and Isabella. Indeed, he and his elder brothers had spent a great deal of their boyhoods rolling their eyes at the antics of their, at times, overly demonstrative parents. It hadn't taken Archer above a few visits home with school friends to realize that not all parents were as happily wed as his own. And though he and his brothers had made a show of being utterly embarrassed when the duke and duchess spoke sweetly to one another, deep down, Archer knew that he would not deign to marry until he knew he loved his prospective bride as much as his father loved his mother.

He'd long ago decided that he'd fulfilled that requirement at least. It was difficult to imagine finding another woman he cared for as much as he did for Perdita. But before he could think of asking her to consider him as a prospective bridegroom, he had to ensure that he would be worthy of her. As things stood now, he was still a younger son without property, but if he had anything to say about it, that situation would change sooner rather than later.

"We need to stop chattering and get to work," he said, turning matters back to the situation at hand. "And I have an idea of what we might do to make things safer for her in London if Perdita cannot be convinced to leave."

Isabella and Georgina were seated at the breakfast table when Perdita appeared the next morning. She'd slept soundly and had awoken with only a goose egg on the back of her head to remind her of yesterday's debacle.

"My dear." Isabella rushed to her side and pulled her into a hug. "I'm so pleased that you are looking so well. I was worried sick."

Perdita couldn't help but notice that her belly had grown in the month or so since they'd last seen each other. She returned the hug, then stepped back to look her sister over. "You are looking well, too, sister. In fact, I'd say that anticipating a blessed event suits you." She tried not to let the pang of jealousy she felt for her sister's situation enter her consciousness. It was not Isabella's fault that she was newly married and happy. If things worked out as Perdita wished, she'd be married and with child soon, too. But there would be nothing like the love of Isabella's marriage in Perdita's. She should be grateful for the knowledge that Dunthorp would never gain the upper hand with her, but at moments like this, she was wistful for the relationship she might have if she would allow Archer closer. Though that was foolish, too, since despite her suspicions about Archer, he'd never come out and declared his affection for her. It was just a hunch.

"Do not try to change the subject," Isabella said, breaking through Perdita's thoughts. "You were very nearly killed yesterday. And we are both concerned for your safety."

"Let her get some breakfast and a cup of tea, Isabella," the ever practical Georgie said, before giving Perdita a quick hug and shooing her to the sideboard.

Once Perdita was seated at the table, with toast and a rasher of bacon, and the footman had poured her a cup of tea, she spoke up. "What are you two planning? For I cannot help but feel that you've been lying in wait for me."

"Don't be so suspicious," Isabella said breezily. "Cannot a sister and friend express their concern for you without being suspected of plotting?"

"Frankly," Perdita said before biting into her toast, "yes."

"We are worried for you, Perdita." Georgie got straight to the point. "And we both know what it's like to be hunted down by someone with a grudge against us. How are you? How are you, really?"

To her shock, Perdita felt tears threatening. She swallowed and concentrated on clamping down on her emotions for a moment, but she could tell that both Isabella and Georgina had guessed what was going on. Finally, when she was confident she could speak without breaking into sobs, she said, "I am as well as can be expected the day after someone tried to run me down in the park. Still a bit frightened, but determined to be strong about it."

"I had hoped so much that this person would stop once he'd finished his business with me," Georgina said, her sincere regret furrowing her brow. "Though I suppose that was a foolish hope given that you were receiving letters from him while we were still in Bath."

"True enough," Perdita said with a sigh. "I had also hoped he would keep to the same leisurely pace as he proceeded to threaten me, but that was a false hope, as well."

"Do you have any guess as to whom it might be?" Isabella asked, fidgeting with her teacup. "Could it have been someone at the Sumralls' ball? A member of the ton, or perhaps one of the servants? Or even a servant hired temporarily for the ball itself?"

Perdita shook her head. "I have no idea. I must admit that I wasn't paying much attention to the servants there, but it's a good guess. And yesterday, I could tell only that my attacker was a man. I have no idea what man, though."

"That is how he works," Georgina said, her lips tight. "He doesn't use the same people every time, so as soon as you try to find the first attacker he's already moved on to using the next one. Or, as with me, he uses a multiperson strategy, so one element of the attack comes from the same person every time, but he uses another for the second prong, and the same for the third. It's impossible to get a grasp on who any of them are while you're trying to figure out what's going on."

Knowing her friend was correct, Perdita tried to separate the threads of attack in her mind so that she might consider the possible attackers at both the ball and the park. But her brain was not quite able to do the work this morning.

"Perdita," Isabella said, reaching over to take her sister's hand. "What about coming to stay with us in Yorkshire for a few months? You know that Trevor and I would love to have you, and the girls would adore seeing you again. Flossie has had kittens again and they will be ready to find homes, too. You know how you said that you wanted one the next time we had some."

Looking at her sister's radiant face, Perdita wished that she could simply accept her offer and return to Yorkshire with them. She had promised to come for a visit soon and it would be a relief to get away from the place where she'd experienced her most frightening attacks. But there was no way she would put her sister and her family in danger. Certainly not while she was with child and therefore at her most vulnerable.

"You know how much I love you." she said aloud, "but I simply cannot go with you just now. I have responsibilities here in London. There is Ormond House to maintain while you and Trevor are away, and you know how many committees I am on for the various charities I am involved with. Not to mention the invitations I've already accepted. It is simply impossible."

"I knew you would refuse," Isabella said with a frown. "But honestly, you mustn't put yourself in danger simply because you wish to protect us. Ormond has very loyal servants at the country house. And there is no question of another threat like my perfidious maid getting into the house."

"Of course you would completely disregard my reasons for not being able to come." Perdita could almost laugh at how quickly her sister had seen through her argument.

"Because your excuses were just that," Georgie said with a sigh. "Excuses. You have never in your life worried about accepting an invitation then not being able to come. And the committee work is just balderdash. You are only on two that I know of and they are hardly stringent about every member being there for every meeting."

Before Perdita could get her back up over it, Georgie continued. "I don't blame you. After all, I didn't want to leave Bath with you all when I was in a similar situation. But don't try to pull the wool over our eyes. Just tell us that you don't want to put us in danger. We are certainly able to understand it."

"It frustrates me like mad that my being enceinte in particular keeps you from accepting my invitation, but I can hardly blame you." Isabella rested a hand over her belly. "I am aware that my condition makes people—especially Trevor—wish to wrap me in cotton wool. But the fact that he expressly wishes me to invite you is a measure of how serious he believes the threat against you is. Do not refuse us lightly, Perdita. You are in very real danger."

"I am quite aware of the fact that I'm in danger," Perdita said, her knuckles white as she clenched her hands in her lap. "And of course I don't wish to put you all in danger. It would be reckless and selfish of me to do so. Besides, it didn't matter if you were buried in rural Yorkshire or in the middle of London or Bath. He still managed to find you. Why on earth would I lead him to your homes when he can strike just as well there as he can here?"

"I don't like it," Isabella said, her eyes filling with tears. "I cannot bear to think of you here dealing with these attacks alone. It is terrifying, but I had Trevor there to help me. To offer me his protection."

"I have Dunthorp," Perdita argued, knowing as soon as she said it that she no more trusted Dunthorp to keep her safe than the man in the moon. He was a nice enough man, but hardly someone she'd put her trust in. Archer's image flashed for a moment in her mind and she knew without a doubt that he would do whatever it took to keep her safe.

As if she'd read her friend's mind, Georgie laughed. "Dunthorp is hardly the kind of man one trusts to protect one from physical attack. I'll bet he ran away from you yesterday rather than to you."

"I don't know," Perdita said with a frown. "I cannot remember anything until just before we left to go to the park. But that's an unfair characterization of Dunthorp. He might well have saved my life."

"Do not be a goose," Isabella said. "We all know very well that it was Archer who shielded you from further harm yesterday. And he will, I daresay, stay by your side through every minute of our mysterious villain's campaign of terror. Because that's what Archer does. He protects. And I think he would cut off his right arm before he allowed something to happen to you again."

"Archer is loyal to the duchy of Ormond," Perdita

said firmly. "And yes, I daresay he would do anything to protect me. But any notion you have of the two of us making a match are simply daydreams, Isabella. I cannot think of him that way. And that's an end to it."

"There's nothing wrong with seeking happiness," Georgie said quietly. "Dearest, we've been in the same position that you're in now. We were afraid of putting our trust into another husband. But not all men are the same. There are dangerous ones, like Wharton, Mowbray, and Gervase, but just because you make the wrong choice once does not mean that you will continue to make bad choices."

The tears that had threatened when she first entered the breakfast room returned, spilling over onto her cheeks. And Perdita, unable to withstand more of Isabella and Georgina's too accurate observations, stood and hurried from the room.

Six

Archer was in the study sorting through the stack of invitations Ormond had received this week—a task he'd ignored since the attacks on Perdita had started—when he heard the door open and shut. Quietly, as if whoever it was wished to keep anyone from hearing them enter.

"Archer," Perdita said, clearly startled to find him there. As he stood he saw that her eyes were wet with tears. Unable to stop himself he crossed the room to her side.

"I'll just get out of here and let you work. I didn't think anyone was in here." She turned to leave, her gown brushing his trousers as she did so.

"Don't go," he said, reaching out to catch her arm before she could open the door. From where he stood he could see one red-gold curl caress the softness of her neck. Could smell the clean scent of her perfume. He swallowed. "Tell me what's wrong. Talk to me."

She gave a bitter laugh. "What isn't wrong? I suppose the attack yesterday has gotten to me. That and the way that everyone is leaping to my defense."

He frowned, calling on every bit of self-discipline to pay attention to her words and not her nearness.

"That bothers you?" he asked once he'd got himself under control. "I should think it would make you feel loved."

"Loved," she agreed with a sigh, her lips twisting into a little half-smile. "But also frustrated because in the rush to protect me, everyone is taking away my autonomy. I am perceived as being unable to take care of myself. And that infuriates me."

He saw that her jaw was set, and he removed his hand from her arm, but indicated that she should precede him to one of the seats before the fire. She gave a sigh, but turned to the chair. And he sat across from her. Wanting like the devil to touch her, but knowing that it wasn't the right time.

He leaned forward and put his elbows on his knees. "I suppose you resent having your choices taken away because of Gervase?" He knew that it was unwise to bring the late duke's name up, but he couldn't help but blame the devil for what she suffered now. His death had been his own bloody fault. And the fact that someone was now punishing Perdita for it was as unfair as unfair could be.

"That's part of it," Perdita agreed, twisting her handkerchief in her lap. "He wasn't overly fond of letting me make my own choices, of course. And now, just as I've become confident again, and able to make choices for myself, I'm suddenly in the position of being dictated to. It's meant to protect me, I know, but I cannot help but feel resentful of it."

"I suppose you refused both Isabella's and Georgina's invitations for you to visit them in the country," he said, part of him disappointed that she'd refused to remove herself from danger, but another part pleased because this would mean that he could stay by her side. Protect her. Which was of course part of what she resented. He didn't let the sigh escape his lips, though he felt it all the same.

"Of course," she replied, leaning back in her chair. The dim light from the window illuminated her from behind, making her strawberry-blond hair glow like a golden crown. He knew that as long as he lived he'd remember this moment in this room. Perdita upset but determined, looking like an avenging angel.

"They simply want to protect you," he said. "They mean well. We all do."

"I know," she breathed out. "I do. But I cannot make my sister and Georgina endure this again. They are beyond it now. And for better or worse, this person seems to have finished with them. He has moved on to the main event now. The job he has been working toward all along: terrorizing me. And I don't mind telling you that I am afraid."

She looked up then, and Archer felt his gut clench as he saw the very real fear in her eyes. If he could have, he'd have leaped up, found the fellow who wished her harm and run him through. But he knew as well as anyone that it wasn't going to be that easy. This man was as conniving as they came. And he wasn't going to let himself be caught without a fight.

Unable to help himself, Archer went to his knees before her chair and pulled her into his arms. He expected her to resist, but to his surprise and relief, she hugged him back, resting her head on his shoulder as he held her close. It was impossible not to respond to the sheer pleasure of feeling her lush body pressed against his. His intentions might be honorable but his body cared nothing for honor when there was a soft female so near.

"What am I to do, Archer?" she asked, the puff of her breath on his neck sending a delicious thrill through him even as he tried to calm his racing pulse. "I cannot put them in danger. I simply can't. But London feels dangerous, too. I daresay I'll feel better in a few days, but right now, I don't know what to do. You are my friend. Help me."

At the word "friend," he felt a bit of the excitement of holding her close ebb away. Still, he reminded himself, friendship was not nothing. And it meant she trusted his opinion, which was something neither Dunthorp nor her late husband could boast of.

"I am going to speak to someone from the magistrate's office this afternoon," he said, his voice rough with wanting her.

She pulled away and scooted back in her chair. "The magistrate's office?" she demanded, her eyes wide with alarm. "Why on earth would you tell them about this? You know how Gervase died. They'll think there was something untoward about his death and begin investigating Isabella, Georgie, and me. Archer, this is the worst thing you could do!"

Realizing that there would be no more embracing between them, Archer dropped his arms to his sides and stood, moving to lean against the mantel. Managing to speak in a measured tone, he said, "There is no reason for them to think something was suspicious about Gervase's death. Because I won't tell them about the threats against you. For all they'll know you're being attacked by some madman with Bonapartist tendencies who wishes to abolish the nobility." And he'd be damned if he'd let her be investigated for what he was convinced had been Gervase's justified killing.

Despite his assurances, however, Perdita still seemed unnerved by the idea of having the magistrate's office anywhere near her. "You can't know that!" she said, standing up and glaring at him. "I can't believe you would risk revealing my secret. What gives you the right?"

Her accusation stung. Especially given how hard he'd worked to ensure that she remained safe. "The right of someone who put his own life at risk yesterday to keep you safe," he said, stepping toward her. "The right of someone who has watched as your sister and friend both suffered the same sort of threats from this same person. Do you think I wish to see you murdered before my eyes? Do you?"

Her eyes widened as she saw how angry he was, but she didn't back down. And her own anger was still there, prompting her words. "I didn't ask you to put yourself in the way yesterday. I didn't even know you were going to be there. It was supposed to be a ride with Dunthorp and myself only."

As he saw the fire in her eyes, he knew she'd said that deliberately to wound him. Well, two could play at that game, he thought. "Dunthorp couldn't protect a mouse from a barn cat," he said with contempt. "And don't think I don't know why you've chosen him as the one man you'll allow to get close to you. I know you quite well, Your Grace. Quite well, indeed."

"Oh, really?" she demanded, her nostrils flaring

with ire. As she sucked air into her lungs, temper making her breath come faster, her bosom rose and fell in way that made Archer long to say something provoking just to see her react again.

Why did she have to be so beautiful when she was angry? It was really quite unfair.

"Do tell," she continued, oblivious to the way her body was distracting him. "I cannot wait to hear your theory on Dunthorp. And my reasons for allowing him to pay me court. I'm sure it will be very enlightening."

He took one step closer, so close that when she inhaled the tips of her breasts touched his chest. "You chose him," he said, leaning in almost until they were nose to nose, "because he can't make you feel like this."

And then, despite all his careful planning, and all his rationalizations about waiting for just the right moment, Archer kissed her.

After all their hot words, Perdita expected his kiss to be punishing. He was angrier than she'd ever seen him. And she knew from experience that Archer was slow to anger. But to her surprise, when he took her in his arms it was with a diffidence and gentleness that nearly took her breath away. She hadn't been approached physically by a man since Gervase had died, and while she knew Archer was nothing like her husband, she'd not expected him to treat her as if she were a priceless treasure, either.

As soon as he pulled her into his arms and leaned in, however, she stopped thinking altogether and allowed herself to feel the heat of his breath on her lips, the strength of the arms that clasped her tightly against his body. Instinctively she opened her mouth as he brought his lips to hers and the moment they came together nearly made her weep.

For years she'd known—deep down in the heart of her where no one could see but her—that Archer could make her feel this way. He'd always been more sensitive to her moods and feelings than any man had the right to be. It was one of the things that made him such a good secretary. He had an innate ability to read people. And he'd been able to see through to her soul from the moment they'd met.

As if he knew she wanted that very thing, he nipped at her bottom lip before sliding his tongue into her mouth, and unable to stop herself, she returned his caress in kind. She slipped her hands up his arms to his impossibly wide shoulders, and then to caress the back of his neck, luxuriating in the soft hair of his nape. How had he possibly known just what to do to make her ache for him?

"Perdita," he whispered, pulling back. And though she wanted more than anything to pull him back down to her, she opened her eyes and saw that his own were wide with wonder. Was it possible that he was just as overwhelmed by this as she was? It was a delicious thought, and one that bore some thinking on, but then he leaned in and kissed her again, sliding his hands down her back and over her bottom, pulling her closer to him. She was aware of every place their bodies touched, and gasped as his hand slid up to caress her breast, his thumb and forefinger plucking the tip, sending a jolt of feeling straight to the center of her. "God, how I've wanted you," he said, his voice low and slightly hoarse with desire.

"Archer," she crooned as his lips found the sensitive spot below her ear. She lifted her chin as he kissed his way down the column of her neck and sucked lightly on her collarbone. If he weren't holding her so close she'd have slid to the floor in a puddle of want, so carried away was she by the sheer power of his touch. She shivered as his slight stubble—so different from her own skin—rasped against her as he slid the arms of her gown down so that he could suckle her through her shift.

It was intoxicating. So much so that neither of them heard the door to the study open to admit Isabella and Trevor, who were in mid-conversation as it happened. "But I don't see why we can't do both," Isabella was saying as they stepped into the chamber, but if she or the duke had more to say, they were startled out of it.

Archer and Perdita were equally as startled.

"We are so sorry!" Isabella cried, and dragged Trevor from the room with as much haste as she could muster while gaping like a madwoman, and shut the door with a thud.

When she heard the intrusion, Perdita's gasp had echoed her sister's and she tried to pull away from Archer. But he'd gripped her tightly and refused to let go. When their audience was gone, he said apologetically, "Sorry, but your gown was half off and I didn't think you wished Ormond to see."

At his explanation her ire cooled. Setting herself to see to the practicalities, she righted her gown as Archer, ever the gentleman, shaded his eyes so that she could do so in some measure of privacy.

When she was done, they both took a moment to get their breath back.

And then, as sometimes happens, they both spoke at once.

"I beg your pardon."

"I cannot believe what just happened!"

They stopped again, suddenly awkward as they studiously avoided one another's gazes.

Archer, his face diplomatically expressionless, waved for Perdita to speak first. She gave him a searching look, but seeing that he gave nothing away, she said, "I am mortified that my sister and Ormond should have walked in on that . . ."

She wasn't quite sure what to call what had just happened between them. Except perhaps a mistake, but even Perdita knew not to say that aloud to a man she'd just kissed like a wanton. When Archer made no attempt to fill in a word for her, she started again. "That is to say, I never expected to be . . ."

How to tell him that the fire between them—which still had parts of her longing to move back into the circle of his arms and pick up where they'd left off—had not only confirmed her fear of getting involved with him, but had been even more overwhelming than she'd feared.

Because what she'd felt in Archer's arms had been more than the infatuation she'd felt for Gervase in the early days of their marriage. Before he became someone to fear. Archer had the potential to break her heart. As well as to make her a slave to her passion. Imagine the aftermath should something go wrong between them. It would be a thousand times more devastating than Gervase. And up till now she'd thought finding out her husband was a monster had been the worst thing that could happen to her.

"I think we can count on them to be discreet," Archer said calmly. "There's no need for you to panic."

There was something about how he said the words that made her wonder how he meant them. "I wasn't going to panic. I trust my sister and Ormond not to spread tales. I was simply . . ."

"Sharing your mortification with me," he said, his handsome face completely devoid of emotion. He ran a hand down his arm and straightened his cuffs. "I understand completely, Your Grace."

Then to her astonishment he returned to the desk and began shuffling through the papers there. Shocked at his coldness, she stalked over to the other side of the chamber and stood across the desk from him. "Archer," she said, looking at the top of his head, his golden hair slightly disarranged, as he leaned over to hastily write a note. "What is the matter?"

Was it her imagination or did his hand tremble just a little when she spoke? It was impossible to tell.

Looking up from his task, Archer said, "I'm not sure what you mean. Let's see." He began ticking off the points on his fingers. "We fought earlier because you resented my interruption yesterday during your ride with Dunthorp. I became angry and kissed you. We were interrupted by your sister and her husband—my employer—then your response to being found kissing me was mortification. Do I have all that right?"

His eyes, which had just minutes earlier been dark with passion, were now cold. She fought the urge to hug herself.

"I suppose, technically, that is correct, but I do think there is a more nuanced way of saying it," she said. Her heart, which had been beating from the excitement of being caught out, now felt as if it were constricting in her chest. "For instance, I wouldn't say that it was being found kissing *you* that was mortifying. I'd have responded in precisely the same fashion if it had been anyone else."

"Dunthorp, perhaps? Perhaps we should send him a note and have him kiss you in the study, as well. I'm sure your sister and Ormond will be more than willing to walk in on the two of you. In fact, I think I will send Dunthorp a note. After all, the man is lucky enough to be the focus of your attention. Why not let him in on the secret?" Archer stood and crossed his arms over his chest, and Perdita couldn't help but remember just how warm and strong it had felt pressed against her own. But that was before something dreadful had happened. Only she wasn't sure what it had been.

"Archer, I don't understand," she said, trying to figure out what had made him so angry. "I've explained to you what I meant. It wasn't intended to be a slur against you or your . . ."—she paused, and felt her face heat—"kisses."

She shifted on her feet, feeling like a green girl in her first season.

For the first time since Isabella and Trevor had left the room, Archer seemed to relax. He looked at her, his gaze intense. Then ran both hands through his hair, clearly exasperated. "I can't keep doing this, Perdita."

He looked tired. And she realized for the first time

that day that he had probably lost sleep last night watching over her. And she'd accused him earlier of intruding on her and Dunthorp. When it had been Archer and not the other man who kept her from getting trampled. Or so her sister and Georgie had told her. She'd been so angry at his high-handedness that she'd lashed out. In a perverse way it had felt good, because she'd never have been able to speak like that to Gervase. He'd have backhanded her.

"Doing what?" she asked in a small voice.

He looked down at the desk, and then back up, his blue eyes intent. "You must have realized by now that I have feelings for you."

Had she? Of course she'd known that he was a good friend. She wasn't sure what she'd have done without him while Gervase was alive. And now, when she was facing almost daily threats from someone who wished her harm, he was the only person she could truly trust to protect her. But surely she hadn't known until today just what it was that he wanted from her. Had she?

"Perdita." He said the word like a prayer. She hadn't noticed that before. What else had she missed? "I have wanted you almost from the moment Ormond—Gervase—introduced you as his blushing bride. And the more I was around you, the more I saw of you, the more I appreciated you. Not just your beauty, but the heart of you." He stepped out from around the desk and stood before her. "I have been head over ears for you for years. So much so that it's become a joke among my friends."

What? She thought back to the worst days of her marriage. To the times when she'd been at her most despondent. Had he loved her all that time? It was impossible. How can it have happened when she was completely and utterly unaware of it?

"I see you are thinking back," he said, his eyes sad. Nothing like she'd expect from a man in love. "It's true enough. I did covet you all that time. If I'd had any clue about how he treated you, I'd have killed him myself."

Gently—oh, so gently—he reached out to touch her on the face. "I knew you were unhappy. Of course I knew that. But when I think of how utterly blind I was to the way he abused you, I cannot help but believe that I don't deserve to have you. Though I am selfish enough to want you all the same."

But that wasn't how she thought of it, at all. He'd been a friend to her when she'd desperately needed one. He'd distracted her when she'd been tempted to bury herself in her unhappiness. She could still remember some of the absurd conversations they'd had when he was at his most entertaining and she was at her most low. She slid her hand up and put it over his where it cupped her cheek. "Please don't blame yourself. Please. I don't think I'd ever have survived if not for you. It isn't your fault that Gervase chose to use his fists on me. And I have no doubt that he'd have had no compunction about killing you if you had by some miracle found out the truth and chosen to step between us."

"You are sweet to say it," he said sadly, "but that regret is something I will have to live with. If I were a better man, I'd have seen to it that he never hit you or anyone else."

He reached up and wiped away a tear from her

cheek, and only then did she realize she was weeping. "What am I going to do with you?" he asked, shaking his head. "You push me away one minute and offer me absolution the next. I know what I want, but you're the one who has been waiting for freedom. Tell me, dearest Perdita, what is it you want from me?"

Seven

It was so tempting, with him standing only inches away from her, to simply fling herself into his arms. Just to avoid the discussion.

She'd spent so much time trying and failing to talk Gervase into some other kind of marriage than they had. But words had been useless when matched against sheer brute force. And it wasn't long into her marriage that she learned to measure each word like a shabby genteel widow measured out her last store of sugar. And it wasn't just the quantity of words. It was which words she chose. But then again, depending on what sort of mood her husband was in, it mattered little which words she chose, because all of them—yes, no, maybe, perhaps, definitely—all of them were wrong.

With Archer, she'd practiced the art of speaking her thoughts again. Nothing too revealing, of course. She wasn't ready for that. But as he let her talk about the little things—how the crocus in the garden reminded her of the flowers in the gardens at Hampton Court Palace; which of Shakespeare's plays she liked most (the comedies); how she disliked the filthy air of London, though she'd been born and raised here. All these little details she shared with him. Without fear that Archer would deride her for her foolish nattering. Or dread that a chance word about the gardener would provoke an attack because her husband was certain she spent too much time with the other man—despite his being happily married and nearly as old as the dowager.

She owed much to Archer and his gentleness. His patience. But it had only been in the last year—when Perdita finally began to feel like a person again—that they had truly become friends. Of course, as before, there wasn't that much time for them to spend together. Even after Gervase died, Archer had continued his work as the personal secretary to the dukedom, and then to Trevor, the new duke who was now married to her sister, Isabella. But they'd managed to maintain their friendship.

Something had changed during their trip to Bath a month or so ago. At first Archer had accompanied her to Bath—as soon as she learned that the coward who had made her sister Isabella's life miserable was now using his power to terrify their friend Georgina, threatening not only her position as lady's companion, but also her very life—and things had been as comfortable between them as ever. But once it became clear that Perdita would be the villain's next target, Archer had overstepped his bounds by demanding that she go into hiding. At least that was how she saw his proposal.

For one who had spent the last five years of her life under her husband's thumb, having yet another man attempt to order her around had been infuriating. Especially because Archer, of all people, should know better. It was not only an annoyance, but a kind of betrayal. Not to mention the fact that she'd grown far too fond of the easy way they had with one another. It would have taken very little for Perdita to allow him to take care of her. As he clearly wished to. But some part of her refused to accept it. To continue her servitude—even if it was to be under the benevolent rule of Archer, her dearest friend.

She'd long thought him to be the handsomest man of her acquaintance, with his delicate features that should have looked silly on a man, but somehow managed to be eminently masculine. As well as his broad shoulders, lean muscles, and shining gold hair. All together, the parts of him added up to a deliciously handsome whole. Made even more impressive by the man inside the beautiful packaging.

All of which was why, when faced with Archer's question of what she wanted from him, she could hardly say. Because if she were absolutely truthful with herself, she would admit that she wanted him—as a woman wants a man—and had done so for some time now. What she didn't want was to embark upon a romance with him that would lead her into the same sort of lopsided marriage as she'd shared with Gervase. In fact, she was quite sure she would rather marry someone for whom she felt none of the desire she felt for Archer. That was what she'd had with Gervase—in the beginning at least, before he turned brutal—and she wasn't sure she trusted desire, or even love anymore.

She thought through each of these things as Archer

waited for her to respond to his question. It was a fair enough inquiry. If their roles were reversed, and he'd carried on a flirtatious friendship with her without ever declaring himself, she'd be within her rights to ask what the next step would be.

"Well?" he prompted, his blue eyes fixed on her face while she tried to decide just how to present her case to him. Because it had occurred to her suddenly that perhaps they could have what they both wanted. It was entirely possible for a widow and an unmarried man to carry on a liaison without raising too many eyebrows in the ton. In fact, as a duchess, even a dowager, she would be forgiven far more than a young widow of good character.

"I think . . ." she began, then simply continued on before doubt could creep in. "I think that I would like for us to be lovers."

Once the words were out of her mouth, she suddenly wished with every fiber of her being that she could recall them. Not because she regretted the sentiment. She actually did want Archer in her bed. In the worst way, she now realized, having admitted it aloud.

No, she wanted to recall the words because she had no idea what his response would be. What if he should rebuff her? Or worse, what if he chastised her? She would die of shame. It was one thing to suffer the cutting remarks of Gervase or even the dowager. She expected it of them. But Archer was special. She'd only ever experienced consideration from him. By suggesting that they cross the line that separated friendship from something so much more, she was allowing herself be to vulnerable in a way that she hadn't since long before her husband had died.

And she wasn't deluded enough to think that they'd be able to go back to their old footing now that this particular cat was out of the bag.

If she'd suggested they strip off all their clothing and dance naked in Hyde Park, the expression on Archer's face could not have been more shocked. Despite her trepidation, Perdita couldn't help but note that his cheekbones and the tips of his ears turned scarlet as he gazed wide-eyed at her. But to her relief, before he hastily looked away, she saw desire in those eyes. He might be shocked, but her invitation was not unwelcome.

At least not to the baser side of him.

She watched as he ran a finger under the cravat that suddenly looked too tight. Then, pulling himself together, he took a step back and surveyed her from head to toe. She'd never seen him look at her like that. If he'd appraised her, and surely he had done so before, she'd not seen it, and it was at once exciting and embarrassing.

When his gaze returned to her face, he tilted his head, watching her. Finally he said, "You want us to become lovers. You'll forgive me if I am somewhat surprised by the suggestion." His mouth quirked up on one side. "I had thought you were determined not to put yourself in the control of another man."

It was a reasonable assertion. Still, she had an answer. "In marriage. And I have a very specific plan where that's concerned."

That surprised him, she could tell. His brow furrowed for the merest hint of time, and then he resumed his controlled expression. "But surely marriage to any man would involve—at least in the eyes of the law—some sort of surrender of power on your part. It's the nature of things."

"But what if I choose not to surrender my affections to the man I marry? What if I ensure that the marriage is little more than a business arrangement? Then I will be free to seek affection elsewhere." She watched him carefully, to see if he understood her. But Archer had always been clever. Of course he understood.

At least she hoped he did.

Because if he didn't, she very much doubted they could ever return to the friendship she'd relied upon these past few years.

And she wasn't sure if she could endure that.

Oh, he understood her well enough, Archer fumed despite the desire that thrummed through him. She wished to take him as a lover, but marry Dunthorp. Or someone equally as biddable.

Which was as foolish a plan as she'd ever proposed.

Not least because Dunthorp wasn't nearly as malleable as Perdita thought him.

Not only would Dunthorp not agree to a marriage in name only with one of the most beautiful women in England, he was a peer. He would want an heir. Surely she didn't think she'd be able to keep them in separate compartments like a man could. Women weren't designed that way. Not to mention the matter of pregnancy. He doubted sincerely that Dunthorp would take kindly to an heir with blond hair and blue eyes.

Of course Archer's body didn't give a damn about

scruples or the possibility of a cuckolded Dunthorp. A certain part of him would like to begin right now.

His hands itched to touch her even as his mind wrestled with the dilemma she'd posed to him.

Then there was the other problem.

Why the hell was he being relegated to the role of mere lover when Dunthorp, or whichever man she chose to marry, was given the proverbial keys to the kingdom? Because no matter how prettily she wrapped this up in a tidy bow, he would be damned if he'd allow her to deny the very real affection between them. And he certainly wouldn't allow her to entangle herself in a loveless marriage simply because Gervase had been a violent, despicable blackguard.

The bastard didn't deserve to have that much power over her. Especially not from the grave.

Aloud, though, he revealed none of this. Instead he asked, "Why me?" And watched as her cheekbones reddened. It seemed they were both at the mercy of their coloring, he thought.

She swallowed, but regained her composure relatively quickly. Looking him directly in the eye she said, "Because I want you. I have for some time. I think we've been dancing around this for some time."

Hearing her say the words was more powerful than he could have expected. And he had to give her credit. It was a brave speech for a woman who hadn't been able to say more than yes or no for months at a time while her husband was alive. Doubly so because she was speaking so boldly about something so intimate.

"But that's not all, I think," he prodded. He wanted the whole reason to be spoken between them. Because he wanted her to admit that there was another difference between him and Dunthorp.

She looked down at her hands, then straightened her back and faced him again. "Because I trust you. There, I've said it. That's what you wished, isn't it?"

"Yes," he said baldly, "it is. Because I think you know that one of the things that will make this work between us is trust. And because I don't agree with you that you must marry someone you don't love because of what Gervase did to you."

Her lips tightened, and she made to turn away from him, saying, "Fine. If you refuse my offer—"

He caught her before she could get far. He turned her face to look at him. "I didn't say I refused your offer," he said mildly, though they were both slightly out of breath. "I accept. But I want you to know that I will not concede the field this easily. You may do what you wish to convince Dunthorp to propose, but I will do whatever it takes to convince you that the only man you should marry is me."

Her gaze was steely, but she nodded. "Fine. But you cannot do anything to threaten or frighten away the men I am considering for a husband."

Archer started to argue that he wasn't the one who was a bully, but decided to simply concede the point. He hadn't planned on using force to make them go away in any event. "And you must agree to listen to me when it comes to your safety."

"That's not fair," she said firmly. "I will continue to make my own decisions about how to handle the matter, but I will agree to keep you informed of my plans. And in return, I wish to be there when you speak to the man from the magistrate's office."

Since the man would likely ask to speak to her anyway, Archer nodded. "Anything else?"

He felt the air change between them, now that their most contentious issues had been settled. And he couldn't help but notice that her eyes had strayed to his mouth more than once. If it was more kisses she wanted, he was more than happy to oblige her. But they should make plans to make that happen. "Shall I come to your bedchamber tonight?"

"So soon?"

It was not hard to see that she had been expecting a few more days in which to think about things. Which was why he had pressed the issue. If it was to be a competition between them, then he'd like to begin as soon as possible so that she'd have the memory of him in her bed fresh in her mind when she began her husband hunting. Still, he did have other reasons for haste. "I've waited a long time," he said with a raised brow. "If your admission earlier is any indication, so have you."

He took her hand and rubbed his thumb over her palm, then leaned in to kiss her softly on the mouth. It was a kiss of comfort, as unlike their earlier embrace as night from day. But there was promise in it, too. "Remember," he said. "You trust me." He whispered against her ear, "I won't forget that."

Before he could anticipate things by doing what he really wished to do and seducing her on the study's leather sofa, he let go of her and walked from the room, grateful that no one was lingering in the hall to see the cockstand his coat didn't quite disguise.

Eight

$\mathcal{P}$erdita waited a long while to make sure Archer was no longer in the hall beyond the study to slip from the room and hurry to her suite of rooms. Once she'd closed the door behind her, she leaned back against it and exhaled the breath she'd been holding ever since he left her.

"What on earth have I done?" she wailed, bumping the back of her head against the door a couple of times as if to shake the memory of the last hour from her head.

"I don't know," came her sister's voice from Perdita's bedchamber. "What have you done?"

With a sigh, she crossed the lush carpet of the chambers she'd chosen after her sister became the new Duchess of Ormond. It was every bit as luxurious as the mistress's rooms. At least Perdita thought so. It also came with the added bonus of possessing very sturdy locks and no threat of being invaded by Gervase in one of his moods, since he'd been dead for months since she'd moved into them.

The locks did not, however, protect against invasions by her sister, whom she found curled up on the chaise in Perdita's bedchamber reading a novel with a box of chocolates on her baby bump.

"What are you doing in here? I thought your own rooms would be adequate to your needs." Then realizing how pettish she sounded, she added, "Not that you aren't welcome, of course."

Isabella popped a chocolate into her mouth and chewed it before she spoke. "My own rooms are perfect, thank you," she said. "But they do not allow me to question my darling sister about the very warm embrace Trevor and I walked in on earlier. I must say, I thought Archer would never make his move. But I am so pleased he's done so at last!" She rolled into a sitting position, rather deftly despite her unwieldy body. "You must tell me everything!"

"There's nothing to tell," Perdita said calmly, moving to her writing desk to pretend to look very carefully at some receipts from the modiste she found there. "I'm afraid that I became overset about what happened yesterday and he was simply comforting me."

"With his tongue?" Isabella asked sweetly. "I don't believe that's called comforting, sister. In fact, that's just how Trevor was 'comforting' me when this happened." She gestured to her belly.

"Don't be absurd," Perdita said with a blush. "He wasn't . . . that is to say, there were no tongues involved."

"That's not what we saw," Isabella chided in a singsong voice. Then realizing that Perdita wasn't smiling, she said, "Dearest, there's nothing wrong with kissing a handsome man. Especially when both the gentleman and the lady are not involved with anyone else. There's nothing wrong with it at all."

"Well, that's not what was going on," Perdita said tightly, "so I wish you wouldn't mention it again."

Isabella, her eyes so much like her own, frowned. "He did offer for you, didn't he? Because I don't know if I've ever seen a man so besotted as Lord Archer Lisle has been with you. Never say you turned the poor man down! Perdy! What have you done?"

It was just the sort of scold that her sister had given her when they were children. The right of every elder sister in the world, she supposed, but Perdita was in no mood for it. "No, he did not offer for me, Isabella. Now please leave it be."

"No, I will not leave it be." Isabella rose from the settee and crossed the room to stand before Perdita's writing desk where she continued to look down. "Perdita, you have a right to happiness. You know that I, of all people, know that. I cannot tell you how reluctant I was to start any sort of relationship with Trevor. Even friendship, for mercy's sake. Because I did not trust him. Or any gentleman. But there is a difference between men like Trevor and Archer and even Con, and men like our first husbands. I know it seems impossible to believe that any man can be trusted after the hell Gervase put you through, but if ever a man was to be trusted, it is Archer."

"It's not what you think, Isabella," she said, lifting her face to look, really look at her sister. To see the glow of impending motherhood that made it almost impossible not to break into a grin. She never would have guessed back when Isabella was at Wharton's mercy that she'd one day be so blissfully happy. And certainly not with any Duke of Ormond. Much less the one who succeeded her own violent husband. "I know what you are saying. Believe me, I do. But I am not as . . ."—she paused, searching for the right word to describe her sister now—"resilient as you are. I don't know that I will ever be completely trusting of a man again."

"But you do trust Archer," Isabella argued. "I know you do. Else you'd not allow him within an inch of you."

Perdita closed her eyes, remembering his expression when she'd told him her plan to keep a husband in a marriage of convenience, and a lover to fulfill her emotionally, sexually. He'd been as angry as she'd ever seen him. And yet, he hadn't lashed out at her. Hadn't flayed her with words or struck out at her physically, either. He'd talked to her about it. As he had always done when there was something they disagreed about. But even Archer hadn't been able to persuade her of the folly of her plan. He might have vowed to convince her of its recklessness, but she knew how to remain resolute when she needed to be.

Besides, the gentlemen of the ton had practiced the same sort of compartmentalization for years. A wife at home to serve as his hostess and bear his children, and a mistress set up in a little house where he would lavish gifts upon her in exchange for her never refusing him in her bed. Why shouldn't it work if a lady were to try it? Of course, the husband and the lover would need to agree to the plan. Or, as most husbands did, she simply wouldn't tell them. Though she supposed that she'd already told Archer. But she suspected she'd be more than able to convince him to keep the matter between them. And she would enjoy the convincing. She hadn't lied when she'd told him that she wanted him. He was a handsome man, and the fact that he wanted her, too, made him even more seductive. He might not be pleased with the terms of her offer, but he seemed more than willing to accept them. A desire she was incredibly grateful for.

"Are you even listening?" Isabella asked, crossing her arms over her belly. "Because as soon as I mentioned him in proximity to you, it seems as if you disappeared into another world."

This was far more than she'd wished to reveal about her discussion with Archer, Perdita realized, but she knew that her sister wouldn't leave her be until she confirmed some of her suspicions. "Fine, yes. I do trust him. And we are going to become lovers."

For the second time that day Perdita was faced with a completely dumbfounded conversational partner. It was becoming tiresome.

"You're going to become lovers?" her sister demanded. "Just like that? No proposal? No promises between you?"

Perdita shrugged. "I trust him. You were right. And I am not quite ready to remarry just yet." She forbore from telling her about the marriage plans. Because she knew that Isabella would never understand. Especially since Perdita herself wasn't even sure she understood. And it was only a castle in the air at this point. Perhaps she'd change her mind about marrying Archer. She didn't think it would happen, but she was honest enough to admit that this was all unknown territory for her.

Isabella studied her face in silence, then, apparently satisfied with whatever she saw there, she grinned. "Lovers, eh? I rather wish I'd tried that with Trevor before we were compromised into marrying."

"So, you don't disapprove?" Perdita asked, not letting on how much her sister's response mattered to her.

"I think I do not, dearest," Isabella said, slipping an arm around Perdita as she stepped out from behind the writing desk. "I couldn't have chosen a better man for you to become involved with. And you know how much I like and respect him. Plus, I think he understands—in a way that many other men simply would not—how difficult it will be for you to let another man touch you in that way. He saw what Gervase did to you. And I think he even blames himself a little. But I also think he appreciates the woman you've become. He doesn't put you up on some pedestal of martyrdom. He is your friend first, and that makes a difference. I think you'll be in good hands, though God knows you were hardly waiting to hear that."

"You'd be surprised," Perdita said, leaning her head on her sister's shoulder. "I think you'd be pleasantly surprised."

Once Archer calmed down, he went in search of Ormond and Coniston. There were a few hours yet before the man from the magistrate's office was expected, and he was in no mood to look at parliamentary business. Besides, Ormond had decided to set his own mark on the dukedom, part of which meant that his involvement with political matters would be restricted to those issues that he found important. Not what the dukedom had historically chosen to be involved in, but what he, Trevor, wished to put the power of the duchy behind. As a result, there was far less for Archer to do as the duke's personal secretary these days. Enough that he'd been giving serious consideration to leaving his post. That had, of course, been before Perdita's attacker had begun to make himself known. He would not leave his position while she was still in danger, and he hoped like the devil that Trevor didn't choose to dismiss him before that.

He found the other men in the billiards room, about to begin a new game.

"Ah, Archer," Con said, the cigar he'd been divested of yesterday once more in his fingers, though this time it was lit. "Come join us, for I fear Ormond offers very little challenge. Comes from growing up with sisters, I suppose. He is likely much more adept at needlework."

Trevor, who was chalking the end of his stick, rolled his eyes. "Not because of the sisters, Coniston," he corrected, "but because I was actually engaging in work on the estates. Something you are not very familiar with, seeing as how you spent your salad days daubing at stretched sheepskin with paints instead of producing something useful to the rest of society."

"Dear God," Con said, grinning at Ormond's obvious annoyance. "If I am forced to listen to yet another tale of your days in the Yorkshire countryside consorting with sheep, old man, I'm afraid I'll be forced to tell your wife."

"You must have me confused with some handsy Scotsman, my lord," Ormond said, leaning over the table to take his shot, winking at Archer while he did so. "I am from Yorkshire, man, but it is still in England by gad!"

As he let the other men's insults wash over him, Archer felt himself grow calmer. Certainly more settled than he'd felt in the study with Perdita. That had been one of the most important conversations of his life, though he'd had no idea it would become so at the time. He'd gone in intending to work, and left with the knowledge that tonight, once the rest of the household had taken to their beds, he'd be taking Perdita into his. Or should he go to hers? They hadn't really discussed the logistics, he supposed. Though at the time he'd have agreed to have her in a rowboat on the Serpentine in Hyde Park with a full orchestra playing on the shore. So long as he could get his hands on her lovely curves.

Somehow, Archer doubted Perdita would feel quite the same way.

"So, tell me about this big to-do in the study earlier," Con said from where he surveyed the table. It looked to Archer as if his words had not been without truth behind them. He was a very good billiards player if the arrangement of the balls on the baize cloth was anything to go by. Still, Con's words brought a curse to his lips.

"Don't blame me," Trevor said, putting his hands up in surrender. "I didn't tell him."

Archer sighed. Which meant that it had probably been Isabella, who told Georgina, who was unable to keep anything from her husband and told Con. "This is worse than the ladies' sewing circle," he said with disgust.

"Actually, they are much worse," Trevor corrected,

frowning as he looked at Con's shot ruin any chance he had of winning. "Ladies' sewing circles, I mean. There's one in our village in Yorkshire. If they were the ones who spread this tale the entire household would have known before Isabella and I had even left the study. They have mysterious ways."

"No one cares about your provincial needleworking ways, Ormond," Con said dismissively. "I want to know what happened in the bloody study. Because for all that you think my wife tells me everything, you are dead wrong. She only told me that Isabella saw something 'shocking in the study.'"

"Better than 'something nasty in the woodshed,'" Trevor said with raised brows. "Not good, that. Not good at all."

Archer, despite his annoyance with the fact that they knew anything at all about what had happened between him and Perdita, couldn't help but laugh. "You do realize that the two of you bicker like an old married couple. I shouldn't be surprised if there is talk."

"Nice try, old fellow," Con said, dropping into a chair in the corner to enjoy his cigar now that it was clear he'd won the game. "You might try to change the subject, but it won't work. I want to know what happened. And if you don't care to tell, then make something up."

Though he considered the out the other man offered, Archer decided he might as well spill the beans. Mostly because although Georgina hadn't told Con yet, he would needle her until she had no choice but to tell him. He could be relentless like that. "Very well," he said, dropping into the chair opposite Con's. "The duke and duchess walked in on me, ah, comforting Perdita in the study."

"Comforting, is it?" Con asked slyly. "Was it 'full comforting' or maybe just a bit of 'light comforting'? Inquiring minds want to know!"

"I want to know," Trevor chimed in.

"You were there this morning," Archer protested. "Unless you've got something wrong with your eyesight, you cannot have missed it."

Ormond shrugged. "I was looking at Isabella's bosom. It's very impressive right now." He raised a finger. "Not that I wish either of you to comment upon it because I'll be forced to throw you in the dungeon."

"There is no dungeon in this house," Archer said automatically. As the duke's personal secretary, he'd know about such things.

"Keep your smarmy bosom-watching to yourself, Ormond," Con said, looking very pointedly at Archer. "Now, I believe there is another question on the floor. Full or light, Lord Archer? It will have an effect on your final score."

"You're a lunatic, you know this, right?"

"As my wife likes to inform me at least once a day. Now tell."

"Fine," Archer said, taking the glass of brandy that Ormond offered him. "Light. It was really just a kiss. And perhaps my hand was somewhere that would not be appropriate were we in a public place."

"Excellent," Con said, clinking his glass with Archer's. "I have a great deal of fondness for those days."

"What days?"

Coniston stretched his legs out before him and crossed them at the ankles. "Before you're quite involved. The exploratory stage, I suppose you'd call it."

Since that was a fairly accurate description of where he and Perdita were—now, but hopefully not five hours from now—Archer didn't argue.

"So, have you talked marriage yet?"

"Con, don't be such a damned busybody," Ormond said with a frown. "It's none of our business."

Surprised to have such faith from Ormond, who by rights should be threatening to blacken his lights and give him a hearty punch in the breadbasket, Archer smiled. "Thank you, Your Grace."

"She's my sister-in-law, Archer," Ormond said with a glare. "You'd better have marriage in mind. Else we will have to do some serious 'talking.'"

God, that's just what he needed. The Duke of Ormond out for his blood. Which of course meant the duchess as well. Frankly he was more frightened of Isabella than her husband. "Of course I mean to marry her. What do you take me for?"

"That's more like it," Ormond said, nodding as if Archer had said just the right thing. "I suppose she'll wish to wait until after the babe is born so that Isabella will be able to stand up with her."

Since Archer wasn't sure if she had given the matter any thought, seeing as how she expected to marry someone else entirely, Archer simply gave one nod. It was not an agreement so much as a "good idea." At least that's what he told himself.

"That will be a long wait," Con said with a raised brow. "Will you be able to endure it?"

"I'm not an animal," Archer said resentfully, though

why he was so annoyed considering that he planned to consummate the relationship later tonight, he couldn't say. It was Coniston's implication he supposed. "I've waited this long. Surely I'll be able to wait a few months more."

"That's what you think," Ormond said. "But once you're betrothed, things change."

"Yes, they do," Coniston said, taking a drink of his brandy. "I don't know what it is precisely but something about knowing you'll be married in the not too distant future makes the temptation that much stronger."

Archer hadn't considered that. Though, again, he had no need to worry about it. Bed. Tonight. Perdita. Hours from now.

"I thought the blasted carriage ride from Yorkshire to Gretna would never bloody end," Ormond said morosely. "It was as if Scotland moved north without telling us."

"Well," Archer said, reminding himself of tonight. With Perdita. In bed. A bed. His bed. Her bed. He didn't really care. "I am sorry you both had such a difficult time of it. But, we are not yet betrothed, so there is no need for worry."

"If you say so," Con said, sitting back in his char. Watching.

"You know best, of course," Ormond agreed, leaning against the billiards table. "Don't let us worry you."

Archer rose. He'd had enough of this, thank you very much. "I've just remembered I need to do something. In another room."

Without waiting for them to say anything, he strode out. Not sure what had just happened.

* * *

"You don't think we frightened him, do you?" Con asked Ormond, who had just dropped into Archer's vacated chair.

"Certainly not," Ormond said, accepting a cigar from the other man. He clipped the end, then allowed Con to light it. Taking a drag, he leaned back. "He'll find out soon enough, anyway."

"Damn right he will," Con said, blowing a cloud of smoke. "Poor bastard."

Nine

Perdita, her sister, and Georgina were taking tea in her private sitting room some time later, when a brisk knock on the outer door was followed by Archer showing a somewhat disheveled man in.

"Ladies," he said, bowing to them. "This is Mr. Josiah Reddington from the London magistrate's office." He looked pointedly at Perdita. "You said that you wished to speak to him when he arrived, Your Grace. Is that still the case?"

Since this was the first time she'd seen Archer since their earlier encounter—the one with kissing and whatnot—she found herself fighting a blush. Hopefully the others would take it for nervousness. "Yes, of course. Thank you, Lord Archer, for remembering."

She turned to her companions, who were watching the exchange avidly. And despite the seriousness of the meeting with the investigator, she knew their interest had nothing to do with him. "Your Grace, my lady," she said, hoping to sound more authoritative than she felt, "I beg you to excuse us while I speak to the investigator."

Perhaps seeing that Perdita was a bit overset by the situation, Isabella and Georgina rose immediately, each squeezing her shoulder in comfort before they left the room.

She turned to the two men and gestured for them to take seats around the tea table. Needing the ritual, she rang for more cups—which arrived in due haste thanks to the kitchen staff's curiosity about the investigator, no doubt—and began to pour for them. "Mr. Reddington," she said to the ginger-haired man, "I appreciate your taking time to speak to me about the incident in the park."

"With all due respect, Your Grace," the investigator said with a frown, "when duchesses are bein' chased down in the park by men in disguise, the magistrate's office takes things very seriously. It just ain't done."

She took in the way his bushy brows moved as he spoke and saw that he was indeed unsettled by it. "All the same, I do appreciate your being here. Now, what may I do to help you in your search for my attacker?"

Perdita didn't look at Archer, who was seated next to her, but she could feel the tension coming off him in waves. He was just as unhappy about this situation as she was.

"Your Grace," Reddington said, holding the dainty china teacup in his large hands. "What I'd like first is for you to tell me everything whot happened when you got to the park. Any little detail might help."

"That's just it, I'm afraid," she said with an apologetic frown. "I don't recall anything that happened from a few minutes before we left Ormond House until waking up in my bedchamber hours later. The entire trip to the park is a blank. I have tried to remember, of course, but nothing seems to help."

If she expected him to be disappointed, she was clearly wrong, however. "Aye," he said, nodding to her, his brows bouncing as he did so. "Lord Archer told me that were the case. I just needed to hear it from the 'orse's mouth." Perhaps realizing that he ought not refer to a peeress of the realm as a horse, he winced, and added, "Not that Your Grace is anywise like an 'orse, o'course."

"I should think not," Perdita said with a smile. The light moment was much needed given the seriousness of the situation. Of which she was reminded at his next words.

"I've spoken to Lord Archer and I'm to speak with Lord Dunthorp later about the events o' that day, but what I need to hear from you is why you think this stranger is tryin' to 'arm you. Most men know well enough the consequences should they do any kind of damage to a member of the aristocracy, but this fella don't seem to care. He must have a real good reason to risk 'is neck like that."

Before she could respond, he continued, his eyes still kind but expressing something else. A statement that she didn't much care for. "Seems to me that your family has suffered a great deal of harm in recent years."

All traces of amusement left her. "I'm not sure I know what you mean, sir."

Turning his teacup around and around in his hands, the investigator's eyes never left her. "Well, it's not many a young man like your late husband that dies so young."

Perdita froze. She had suspected this was where he was headed, but hearing the words sent a jolt of fear through her the likes of which she'd not experienced since Gervase died. Still, she managed to maintain her composure. Taking a sip of tea, she then lowered it to the saucer in her hand. "I fear it was an accident while he was cleaning his gun, Mr. Reddington. Things like that happen in even the noblest of households, I'm afraid."

She resisted the urge to turn to Archer for support, but couldn't help but feel his reassuring presence beside her.

"Aye," Reddington said slowly. "It does happen from time to time. It's just there was a rumor at the time that everything wasn't as it seemed with that 'accident,' if ye know what I mean."

"Is there a question for the lady there, Reddington?" Archer asked amiably. "For I can assure you that she is more than willing to answer them. But I don't quite see the connection between His Grace and what happened to the duchess yesterday."

But whatever he'd been searching for with his questions seemed to have been answered, for Reddington nodded, saying, "If you want my 'onest opinion, my lord, I don't think one has anything to do with the other. But an investigator must cover every possible line of enquiry."

The knot in Perdita's stomach loosened a bit and she was able to breathe again. "As far as I know, Mr. Reddington, I don't have any enemies. At least none that I am acquainted with. There was talk when my husband died, suggestions that he took his own life or perhaps that my sister and I had done it so that she could then seduce and marry the heir to the dukedom. But that was ludicrous of course. She had never even met the current duke then. Though they are married now."

"You'd be surprised just what sorts of things folk will come up with to explain deaths, Your Grace," Reddington assured her. "But right now, concentrating on your attack, I've taken as much information as I can from you. If you find you've recalled something about that day, no matter how small, I should like for you to contact me." He handed her a calling card with the address of the magistrate's office on it.

He rose, and Perdita and Archer did so as well.

As he neared the door, Perdita said, "Oh, Mr. Reddington, if at all possible, I do wish that you would try to keep the news of my attack out of the papers. I shouldn't wish for something like this to become public knowledge."

At that, the man turned back again, and exchanged a speaking glance with Archer. At the other man's nod, he said, "Your Grace, I'm afraid that won't be possible."

Unused to having her requests refused, she frowned. "Why not? There's no reason to even speak of it when we have no information on who the man was anyway."

"You misunderstand me, Your Grace. It's not that I'm unwilling to keep the attack quiet. It's that the papers have already got hold of the story. It was on the front page of the *Times* this morning."

Perdita's mouth dropped open. "No! Why haven't I heard anything about it? I should think we'd be pestered with journalists at every turn."

"As to that," Reddington said with a shrug, "I cannot tell you."

Taking his leave of her, he saw himself out.

Archer, who had been standing just behind her, spoke first. "Before you rip up at me," he said, "I did not keep the papers from you. As it happens, since the duke is in residence they were taken to him in his study."

She turned to look at him, gauging his sincerity. Which seemed honest enough. "And the journalists?"

"The staff has been told not to disturb you. And all journalists have been refused entry."

"Thank goodness for that," she said with relief. "I should have run mad. They are persistent."

"You aren't angry?" he asked warily. He looked at her as if she were a snake about to strike.

"Should I be?" she asked, wondering what was bothering him.

He thrust a hand through his carefully coiffed hair. "Not angry, I suppose," he said, "but you were quite upset this morning at the news I'd called for the magistrate's man. I assumed that you would be equally annoyed that decisions had been made about who got to see you."

She must have really been awful this morning, Perdita reflected. She walked closer to him, until they were almost chest to chest. Looking up at him, she said, "I have no problem with your saving me from distress while I was unwell. And I certainly—as you know—have no interest in speaking to journalists about an event I cannot even remember." She leaned up on her tiptoes and kissed him lightly on the mouth, but slipped away when he tried to pull her closer. "Ah, ah, ah. No more until tonight"

Now a few feet away, Perdita grinned at him.

"You're trying to kill me, aren't you?" he asked, with a mock frown.

"Not yet, if you please," she said with asperity. "At least not until I've had my wicked way with you."

"Have you noticed that this entire relationship is upside down?" He arched one blond brow. "I am the one who should be having my wicked way with you."

"Only if I were some naïve innocent," she said with pursed lips. "Which I most certainly am not."

He took a step closer. "Nor, madam," he said with a bit of a growl, "am I."

Oh, she liked this possessive Archer. Despite her fear of marrying again, she could not deny that some part of her enjoyed the idea of being possessed by him. Perhaps because she knew that he would let her go if she wished.

Dancing back a few steps, she held out a restraining arm. "I never said you were, sirrah. In fact, I'm counting on it."

At her words, she saw his eyes darken. This was fun.

And dangerous.

"Now, be off with you," she said. "I must decide what to wear this evening."

He frowned. "For dinner?"

"You've forgotten, haven't you?"

At his nod, she said, "I am promised to the Elphinstone rout. And so are you, I daresay."

"Ugh," he said, not bothering to hide his disgust.

"I forgot. I don't suppose you will agree to stay in and rest your poor head?"

"Of course I won't," she said. "Our guests wish to go, too. And I should like to see what those in attendance have to say about my attack."

"Surely they will offer some sympathy and be done with it?"

She shook her head. "I cannot help but feel that our villain will wish to see the results of his handiwork. If not bruises, then fear."

"You think he'll be there?" Archer asked, his gaze intent.

"I cannot know," she said. "But I'm curious. Very, very curious."

The Elphinstone rout was, by anyone's estimation, a crush.

Archer had hoped he would be able to use the occasion to gauge reaction from those in attendance to Perdita's attack in the park, but there were so many people crammed into the rooms of the Elphinstone town house that it was difficult to gauge where he would take his next step, much less look about him as he walked.

"I've never understood the entertainment value in packing as many people as one can into airless rooms," Con muttered from behind him. The Duke of Ormond had taken one step into the entrance hall and turned right back around, Isabella in tow, and left. Archer didn't blame him. It was enough to make him want to swoon, so he had no surprise that the other man would wish to keep his pregnant wife away.

"Surely there are some less crowded rooms the farther back we go," Perdita said from beside him. "I think I recall there is a parlor to the right with French doors."

He allowed her to leave, and watched as the crowd seemed to separate a bit as they realized it was she who wished to get by. More than one lady stopped fanning herself to whisper behind the accessory to a companion. No one offered her a greeting, though Archer wasn't sure if that was because of Perdita's notoriety or simply the heat. They finally reached the parlor she'd spoken of to find that it was indeed cooler than the entrance rooms had been, and some clever soul had opened the doors leading into the garden. The fresh air was a welcome relief.

"I was afraid we'd spend the entire evening trapped in that heat," Georgina said with relief. "Thank goodness you knew to keep going, Perdita."

"I've been to one of the Elphinstones' routs before," Perdita responded. "For some reason people seem to go only so far and then stop. It's quite odd, really."

"Now that you two are settled," Archer said, "Con and I will go in search of refreshments. This room is cooler, but I should like a drink for my trouble. And I do not mean to settle for that insipid lemonade Lady Elphinstone tries to pass off as punch."

"Excellent notion, that," Con said with a nod. "Lead the way."

When the two had left the room, Georgina pulled Perdita toward a small settee near the open doors. Both ladies sat and appreciated the fresh air for a bit before Georgie spoke. "I don't suppose you'd like to tell me about what happened earlier today." She kept her voice low so that they'd not be overheard by the others in the room. Which was unlikely since there were still a lot of people there, just not as many as in the rooms closer to the entrance hall.

Perdita had been hoping that her explanations for what happened that morning in the study were over. But she shrugged and said, "Not really. I've already been interrogated about it by Isabella. Can you not ask her?"

"I did," Georgie said with a frown. "But she said that only you and Archer were there."

Something about the way Georgie said the words made Perdita pause. "Wait. What are you talking about?"

"The meeting with the man from the magistrate's office," Georgie said. "You didn't think I'd be so forward as to ask what happened in the study, surely? Con would probably do so, but I think some things should be kept private."

Perdita hugged her. "Have I told you lately how much I adore you?"

Georgie grinned. "Not nearly enough."

A disturbance near the pocket doors leading into the parlor interrupted them.

"The Duchess of Ormond," a well-dressed gentleman slurred as he pushed forward toward them. "As I live and breathe."

Perdita recognized him at once. Lord Vyse, one of her late husband's boon companions. Up to any sort of vice, Vyse had been by Gervase's side for his most debauched entertainments. From whorehouses to gambling hells, nothing was too unsavory for them.

He had not been a favorite of Perdita's, though he had enjoyed casting lascivious looks her way when her husband wasn't looking. She'd never told Gervase, unsure whether he'd have become angry at Vyse, or as she suspected, turned his anger against her.

"It is the dowager Duchess of Ormond, Lord Vyse," she said calmly, "as I believe you know."

His cruelly handsome face darkened. "Yes, I do know, Your Grace." He made the courtesy sound like an insult. "It is hard to forget that one's dear friend is dead. I wonder that you even remember he existed, madam, for all the mourning you've done."

"It has been over a year, my lord," she said, wishing she could think of something that would make him leave her be. Unfortunately, they'd attracted the notice of everyone in the room, and guests from the rest of the house began to slip in, as if in hopes of a brawl. "I have mourned my husband as decreed by society, I think."

"Oh, listen to her," Vyse said to the room in general. "As if she's been weeping over poor Ormond this past year and more. It's enough to turn my stomach."

"I should think that's just the overabundance of alcohol you've put in it," Georgie said coolly. She took her friend's hand and Perdita nearly wept with gratitude. "Perhaps you should go home and let the spirits wear off, my lord."

"Who asked you, you nosy bi—" Vyse swayed on his feet a bit, but managed to stabilize himself by grabbing hold of the mantel. It was impossible not to notice the enormous signet ring he wore on the hand that clutched the ornate stone fireplace. Vyse had always been rather vain about his lineage, which he claimed connected him to kings on both sides of the Channel.

"That happens to be my lady wife, Vyse," came Con's silky tones from the entrance to the room. "I suggest, although I know it will be difficult, you reconsider finishing that word, else I shall have to call you out. And to be honest, I would rather not spend the wee hours of the morning putting a bullet in you. Much nicer places to be at that hour, don't you think?"

It was indeed a difficult matter for the drunk man to take in what Con was saying, but since he was incapable of maintaining more than one thought at a time just now, he simply shifted his attention to Con. As if he hadn't just threatened to shoot him. "Con'ston. You knew Ormond, di'nt you? Bet you think she did it, too, don' you?"

But Archer, who had been waiting beside Coniston, taking in the scene, stepped forward. "I believe you'd best stop this line of conversation, else you'll be facing more challenges."

Vyse tried to focus. "Who're you?"

Archer bowed, not nearly as low as the other man's rank demanded, but Vyse was too far gone to notice social niceties. "I am Lord Archer Lisle, and I was acquainted with the late Duke of Ormond. I should like it if you refrained from discussing him any further."

Like a small child denied a treat, Vyse stamped his foot. "No I won't. He's dead and it's all her fault."

"Surely you can't think that she shot him herself?" Archer asked icily. Perdita was shocked at how close to the truth he'd come, and for a moment, she feared that the others in the room would all shout out that yes, they did believe she'd shot him.

But the ploy worked just as Archer must have planned, for the room at large gasped, and she could hear a few of the ladies murmur, "Surely not!"

"No," Vyse protested. "Not . . ." His brows knitted together. He was clearly having difficulty thinking. About anything.

Before Vyse could continue, or Archer could attempt once more to make him stop talking or leave, another voice sounded from the doorway, and to Perdita's extreme discomfort Lord Dunthorp elbowed his way past the onlookers. "My dear duchess," he exclaimed, so loudly that Perdita suspected they'd heard him on the front steps of the house. "Pray tell me you are unharmed by this ruffian! First the attack yesterday in the park and now this! It's not to be borne." He knelt before her and took both her hands in his own.

Perdita kept from snatching them away by sheer dint of will. But every fiber of her being wanted Dunthorp to get away from her. Now.

At the mention of the attack in the park, the room erupted with conversation as everyone who had been too well bred to ask about what they'd all devoured in this morning's papers took the opportunity afforded them by Dunthorp to have their curiosity satisfied.

Vyse, no longer the center of attention, and likely overcome by drink, slumped against the wall, and was escorted from the room by two other gentlemen who were either friends of his, or saw his removal as a good deed.

"You must have been terrified," Lady Gowan said from the French doors.

"Have they caught the ruffian yet?" Lord Goodnight demanded, his walruslike mustache communicating his worry.

"Could it have been the ghost of your husband?" whispered old Lady Moreton, who was known to hold séances fortnightly. "If it was a violent death his spirit could be unsettled."

When Archer stopped just behind where Dunthorp knelt clasping her hands, Perdita nearly wept with relief. Perhaps she would have to rethink the idea of marrying Dunthorp, she thought, wishing he would back up. He'd clearly had onions for supper and the smell was making her nauseous.

"I beg your pardon, my lord," Archer said in that tone Perdita knew meant he was not to be gainsaid. "But I think it would be best for Her Grace to leave." When Dunthorp made no move to get out of the way, Archer added, "Sooner rather than later."

Still the other man ignored him, saying to Perdita, "I knew something like this would happen as soon as I learned you were coming tonight."

"How could you possibly have known?" Perdita asked, wondering if she'd mentioned it in conversation sometime earlier in the week.

"I called at your house this evening shortly before the dinner hour," he said calmly. He'd been trying to wangle a dinner invitation, she thought with annoyance. "As I was concerned about your health after yesterday's—"

Perdita cut him off, "My lord, as you can see, I am well. And I agree with Lord Archer that we should leave now. I no longer wish to be here and endure being the center of attention."

"Of course we must leave," Dunthorp said indulgently. "If Lord Archer would just have my coach pulled around, we can be gone at once."

Behind him, Archer raised a brow and Perdita returned the look with widened eyes. Clearly Dunthorp was ascribing more importance to their relationship than she was. "Lord Dunthorp," she said firmly, "I should like to return home with my own party. Thank you all the same."

But to her surprise, Dunthorp would not take no for an answer. She could see that Archer was losing patience, but thankfully, Con stepped forward and addressed the kneeling man. "Dunthorp, old fellow. I should like to talk to you about putting in some protection measures at Ormond House. The duke has asked me to do so and I thought since you are clearly concerned about Her Grace's safety, you might wish to discuss it with me."

Clearly liking this line of thought, Dunthorp rose. "Of course. An excellent notion." Turning to Perdita, he said, "I will exchange a few words with Lord Coniston before we go. I won't be but a few minutes."

When he turned he saw Archer was still standing there, and his brow furrowed. "I thought I asked you to have my carriage brought round."

Archer didn't blink. "I'm afraid you've confused me with one of the servants, Dunthorp. I am the son of a duke. A younger son to be sure, but fetching carriages is not something I do. Especially when it goes against the wishes of a lady."

Dunthorp stood up straighter, though he was still half a head shorter than Archer. Perdita rather thought Archer made Dunthorp look much worse by comparison. "Now see here," he began, before Con slipped an arm around his shoulders and led him away. Perdita could hear him saying, "Now, personally, I think armed guards are the way to go, but Ormond disagrees. Where do you stand on the issue?"

To Perdita's relief, Dunthorp forgot his annoyance with Archer in the onslaught of pride brought on by Con's trust.

"You've got a problem there," Georgina said from beside her. "I thought I was going to have to use my pistol."

"Good God," Archer said, gaping. "You carry it with you to routs?"

"One never knows when someone will need to be shot," Georgie said with a shrug. "I think I'll go see where Con took Lord Dumbthorp."

Perdita giggled at the wordplay, and then saw that she was about to be accosted by a very large lady whose avid expression marked her as someone who wished to discuss something with her that she'd find unpleasant. Perdita wasn't sure what, but she didn't want to find out. "Get me out of this place," she told Archer, who took her arm and protected her from all importunity as they made their way to retrieve their cloaks and wait for the carriage.

Ten

The ride back to Ormond House was blessedly swift, despite the number of other vehicles making their exodus from Elphinstone House.

Everyone headed up to bed, and though he'd exchanged a look with Perdita, he wasn't quite sure whether what they'd planned earlier in the day was still on after what had happened at the Elphinstones'.

Still, when he knocked on her bedchamber door once everyone at Ormond House was abed, Perdita opened it almost before his knuckles hit the wood.

"Hurry," she whispered, shooing him in. "You weren't seen, were you?"

"Not that I'm aware of," he responded, as she shut the door behind him. He turned to look at her—really look—and he caught his breath as he saw how beautiful she was. She'd donned a nearly transparent gown that left very little to the imagination when it came to her lithe curves. He could see the shadow of her nipples through the thin fabric as well as the hint of triangle at the juncture of her thighs.

It was the most sensual garment he'd ever laid eyes on.

Seeing the direction of his gaze, Perdita crossed her arms over her chest. "I'm sorry about the gown. I've never engaged in an affair before. I wanted to be alluring for you. Though I'm not sure alluring is something I can do."

"There is absolutely nothing wrong with your gown," Archer said, hoping his eyes conveyed that as well as his words. "I've never seen a more beautiful sight than you in that gown, Perdita. In fact, I think I should like to have a painting of it to keep in my bedchamber."

"Really?" The words came out in a whisper as he crossed to stand before her. "I thought it was perhaps a bit too . . ."

"It's not a bit too anything," he assured her, caressing her face. "You are beautiful, my dear. You don't need a thin nightrail to tell me that, but I am a man, after all. If I were immune to what that silk does for you I think I'd have to be dead."

"Really?" she asked in a surprised voice, stepping into the circle of his arms.

"Really," he said on a whisper as he kissed her. Softly, oh so softly, he moved his mouth on hers, kissing and lightly sucking as she opened her mouth and let him in. Perdita answered the first thrust of his tongue with a lick of her own.

"Why am I nearly naked, when you are still almost fully clothed?" Perdita asked as he brought his lips down over her chin. Her hands moved restlessly over the lawn of his shirt. "It's not quite fair, sir."

"I'll disrobe just as soon as I do this one thing," he said against her skin. He was intoxicated by the smell, the feel, the taste of her. As he kissed down her chest, he felt her fingers in his hair. And when he bent to suckle her through the thin fabric of her gown, she made a sound that sent all of his blood southward.

"Oh, that. That's divine," she said in a low voice that thrummed in his belly. And when he lightly pulled at her nipple the hands in his hair pulled him closer. "Archer, my God."

"No," he whispered, "just a man." Kissing his way back up to her mouth, he bent slightly and slid his right hand beneath her knees. "I think this would be much more comfortable on a soft surface," he said as he lifted her into his arms.

Surprised, Perdita made a little squeak. "I could have walked, you know," she said in a faint voice. "But this is much nicer."

"I'm glad you like it," he said, lowering her onto the large bed, which had been turned down earlier. He leaned down to kiss her again, craving the warmth of her mouth, her skin.

She scooted over to make room for him, and Archer climbed up alongside her, propping his head up on his hand. "Perdita," he said, trying to keep his voice level while his body warred with what his heart and mind told him was necessary before anything more happened between them. "I don't know what sort of things Gervase . . ." He paused, searching for the right words. "If he was rough with you," he said, "or if there is anything from your time with him you find uncomfortable or unsettling, you must tell me.

Please. Tonight is for pleasure. Yours is paramount. Mine will happen no matter what, simply by dint of my sex."

At his words, her face lost the glow she'd had a moment ago, and he thought perhaps he shouldn't have said anything. But then she spoke. "You are the sweetest man I've ever met, Archer Lisle." She leaned forward to kiss him softly, and to bring her body flush with his. From head to toe. Archer felt each and every point of connection. "Gervase was rough with me at times," she continued, her face serious even as she stroked his arm, slid her hand down to clasp her hand with his. "I thought then that I would never, ever want to be with a man again."

Archer fought to keep from showing his disappointment.

"But," she said, leaning in to kiss his neck, "I have had a great deal of time to think about it. And I've . . ." She ducked her head under his chin, hiding her face, "I've found myself watching you, wanting you for some time. And if ever there was a man I could trust to be nothing like Gervase, it's you."

A sigh escaped him as he pulled her against him and kissed the top of her head. "My dear girl, I have felt much the same way about you. But I beg you to let me know if anything I do bothers you. All right?"

"All right," she said as he pressed his lips against hers again. He stroked into her mouth again and again, allowing his hand to wander down over the silk of her gown as he did so. Inch by inch he slid it up until he could touch the soft skin beneath, and Perdita, not to be outdone, began pulling his shirt from his breeches. When her hand slipped beneath to caress bare skin, Archer hissed a breath in at the sensation of her soft hands on him.

While she explored his back, he slipped the arm of her nightrail down until her breast was exposed, and went back to it, kissing, sucking, scraping it with his teeth. With each touch Perdita grew more restless, and when he caressed a hand up from her calf to her knee to her thigh, to the place between, she panted a little. "Easy," he whispered, stroking a finger over her, into her, grateful for her body's readiness. When he slipped a finger into her, she made a whimpering sound. "Alright?" he asked, though he didn't remove his hand. "Alright," she said, nearly breathless, "more than okay." When he began stroke in and out of her, she grew even more excited, lifting her hips to meet him, and when he added another finger she moaned and continued to move against him.

Unable to resist, Archer removed his hand, and began to slide down the bed. "What are you doing?" Perdita asked. Her voice was plaintive.

"Something you'll like," he said, parting her knees and sliding first one leg, then the other over his shoulders.

"Are you . . . ?" She sounded puzzled. "Are you looking at me?"

"Yes," he replied, amused. "And then I'm going to taste you."

Before she could say anything else, he suited words to action and licked her luxuriantly, and Perdita let out a sound, half moan half sigh. Smiling to himself, Archer savored the scent of her wanting, using his tongue to caress her outer folds, and then stroking up over the sensitive bundle of nerves that brought the most pleasure. As he caressed her, Perdita began to shift her body, lifting her hips in the rhythm he set with his tongue, and soon he brought first one and then two fingers up and pressed them into her as he sucked lightly on her bud. Stroke by stroke, moment by moment, Perdita grew more and more aroused. And by this time Archer was almost painfully hard as he held off on his own pleasure to stoke hers.

Finally, she hit a point of no return and as he stroked faster and faster into her, and suckled her one last time, she let out a cry and lost herself, her hips jerking uncontrollably until finally, her tremors subsided and she collapsed on the bed, spent.

Perdita had never felt anything more blissful in her life. She'd supposed that Gervase had tried every sort of lovemaking on her. First to woo, then to punish. But she hadn't known the half of it.

"What do you call that?" she asked, her voice breathless.

She heard him chuckle as he kissed her stomach and climbed up to kiss her mouth. She tasted something—herself? It was strangely exciting.

"The technical term is 'cunnilingus,'" he said with a half-grin. "And you may rest assured that every schoolboy in the nation spends a great deal of time thinking about it."

"I liked it very much," she said with what almost sounded like a purr. When had she learned to purr?

While they talked Archer divested himself of the rest of his clothes and Perdita did the same. When he turned, Perdita saw just how beautiful a specimen of manhood he was. And there springing up from a nest of gold curls was a very large, very insistent erection.

He didn't linger, but climbed up onto the bed, and as he stretched out beside her, Perdita couldn't stop herself from sliding her hands over the hard muscles of his chest. He was so well made, she thought. She'd always known he was handsome, of course, but without clothes he was somehow more primitive. More animal. The thought made her breath catch in her throat.

And at just that moment, Archer gripped her by the arms and flipped onto his back bringing her to sit astride him. As they moved, his erection slid against the center of her, sending another pulse of pleasure through her as it did.

"Oh," she gasped as Archer's hands gripped her hips. In this position, she felt powerful. Experimentally she lifted up onto her knees, bringing herself into contact with his member again.

"Easy," he said, pulling her back down. "Not yet." Curiously she watched as he sheathed himself with something, his fingers brushing against her as he did so, stealing the breath from her. He muttered something, and she wanted to ask him to repeat himself, but when he gripped her hips and brought her forward and up she lost her breath again. Perdita lifted up on her knees a bit and guided the tip of him to her opening. Without further conversation, she lowered herself onto him.

At first, there was some resistance, but when Archer thrust up, she took him in until he was fully seated and they both moaned.

"You can control things this way," he said after a silent moment where they both savored the sensation. "Better."

And to her great delight, Perdita learned he was right. Using her thigh muscles she set the pace, raising and lowering onto him, while Archer followed the pace she set and thrust upward on her every downstroke. With each movement, Perdita felt needier and needier, wanting more of him, more friction, more motion. As she moved, Archer leaned forward and took her breast into his mouth. To Perdita's shock the sensation sent a jolt right down to where they were joined. She kissed him, and felt the same overwhelming sensation his mouth on her mound had brought, only this time it felt stronger. As if they were more fully connected.

As her excitement built toward a crescendo, she became mindless to what was going on around her, so when Archer flipped her neatly onto her back, she was only annoyed until he began to stroke harder, and faster into her. The increased intensity, and his hot breath on her neck brought her even higher. And when she felt his thumb on her where they were joined, she tipped right over the edge from excitement to ecstasy, her body on fire as she heard Archer's hoarse shout, and they both were lost to a moment's oblivion.

Eleven

*A*rcher came back to himself with the realization that he'd collapsed on Perdita's chest like a green boy. "Sorry," he murmured as he rolled off her. "Be right back," he said and padded to where he'd left his cravat and with his back to her removed the French letter and wrapped it in the neck cloth. It wouldn't do for Perdita's maid to find it among her things. They had enough eyes on them thanks to the threats against her.

He'd been waiting to have her for such a long time that he'd feared their first encounter would be awkward. They were friends, after all, and when friends became lovers trouble often followed. But Perdita had far surpassed his expectations. Despite what she'd gone through in her marriage, she'd managed to retain a fresh and natural sensuality that made her every touch and response as exciting as if she were a practiced courtesan.

He'd expected things to be good between them. It was rare that he felt such a spark with a woman—and he wasn't sure he'd ever experienced a connection as

..ong as the one with Perdita. This was very different from the lackluster couplings he'd had with other women. Once more he wished like hell that he could persuade her out of her foolish determination to marry someone else. But patience was a skill he'd learned over his career working with the House of Lords, so he would simply rely upon it to help him to either convince her to marry him, or to wait her out.

When he climbed back into the bed and pulled her against him, Perdita slipped her arm over his chest and said, "I didn't mind."

At his questioning glance she clarified. "Your weight. I like the feel of it."

"Do you?" he asked, curious. "I thought ladies disliked being crushed."

She raised one brow, in a mockery of himself, he guessed with an inward smile. "I don't know what other ladies you might have been consorting with," she said with asperity, "but this one feels differently."

Her words made him wince. "I haven't particularly been a saint, you know. There have been others before you."

She tucked her head beneath his chin and began to draw circles on the surface of his chest. "I know that. I know how gentlemen are. I didn't expect you to come to me untouched."

He wasn't sure he liked her comment about "how gentlemen" were. Because he knew much of her understanding of men had been formed by her husband and her father. Neither of whom were particularly fine examples of the breed.

"I wish I could have," he said, knowing the statement made him sound like a ridiculous romantic fool, but he truly did wish he could have come to her without the memories and knowledge of the others. It wasn't that there were so very many. It was more that he felt Perdita deserved more.

She looked up at him, from this angle her lashes long and lush and catching the candlelight. "I don't mind," she said. Her face turning sly, she added, "If you'd come to me without ever having done this before, you wouldn't have known some of the things that I found the most . . . delightful."

That was one way to look at things, he supposed. Though he could have done rather well with only books as his tutor. Even so it was a moot point now, so there was no going back.

"About the . . . French memo, was it?" she asked, returning to her exploration of his chest.

"Letter," he corrected with a grin he was grateful she couldn't see. He'd imagine the Foreign Office would be quite unamused if they found a stack of French letters had replaced their French memorandums.

"Yes, that's it, 'letter,'" she said with a nod that tickled his chin. "Where did you learn about those?"

This had turned into rather more of a discussion than he'd anticipated. But Archer was glad she trusted him enough to ask. And since these issues involved her own body she was entitled to answers.

He thought back to when he'd first heard about the lambskin sheaths. It felt as if he'd known forever but that couldn't be true. "I suppose in school," he said, frowning. "Or perhaps from one of my brothers. They were good about lording their knowledge about such things over my head."

"Ah," she said, laughing softly. "Siblings can be that way, can they not? Isabella used to do the same kind of things to me."

"Boys can be especially annoying, though." Which was an understatement. He knew Isabella and she could not possibly have acted as superior as his brothers had. There were advantages to being the youngest, but there were also drawbacks.

"How many are there?" Perdita asked. "Brothers, I mean. I knew you were the son of the Duke of Lisle but I didn't realize you had lots of brothers."

"Not so many," Archer said with a shrug. "Four. We get along well enough now, but when we were children we tormented one another."

"Tell me about them," she said, looking up at him.

"Well," he said, resting his chin on her head, "the eldest is Rhys, he is eight years older than me. He's the Marquess of Duclair, and to my mother's great distress has not married and filled the nursery with a passel of boys."

"Goodness," Perdita said, "it isn't as if there is shortage of them already in the family."

"One would think," Archer agreed, stroking his hand over the soft skin of her back, "But I think they live in fear that something will happen to Papa and Rhys and things will be left in the hands of Benedick. He's a bit of a black sheep."

"Oh, dear, is he a terrible rakehell?" Perdita's voice sounded sympathetic.

"Nothing like," he said, reassuring her. "He's a clergyman, actually. He left his position as a don at Cambridge to come home to Lisle Hall and take up the living on the estate."

Perdita sat up so that she could look at him. "You're funning me," she said skeptically.

"Not a bit of it," Archer said, raising his hands in defense. "My parents wanted him to go into the diplomatic corps, but Ben preferred the church. He's the cleverest of us all. And I thought he was happy enough at college, but I think he came back to Lisle Hall simply to give my parents a hard time. Especially my father. He wished to have a son negotiating treaties and traveling the world, so that he could live vicariously through him. At least that's my guess."

"Your poor brother," Perdita said with a shake of her head. "He must be miserable."

"Actually he's quite happy, I think. He really does enjoy the life of a country vicar. And he teaches Latin to some of the village boys so he is able to teach, too."

"So that's two," Perdita said. "What of the others?"

"Next is Frederick," he said, "who is an actual rakehell. He's been in Paris for the last several years so you would not have seen him in town. But he is quite good company, and amiable. So there's that."

"Do you miss him?" Perdita asked.

Archer tried to decide if he did or not. "I suppose in a way I miss all of them. Though it's not as if we all have similar interests. When we're together we have fun, but it doesn't take very long before someone says something that riles another and we are ready to separate again."

"Next?"

"That would be Cameron."

"And what does Cameron do?"

"What does Cameron do?" Archer repeated. "I suppose you could say that he collects things."

"You mean like antiques or Limoges boxes?" she asked, clearly puzzled by that description.

"Stones mostly," Archer said with a shrug. "And bits of fossilized bone. Things like that. He is a member of the Royal Society and presents papers on his findings. Something to do with beasts from long ago. Exploring."

"How odd," Perdita answered. "Though I suppose it can be interesting for some people."

"Indeed it can," Archer responded. Pulling her up so that he could kiss her. Properly.

But before he could touch his lips to hers, Perdita's hand came up and touched him on the chest. Staying him. "You've told me what your brothers do," she said, her eyes intent in the light of the guttering candle. "But what do you do?"

He thought to fob her off with some glib words about dreaming of being a duke's personal secretary from a young age. But he knew she deserved the truth from him. "You of all people know that I am Ormond's personal secretary. As I was to the duke before him."

"But?" she said, waiting.

"But," Archer conceded, "as you have perhaps guessed, I have other ambitions. Ambitions that have nothing to do with hanging about Parliament waiting for bills to be drafted or writing Trevor's correspondence on his behalf."

A line appeared between Perdita's brows. "If you have other ambitions," she said carefully, "then why have you remained here? You might have left when Gervase died. Indeed, it would have been perfectly understandable. Expected even."

He paused for a fraction of a second too long,

which allowed her to draw her own conclusion. One that wasn't so very far from the truth. Her gasp let him know as much. "Dear God, Archer," she exhaled. "Never say you stayed because of me."

The words hung in the air between them as Archer tried to school his features into some semblance of normalcy. The truth of it was that he had stayed because of her. And he would be a fool to deny it. So he shrugged.

"Oh, Archer."

"It's not as pathetic as you make it sound," he said stiffly, rolling onto his back to look up at the bed hangings overhead. "I wasn't ready to leave when Gervase died. And I could hardly just go haring off without overseeing things in his absence. No more than I could have left things to waste away while the dowager tried to convince Trevor to take up the reins."

"Not pathetic," she said fiercely, pushing up onto her elbows so she could look down at him. "Never pathetic. It's just that I never got the feeling that you really enjoyed the work."

"It wasn't all bad," he argued, knowing even as he spoke that the words were hardly convincing. "In truth, it was never my dream to be a secretary. It was my lot as the youngest son. I was smart, fairly politically minded, and I was familiar with the workings of a ducal household. It was a natural fit for me to accept the position when my father began prosing on about all of us finding our own lot in life."

She was silent, and he could tell she wanted to ask questions, but he was grateful for her self-control. He needed to get the story out or he'd never have another opportunity.

"But, yes, when Gervase died I'd got to the point where I could have left and bought a small farm for myself and started to put some of the newer farming methods I'd been reading about into practice."

"You want to be a farmer?" she asked, looking more shocked than if he'd admitted a fondness for opium eating. "A farmer? You?"

"What's so surprising about that?" Archer asked, puzzled by her reaction more than anything else. "It's hardly as if most gentlemen of property don't need to know something about the land their tenants are farming."

"Yes," she said with a bemused shake of her head. "But it's just that you're so . . ."

"Soft?" he asked with one brow raised.

At the innuendo her cheeks turned pink. "Hardly," she said with a grin. "But you just don't seem like someone who would long to feel the soil between your fingers."

Archer shrugged. "I always enjoyed going to visit the tenants with my father and his bailiff. And when I was younger I had hopes that Papa would allow me to take over for Vickers when he got too old to do it. But that wasn't smart enough for my father. So it was off to London and into Gervase's employ I went."

"I wonder why it is that our parents often wish things for us that we ourselves would never choose? I certainly had no ambitions to become a duchess. That was all *my* father's doing. I fell in love with Gervase, but it was really only after my father made it clear to me that I would wed him whether I loved him or not."

Archer thought about what young Perdita must

have been like, before she was exposed to the toxic influence of the late Duke of Ormond. "I'm sorry," he said softly.

"And I'm sorry your father didn't allow you to follow your own inclination," she said, leaning over to kiss him.

"I'm not," Archer said, realizing that it was the truth. "If he'd allowed me to have my way, I'd never have met you."

A smile not unlike that of a cat who's just been in the cream turned up the corners of her mouth. "That's true," she said thoughfully. "And painful though it is to admit, I wouldn't go back and change anything from my past—even the bad things about my marriage. Because one small change might mean that I wouldn't have this moment here and now, with you."

Archer wanted to argue. But he knew there was a rightness to what she was saying, even though it went against the grain to admit as much.

"I like being with you here," he said softly. "And now."

He reached up and cradled her face in his hands, bringing her mouth down to meet his own.

When they were both breathless, he said, "I think perhaps we should spend a little time exploring the here and now."

She kissed him again. "Good idea," she said, slipping her hand downward to stroke his burgeoning erection.

He sucked air through his teeth. "Easy, unless you want this to be over rather more quickly than would be enjoyable for you."

"I wouldn't mind," she said, lightly scraping her teeth over his bottom lip. "I'd like to watch you lose control."

Of course her words had the expected effect and she gave an evil laugh. "You did that on purpose," he said, flipping her neatly onto her back. "I think I'm going to have to get used to this naughty side of you, Perdita. I had no idea you had it in you."

"I can think of something I'd rather have in me," she said against his mouth as he pressed his legs between hers and pressed himself home. "Ahhh, yes, that."

Archer brought her right knee up and sank into her even more deeply, the sensation of her warmth and tightness around his cock nearly bringing him off then and there. He struggled to think of something else. Conjugated a few Latin verbs before he felt his control return and then looked down into Perdita's face. She was watching him, her lips parted, her arms clasped around his lower back, as she held him to her. "What you do to me," she breathed.

He slowly pulled out and then just as slowly pressed back into her. Every inch stringing out the breathless moment between them. Their eyes held as he did it again and again, until Perdita wrapped her other leg around him, pulling him closer, and Archer lost control and began to thrust into her again and again. Perdita, in turn, began her ascent into the maelstrom and not long thereafter cried out her pleasure. Only moments before Archer cried out, spilling himself into her. One word repeating itself again and again in his consciousness.

Mine.

* * *

It wasn't until he was pulling his clothes back on in the wee hours and found his cravat with the French letter that he realized he'd forgotten to use one the second time they'd joined. Cursing himself for a fool, he pulled his shirt on over his head and slipped from the room.

Perdita awoke the next morning much later than her usual time. Immediately she regretted that Archer had had to leave before the tweeny came to make up the fire. But she didn't wish for them to generate talk among the servants. They would likely figure things out at some point, but she would rather it be later than sooner.

Stretching, she felt some twinges in places that hadn't been used in a while. But she could have no regrets for what had happened between her and Archer the night before. Not only had he been tender, he'd also been exciting in ways she'd not anticipated. She wasn't sure why, but she'd expected making love to him would be rather sweet. She certainly hadn't expected him to make her feel like such a wanton. He'd brought her the kind of pleasure she'd always hoped to achieve with Gervase, but now she realized that her husband hadn't been capable of such a thing. Now that she knew what it meant to have a man take care to ensure she achieved her own pleasure before he did, she knew that nothing she'd experienced before compared.

Archer had surprised her in other ways, too, she thought as she rose from her bed and pulled on her dressing gown. She'd known he was well muscled beneath his eminently civilized clothing, but she hadn't expected to see such a perfect specimen of manhood when he removed them. From his broad shoulders to his taut middle and lean flanks, he was like the Elgin marbles come to life. All except for one particular part of him, which was much, much more impressive than anything she'd seen in the British Museum. She closed her eyes as the memory of all that male glory moving inside her sent a spasm through her. Oh, no, there was nothing about Archer that could be called unimpressive. She grinned, the euphoria of the night before washing over her as she rang for her maid.

When her maid arrived, she didn't seem to suspect that her mistress had spent the evening before fornicating with the Duke of Ormond's private secretary. Instead she was frowning as she brought a card forward and said, "Your Grace, Lord Dunthorp is here and wishes to see you. I tried to explain that you weren't yet receiving, but he insisted. Shall I let His Grace or your sister know so that they can send him about his business? And you not feeling well." She pursed her lips.

What could Lord Dunthorp want of her at this hour? Perdita wondered. He wasn't the sort to press himself upon servants so there was likely a good reason that he'd insisted upon seeing her. She wondered if there was some problem relating to the Elphinstone rout.

"I'll see him. It's no bother. And I'm not unwell, I just wanted to sleep in since we were out so late last night."

She allowed the other woman to dress her, and

though she was famished, she went downstairs and entered the parlor to find Lord Dunthorp being entertained—though from his expression he didn't find it particularly amusing—by Isabella and Georgina, who were chatting about the latest on-dit involving an elderly marchioness who'd run off with her footman.

"Lord Dunthorp," she said, when the ladies stopped for breath. "To what do I owe the pleasure of this visit?"

"Your Grace," he said, springing to his feet and hurrying forward to bow and kiss the back of her hand. "I am sorry to see you looking so wan this morning. I have no doubt you were sleepless over what happened at the Elphinstones' last evening."

Well, Perdita thought, that was certainly forward of him. Aloud she said, "Actually, I slept rather well, Lord Dunthorp." In between bouts of strenuous lovemaking, that is. She wondered for a second what he would say if she actually told him that. The idea nearly caused her to laugh aloud. Instead, she continued, "There is no need to fuss over me."

"There is no shame in it, Your Grace. After all, every well-bred lady is entitled to a case of nerves when she encounters the sort of incivility that you did."

"I assure you," she said silkily, becoming annoyed at his insistence, "that I am well. I thank you. Now please, let us sit down and discuss what brings you here." This did not bode well for her plans to marry the man.

Isabella and Georgina, who watched the exchange with varying degrees of shock and outrage, schooled their features and made a place for Perdita on the long sofa where they were ensconced. Seeing that he would get no farther with that tack, Dunthorp took a seat in the chair opposite.

"Your Grace," he began, "I am here to discuss your protection. Last evening I had quite a productive conversation with Lord Coniston about what might be done to ensure your safety both while you are here at Ormond House and while you are away in other places in town. Obviously you will need to curtail those visits as much as possible, for leaving home will expose you to further attacks."

"My dear Lord Dunthorp," she said with a touch of asperity, "while I do appreciate your concern, I have not agreed to any of this, so perhaps I should discuss it with Lord Coniston and His Grace before we begin making plans."

But Dunthorp waved her concern away. "There is no need for you to worry yourself over it, my dear," he said with as much condescension as she'd ever encountered from a man she wasn't related to. "I simply wished to inform you that you mustn't embark on some shopping trip or otherwise silly errand, until his lordship and I have put these measures in place."

There was a cough from the doorway as Archer and Con stepped into the room and gazed with equal displeasure on Dunthorp. Before they could speak, however, Perdita said, "Lord Dunthorp, while I appreciate your concern for my safety, I will remind you that as a duchess, even a dowager one, I am to be addressed as 'Your Grace,' not 'my dear' or any other inappropriate endearment you might wish to use. I have perhaps allowed you more latitude in these past weeks than was warranted, but I thought that we were growing closer. Unfortunately, it seems that I was mistaken. I have quite enough gentlemen to look after me at the present time, and accepting direction from a man who is neither my husband, my brother, or even my fiancé is something I simply cannot do."

As she said all this, Dunthorp gaped at her. Whether he was shocked to have been given such a set-down or surprised that she had the cheek to do so, she didn't really care.

"I fear you've outstayed your welcome, Dunthorp," Con said, as he and Archer moved to stand on either end of the sofa, clearly in a protective move. "Shall I call a footman to see you out?"

"I'll do it," Archer said with more relish than Perdita liked. She didn't want him or anyone else to waste their fists on the man. He was simply a boor, something she'd only begun to suspect in the past few days. "I believe the footmen have other duties to attend to."

"Your Grace, you will regret this," Dunthorp said tightly. "I know what's best for you. It's already assumed that we are all but betrothed. Don't let a little missishness ruin things between us."

Really, did the man not take no for an answer?

"I admit there was a time when I did consider a possible match with you, Lord Dunthorp," Perdita said sharply. "But it was not long into our acquaintance when I changed my mind. I will not stand for one more minute of your telling me what I should and should not do. Now, kindly take yourself off."

"Come on, Dunthorp," Archer said, taking the other man by the arm.

But Dunthorp wasn't having it. "Take your hands

off me, Lisle. I don't need you or any other servant to see me out."

His insult made Perdita's blood boil. She got to her feet and walked over to where Archer was about to lead the man away. "For the last time, his name is Lord Archer Lisle. He is the son of the Duke of Lisle. And a far better man than you have shown yourself to be. Now, please leave."

Dunthorp's face was red with fury as he allowed Archer to almost drag him from the room.

"Well—" Con began to say before they heard a scuffle in the hallway. "I'll go see what happened," he said, hurrying out.

"What a nasty little man," Isabella said, wrinkling her nose as if she'd smelled something bad. "Did you really plan to marry him, Perdita?"

"Not one of my more rational moments," she said with a moue of distaste. "He seemed much nicer when we first met. I thought he was a gentleman."

"Some men are like that," Georgie said. "They will pretend to be perfect until something lifts the mask of civility and you realize that they are just awful."

Perdita rubbed her forehead where a headache was burgeoning. "I cannot believe I almost did it again."

"Did what?" Isabella asked with a frown.

"I almost married another man who masks his true self beneath a gentlemanly mien. Dunthorp is just a different version of Gervase." She shook her head in disbelief. "How could I be so foolish? I am not to be trusted with choosing a husband."

"Darling," Georgie said, rubbing her on her back, "you didn't really intend to marry Dunthorp. You simply chose him because he seemed safe."

"Safe?" Perdita asked.

"I think she means," Isabella said, "that he is not the sort that you were likely to fall in love with. Which if I recall is completely different from what happened between you and Gervase. You were head over ears in love with him."

"Yes," Perdita said, "but—"

"You were able to see through Dunthorp because you aren't in love with him, you goose," Georgie said. "You figured it out. And when you do fall in love again, it will be with a man who is about as far away from being like Gervase as is humanly possible."

"How do you know?" Perdita turned and looked at her friend. Hoping to read some sort of reassurance in her face.

"I know because you are more canny than you think," she said simply. "You've already been with a Gervase. You know how his sort operates. You know all the tricks. You'll never truly fall for another man like that again."

They were saved from further conversation by the return of Archer and Con, followed by Ormond.

"What happened out there?" Perdita asked, noting that Archer's cravat seemed a bit askew.

"Dunthorp tripped," he said with a shrug, taking the chair vacated by the other man and stretching his legs out before him.

"And fell onto Archer's fist," Ormond said with a smirk as he took the chair beside Archer's. "It was really quite magnificent to see."

"Lord Archer," Perdita chided. "You shouldn't have done that. He might call you out now."

"Doubt that, since he seems unable to remember

I'm a gentleman and not a servant," he said cheerfully, gazing at his bruised knuckles.

"Still, that doesn't, excuse—" Perdita continued.

But Archer cut her off. "Enough. He was speaking out of turn and I made him stop talking."

"About me?" she asked her lips tight.

He nodded once. His eyes met hers and she felt as if they were alone again in her bedchamber. She remembered at some point that he'd said "mine." She knew now what that meant. And what it might mean for anyone who tried to harm her.

She hadn't intended to become seriously involved with him. But now she realized that had been a foolish hope. There was no way to share what they'd shared last night without becoming involved. And by defending her against Dunthorp, Archer had just shown her that he was involved. What's more, he saw himself as her champion.

"All right," she said, suddenly realizing that the room was silent. As she glanced around, she saw that each of the others had found somewhere to look besides at Perdita or Archer. She felt her ears redden. Silly fair skin, she inwardly moaned.

"So," she said brightly, "what does everyone have planned for today?"

It was perhaps a bit awkward, but the others went with it, and they began to chat.

Archer, she noticed, didn't take his gaze off her.

Twelve

Gaslight winked from the torches of Vauxhall as Perdita strolled along the meandering main path on the arm of Sir Lucien Blakemore, a friend of Ormond's from Yorkshire. She'd have been happier to come on the arm of Archer, but since she was trying desperately to be discreet about their affair she'd agreed to Blakemore's escort when Isabella suggested it.

Thus far, Sir Lucien had proven himself to be an amiable companion, and trying to keep to her plan for a marriage of convenience, she vowed to give the man a chance. Especially since despite his good looks and pretty manners he had no effect upon her heart at all.

"What is it you most enjoy about the pleasure gardens, Your Grace?" Sir Lucien asked as they neared the pavilion. "I vow that I cannot resist the ham, though that perhaps doesn't count as a feature of the gardens themselves."

"Perhaps not," Perdita acceded, "but I enjoy it as well. My favorite part, though, would have to be the music. I can never resist the lure of a beautiful song. I never could."

Before Blakemore could respond, another couple, deep in conversation, came walking toward them, and Perdita felt her stomach knot as she recognized Archer with Mrs. Alicia Fitzroy, a widow with as scandalous a reputation as Perdita's was sterling. She'd known he would be in attendance tonight, but he hadn't mentioned that he'd be coming with the blowsy Mrs. Fitzroy. She felt the unfamiliar sting of jealousy as she watched their two golden heads lean together as if their words were private and not meant for the ears of others.

She'd have suspected Archer of many things, but she'd never imagined he could be swayed by the likes of Mrs. Fitzroy. She'd had enough experience competing with that sort of woman during her marriage to Gervase, and if Archer thought she'd sit idly by while he flaunted the other woman under her nose he was sorely mistaken.

The couples exchanged greetings. Blakemore and Archer bowed and discussed a mutual acquaintance who was in town, while Perdita and Mrs. Fitzroy smiled coolly at one another.

"Your Grace," Archer said to Perdita while Blakemore and Mrs. Fitzroy chatted, "I hope you don't mind our imposing on your party. I found I simply could not stay away once I learned you all would be here." Beneath his words was a message Perdita had little difficulty reading: *I came here because you gave me no choice.*

She wondered if that applied to his bringing Mrs.

Fitzroy, as well. "I'm so pleased you were able to join us. And Mrs. Fitzroy of course." *Really? Mrs. Fitzroy? Could you not have found someone less possessive of you?*

"Thank you," he said, showing his teeth. "I thought of her as soon as I decided to come." *As soon as I learned you'd be escorted by another man.*

"How pleasant that we were both able to come with such amiable partners," she said stiffly.

Perhaps it had been impolite of her to accept Blakemore's invitation so soon after she'd taken Archer into her bed, but really. She had told him about her plan to marry elsewhere. And despite their short acquaintance, Blakemore was a good prospect. A baronet with a reputation for fair dealings in business as well as with ladies, he was just the sort of man she'd been looking for. Especially when it came to her own response to him. She was not in the least danger of falling in love with him.

And if Archer couldn't accept that, then perhaps they'd best bring their liaison to an end.

A small voice within her, however, shrieked at the idea of giving up the one thing that had brought her true pleasure in the past five years. Mercilessly, she ignored the voice.

The two couples were chatting amiably, if a bit stiffly, when a young man, clearly the worse for drink, stumbled into Perdita, grabbing hold of her arm in a firm grip as he fell forward. She gasped in surprise and tried to throw him off, but he held tight, putting his whole weight into pulling her down.

"Watch yourself, man," Blakemore said sharply as

Archer leaped forward to disentangle her. As Blakemore gripped the man, he giggled and mumbled something that Perdita was unable to hear.

"Are you all right?" Archer asked, his tight hold reassuring as Perdita brought her breathing under control.

"Get off!" Mrs. Fitzroy shrieked, shoving the young man, who had run into her in his attempt to evade Blakemore. "You drunken lout!"

"I know," the young man sang out, like a child with a nursery rhyme. "I know, I know . . ."

Archer had to let Perdita go as Mrs. Fitzroy grasped onto his free arm like a limpet. "What a horrible person," she said with disgust.

"I know," the drunkard said again, this time with more force. Now Blakemore had hold of him, though the man still seemed to be in control of his movements enough to keep the other man from holding him fast. "I know, I know . . ."

"Yes, indeed," Blakemore said in exasperation, "you know. Now come along." He hauled the man up by the arm as he continued his wailing.

"I wonder where the rest of his party is," Perdita said with a frown. "Young men usually travel in packs."

"Like wild dogs?" Archer asked with a grin.

Mrs. Fitzroy giggled, and Perdita would have laughed as well, but the words of the drunken man had finally penetrated her awareness and she stilled to listen more carefully.

"I know what you did," the young man said in a singsong tone, and Perdita turned to him, her mouth agape in horror. "I know what you did," he said again. "Last season," he sang out. "Last season."

"I know what you did last season . . ." he cried out, and wrenching himself away from Blakemore, the youth removed a flask from some hidden pocket and flung its contents at Perdita. "Murderer!" he cried. "Murderer!"

Shocked, Perdita looked down at her pale pink gown and realized at once that it hadn't been brandy or some other potent potable the fellow had poured on her.

It was blood.

She wasn't sure if it was she herself or Mrs. Fitzroy who screamed the loudest.

Archer swore when he saw the drunken lout pour blood all over Perdita. Ignoring Blakemore, whose response was to grab the young man by the arm and demand to know just what he thought he was doing, he gave Mrs. Fitzroy a little shake to stop her from screaming like a bloody banshee, and went to Perdita. She was shaking visibly and he was unable to hide the condition of her gown from the crowd that was already gathering around their little tableau.

"Good heavens!" he heard a plump matron declare. "Has it come to this? Are we to be accosted in the street by such lawless ruffians as this?"

"Take me home," Perdita said tightly. "Please, Archer." The look of desperation in her eyes sent his protective instincts, already in a high state thanks to the attack upon her, into orbit.

"One minute," he promised her. "I need to ensure that this fellow is taken care of properly."

It was perhaps a measure of Perdita's shock that she didn't argue, but nodded and wrapped her own arms around herself, like a child seeking warmth.

"What's the to-do?" Con along with Ormond hurried forward. "We heard shouting and saw the crowd gathering. If Georgina hadn't recognized Perdita in the middle of it all we should have left before things got out of control."

Archer was grateful to see that Georgina and Isabella were comforting Perdita. "It would appear that the stalker has struck again," he said, his jaw tight. "This fellow stumbled over muttering something about knowing what she did last season and tossed a flask full of what I very much hope was animal rather than human blood on her."

Both men cursed and Archer heard Isabella gasp behind him. "You poor dear," Georgie said to Perdita. "Con, we should take her away from here."

Before they could discuss the matter further, however, Blakemore turned to them. "I escorted the duchess this evening and would be happy to see that she returns safely home."

Which would happen, Archer thought, over his dead body. He would accompany Perdita home whether Blakemore liked it or not.

Aloud he said, "What about the fellow who did this?" Looking behind the other man, he saw that the crowd had thinned and the young man who had attacked Perdita was nowhere to be seen.

"I had the watch take him away," Blakemore said with a dismissive wave of his hand. "It was clear the fellow was drunk out of his wits. Clearly he must have been to do something as absurd as pour wine all down the front of Her Grace's gown."

"It was blood," Archer corrected. "And I wished to question the man further."

Blakemore winced. "My apologies, old chap. I didn't realize he was anything more than a common ruffian. I'm sure you'll be able to find him at the nearest magistrate's office tomorrow. It's not as if he will be walking the streets free for the next couple of days. One does not accost a duchess without feeling the full weight of the law, after all."

Conceding the man had a point, Archer turned to check on Perdita, who was still shivering. "Blakemore, I think the duchess would prefer to have her sister and Lady Coniston accompany her home," Archer said with more diplomacy than he felt. "Her gown is, after all, not quite decent what with being covered in blood and whatnot."

"And what of me?" Mrs. Fitzroy, who'd been pouting off to the side while the others hovered over Perdita, demanded. "I was almost splattered with blood, as well!"

Mentally rolling his eyes, Archer said, "Of course, Mrs. Fitzroy, you are clearly overset by this business, as well. Perhaps Blakemore will see to it that you are returned home safely."

Archer expected the other man to protest, but the baronet must have read more into Archer's relationship with Perdita than they'd intended, for after a thoughtful look from one to the other he said, "Of course, delighted, I'm sure." Turning to the widow he said, "Mrs. Fitzroy, will you allow me to see you home?"

The widow frowned, but allowed Blakemore to take her arm. "Thank you, my lord," she said haughtily, "for being such a gentleman." The implication being that her original escort was not. Though Archer could not possibly have cared less.

When they were gone, Archer and the others led Perdita to the gates of the pleasure gardens where Ormond's carriage, which was quite large, awaited them.

Once they were on their way, Archer turned to Perdita, who had finally stopped shivering though she clung to Isabella's arm for support. "Tell me exactly what happened," he said quietly.

Looking up, he could just see Perdita's frown in the dim carriage light. "What do you mean?" she asked. "You were there. You saw everything I did."

"But you might have seen something that I missed," he said patiently. "So tell me from the beginning."

So, with a sigh, Perdita related step by step exactly what had taken place just before and when the young man had come upon them and accosted her. "And then he threw the flask of blood on me and laughed in that maniacal way." She shivered as she said the words. "It was as if he were in some sort of trance," she said with a shudder.

"I thought the notes were awful," Georgina said, rubbing Perdita's arm. "But I think receiving the message in person is much worse."

"It's certainly a more personal approach than our friend has tried in the past," Archer said grimly. "I don't like it. It seems to indicate that this person has decided to stop playing nice."

"If you call trying to make Georgina think her dead husband was alive, then making an attempt on her life, 'playing nice,'" Con said bitterly. "As far as I'm concerned this bastard has been playing dirty from the beginning, he's just started out with more force when it comes to Perdita."

"I suppose it's because he thinks I deserve it," Perdita said quietly. "Perhaps I do. I am, after all, the reason that Gervase is dead. And that's what this person is so angry about."

"The only reason the late duke is dead," Archer bit out, "is his own miserable hide. If he hadn't threatened your life, then you wouldn't have been forced to defend yourself."

"Amen," Trevor said fiercely. "I have a hard time believing anyone mourns the fellow. Though I suppose the dowager must."

"Which is why I believe she's the one behind all of these attacks," Archer said carefully.

"I don't know if I can agree," said Perdita with a shake of her head. "She is ruthless, but I don't see her setting someone upon me to do something like this. I know her, and she is too fond of seeing her own handiwork to ever rely on someone to follow her orders out in the world. And that includes what happened to Isabella and Georgina, as well. I think it must be someone else. Someone who is comfortable giving orders and relying on his surrogates to follow them."

"Like a general, you mean?" Georgina asked, brow furrowed. "I must admit that it makes some sense. Not having spent much time with the duchess myself, I cannot speak to a great deal of knowledge of her character. But she does strike me as a hands-on sort of person, if that is what you mean."

"Exactly," Perdita agreed. "She adored Gervase, and I cannot imagine that she would seek revenge against anyone who might have hurt him without seeing it with her own eyes."

"Whoever it is that has you in their sights," Archer said with a shrug, "it is clear that he means to go all out, so to speak." Turning to Perdita, he frowned. "How many threatening letters have you received thus far?"

Her mouth dropped open. "How did you . . . ?"

"You told us in Bath that you'd already received several of them. It stands to reason that you've gotten more since then."

Her mouth tight, she said, "Five. I have received five threatening letters and one was included with a bouquet of roses."

"What?" Georgina demanded. "You didn't tell me that! Why roses?"

"They were what Gervase always sent the day after . . ." Perdita paused, her eyes revealing her discomfort.

"You don't need to finish," Archer said quietly. He was as aware as anyone of just how Gervase had stripped her of her dignity time and time again. "What did the note say? Was it the same as the others?"

"It was a bit different," Perdita said, twisting her hands before her. "It was a reminder, more than anything else. Of the anniversary."

"Of your wedding?" Archer asked.

"Of his death," Georgina guessed. "Oh, dearest, what a horrible thing to remind you of."

"When is it?" Archer asked, his every sinew on alert. What if this person were merely teasing Perdita as he led up to some spectacle of revenge to occur on the actual anniversary of Ormond's death? It made a sick sort of sense.

"In five days, on April 25," she said. "On April 25 it will have been two years since I killed my husband."

"Do not say it like that," Isabella protested. "You make it sound as if you set out to do it. And I will remind you that both Georgina and myself were there and might have killed him just as well."

"You're a dear, Isabella," Perdita said, squeezing her sister's hand. "But even if you were both there it doesn't mean that I didn't have a hand in his death. Whoever it is that seeks to punish me is right."

"By that rationale then he was also right to punish Georgina and Isabella," Trevor argued. "This is the work of a madman and nothing more. None of you is to blame for his insanity."

"What's to be done?" Archer said, cutting to the chase. "We are clearly seeing some sort of intensifying of this person's agenda as the anniversary approaches. I think it means that we need to take drastic measures."

Perdita's fine auburn eyebrows drew together. "What do you mean, 'drastic measures'? I warn you now that I refuse to live shut up in Ormond House like some sort of prisoner."

"I wouldn't ask that of you," Archer said firmly. "Not least because it would be too difficult to maintain security in the middle of London. We have no notion of whether any of your servants are in this person's employ, and I refuse to take chances with your life like that."

"Then where?" Con asked. "You are more than welcome to come to us in Kent," he said to Perdita. "I'm sure Georgina would be pleased as punch to have you."

"I shouldn't like to put you in danger, as well," Perdita said with a shake of her head. "It's why I haven't gone to Isabella and Trevor. Especially with Isabella's condition. I don't know how I'd live with myself if I somehow endangered the child."

"I was thinking of someplace altogether different," Archer said firmly. "A place where you are a complete unknown. A place where you can come and go as you please without feeling as if you are in the sights of some madman constantly."

"Well?" Perdita asked, her attention trained upon him. "Where is this magical place?"

"I cannot tell you," he said with an apologetic tone. "It must remain a secret to all but a very few until we get there."

"But what am I to tell my maid?" Perdita asked, frowning. "She will need to know what to pack."

"I'm afraid you won't be bringing your maid," he said. "And I will forgo my valet."

"This sounds like a scandal waiting to happen," Georgina said with a grin. "I like it."

"Well, I do not!" Perdita said, glaring. "It's completely improper. And impractical besides. How are you supposed to perform your duties as the secretary to Ormond? It's not as if you can simply take off for a few weeks and expect Ormond House to simply go on without you."

"Actually, that's exactly what I mean to do," Archer said with a grin. "Or I shall tell Trevor that he is welcome to dismiss me."

"I can do without you for a few weeks," Trevor said with a shrug. "It's not as if I cannot write my own correspondence in the name of protecting my sister-in-law."

"But . . . but . . ." Perdita looked around and found them all smiling like little children at a traveling fair. "You're all mad!" she said, throwing up her hands. "Utterly mad."

"Not mad, dearest," Georgina said, patting her friend's hand. "I think it might be quite sane, in fact. You certainly don't wish to sit about here in town waiting for some calamity to befall you. This way, you can wait in safety and seclusion for the anniversary date to pass, then return to town with no one the wiser."

"But what are we to tell people?" Perdita demanded. "It's not as if I can simply disappear and expect no one in the ton to notice that I have not been seen in days. I have responsibilities. And social obligations."

"You let me take care of those," Georgina said with a reassuring smile. "I will see to it that a story is passed around the ton that you've been taken with the measles. Dreadful, but it does happen. And you are quite likely to contract them what with all your charity work in foundling hospitals."

"An excellent idea," Archer commended her. "I must admit that's much better than my plan for her to simply go away to the country for a bit. This way no one will be able to find her out with a well-placed letter to a country neighbor."

The carriage having slowed to a stop, Archer turned to Perdita. "What say you, Your Grace? Will you trust me to keep you safe?"

In the dim light of the carriage lamps, he was unable to read her expression, but the shake of her head was obvious enough. "I cannot do it," she said sadly. "I cannot go someplace else and put those people in danger, as well. And if I were to leave, this person— whoever he is—would think he'd won. And I will not let him think it."

Archer bit back a curse of frustration. If she was

still unwilling to concede that she should leave London for her own safety at this point, with her sister and Georgie adding their voices to his own, then it was unlikely that she could ever be convinced.

Knowing he could do little to add to his previous arguments, he left off trying to convince her the whole way back to Ormond House.

He was still fuming, hours later, as he tried and failed to fall asleep. He'd asked her quietly once they were inside whether she'd like company, but she'd rebuffed him, saying she needed to be alone. He wasn't sure if it was because she thought he'd try again to convince her, or because she was angry about Mrs. Fitzroy, but whatever the reason, he went to bed alone, in his own bedchamber.

"If this keeps up I'm going to have to kidnap her and take her to safety myself," he muttered, punching his pillow into a more comfortable position. Then as he laid his head down, he thought about what he'd just said. Kidnap her. Kidnap her?

He sat up, the sheets falling down to his waist. "Of course!"

To the room at large he said, "I will simply have to kidnap her."

Thirteen

After a long night, Perdita arose the next morning not long after dawn. Again and again, she'd fallen into a fitful sleep only to be jolted awake again by the memory of the young man from last night dousing her gown with blood. Exhaustion had overtaken her sometime after three, but the noise of the street vendors had penetrated her light sleep as they began their day, and so she rose and dressed.

She should probably have agreed when Archer intimated that he could come to her last night, but she'd been unwilling to face another argument with him despite her suspicion that having him with her would have allowed her to sleep. Then there was the matter of Mrs. Fitzroy. His concern for her after the attack last night had been all she could have wished, but that he would bring that woman to Vauxhall and parade her in front of the ton like that made her more angry than she was willing to admit. Blakemore, she fumed, was entirely different, and she was not willing to entertain the idea that what was good for the goose was good for the gander.

Geese were silly creatures anyway.

She went down to breakfast, expecting to find the table empty, but was surprised and, despite her pique, pleased to see Archer there. He was often long gone by the time she came down.

"Your Grace," he said, rising as she entered the room. "I hope you were able to sleep better than I was."

"Little, I'm afraid," she conceded once she'd asked the footman for a cup of tea and chosen a rasher of bacon and some toast from the sideboard. "For all that that ruffian didn't actually harm me, he certainly was able to upset my mind."

"That's the point," he said tersely. "He wishes to steal your peace of mind. To make you jump at every little noise or jostle."

"Well, he's certainly succeeded," she said morosely. "I thought I had more fortitude than this. But it would appear that I am just as mortal as anyone else."

"Do not be too hard on yourself," Archer said, putting his teacup down. "Even grown men have found themselves unsettled in such situations. I think you handled the events of last evening admirably."

"I thank you, my lord," she said. Then, deciding that they needed to clear the air between them, she indicated that the servants should leave the room. Once they were gone, she said, "I regret not allowing you to come to me last night," she said, not daring to look at him lest he see the emotion that was sure to show in her eyes. "It was stubborn of me, and I think I robbed us both of some much needed solace all for the sake of my pique."

She looked up and saw that he was smiling. Since there were no witnesses, she supposed, he put his hand over hers where it lay on the table. "I am sorry about Mrs. Fitzroy," he said wryly. "I admit that I was a bit . . . well . . ."—he looked sheepish—"jealous that you'd agreed to accompany Blakemore to Vauxhall. So I sent round a note to Mrs. Fitzroy. But you must know that there is nothing between us."

Perdita felt a weight lifted from her heart at his words, but she also knew that she had to stop this if they were to remain friends. "Archer, you cannot continue to pretend that we will live happy ever after. I am determined that when I marry again it will be to someone who cannot possibly break my heart. And that will be someone like Blakemore, if not the man himself. I must have your promise that you will not cut up rough every time I am seen in public with another man."

She saw his frown at her words and knew that he was not convinced.

He pulled his hand away, but though she expected an argument, he only said, "I will agree to let you go to another man only when you have agreed to give us . . ."—his eyes flashed with emotion—"give me a chance. Until then, I fear we will have to agree to disagree."

Disappointment flooded her, but she knew that it had been a foolish dream to think that a man as passionate as Archer would take kindly to sharing her with someone else. His loyalty was one of the things she liked most about him. "Then I suppose we will," she agreed. Then, hating what she had to say but knowing it was the only fair thing for both of them, she continued, "I think that until we reach some sort of agreement, we should not sleep together again."

She'd expected him to balk, but instead he simply nodded. Though his jaw did clench, so she knew he wasn't entirely unmoved.

"If that is all," he said, standing, "I have work to do."

Alone in the breakfast room, she allowed herself to shed a tear over the dissolution of their liaison.

Any hopes Perdita had of the incident at Vauxhall being ignored by the gossip sheets were dashed when soon after breakfast, while she was writing letters, one of the maids appeared at her door bearing a note from the dowager accompanied by a copy of the most lurid of scandal sheets, *The Daily Whisper*.

The note was short and to the point:

> *Perdita,*
>   *How dare you make a spectacle of yourself?*
> *Come to me at once.*

She knew the dowager was especially overset because she'd not even bothered to sign her name—something she rarely omitted since she enjoyed using the power of her title if at all possible. It was tempting to ignore the summons. After all, Perdita was not a child, and since her sister had succeeded her as the duchess, she need not answer to the dowager any longer. Well, she amended, to a point.

Putting off the inevitable, however, had never been something Perdita was very good at. She'd much rather get the meeting over with than to have it dangling over her head all day. Calling for her maid, she had the carriage brought around, donned a pelisse and hat, and set off for the lavish town house the dowager Duchess of Ormond now called home.

Though there were but a few streets between Ormond House and the dowager's new abode, the traffic was such that it took nearly half an hour for the carriage to pull up before the elderly lady's town house. Clearly the butler had been instructed to expect her, for no sooner had she been handed down from the carriage by the dowager's footman, than she was being ushered into the entrance hall, with its gleaming white and black checkerboard-patterned marble floors.

"Her Grace awaits you in the front parlor, Your Grace," Jennings said as he took her things. Perdita had long become accustomed to being the second dowager Duchess of Ormond. Though it did feel a bit redundant at times. It was a rarity among the ton, simply because it was a rarity for a duke to predecease his grandmother as Perdita's late husband Gervase had done. And it was the circumstances of that death which had caused so much trouble for her. Including the frightening assault she'd endured the evening before.

Following Jennings upstairs, Perdita reflected that she might be able to better explain why she'd been accosted at Vauxhall if she were at last to tell the dowager about the threats she'd been getting since Gervase died. But when the threats had begun—first with Isabella, and then a few weeks later with Georgina—it had been decided that none of the three ladies would tell the dowager why they were being threatened. The dowager still thought that Isabella's maid had simply gone mad and threatened her mistress. And she had had no reason to be informed of what had occurred with Georgina in Bath, though there had been some talk of it. She'd never thought Georgina, as the daughter and widow of mere army officers, was worth the notice of a duchess in any event. That both Isabella and Perdita counted her as a friend, and the Earl of Coniston had wed her a few weeks ago, was neither here nor there.

As they reached the doorway to the parlor, Jennings announced Perdita and then discreetly disappeared. Perdita found the older woman seated before the fire, her feet up on a footstool, and her color better than the last time they'd seen one another. An apoplexy had left the dowager in a weakened state some months ago, but she seemed to be recovering. Especially now that she no longer had to share a house with Isabella, whom she saw as a snake in the grass for having tempted Trevor into marriage before his grandmother could parade him before the ton like a prize cow. Or bull, Perdita corrected herself with an inward smile.

"Grandmamma," she said, leaning down to kiss the dowager's cheek, "you're looking well. I trust you've been resting as the doctor has advised."

"Tcha," the dowager spat, "that ninny would have me an invalid if he had his way." As Perdita pulled away, the old woman looked up at her through narrowed eyes. "I'm glad to see I can still have you at my side when I wish to," she said with some degree of satisfaction.

"You know there is no need to test me, Your Grace,"

Perdita said mildly as she sat down in the chair across from her. The room was oppressively warm, but she chose to bear it since the dowager often complained of being cold. "I will come to you when you summon me, if I am able, of course."

"And why wouldn't you be able?" the dowager asked with a frown. "Perhaps because you've been cut down in the street by some madman?"

"I hardly think that is likely, do you?"

"Who is to say, Perdita? When the widowed Duchess of Ormond is accosted before a crowd of onlookers at Vauxhall, anything might happen!" She pounded her walking stick upon the floor for emphasis. "I don't suppose you saw fit to inform me of the assault last evening? Before I was forced to read about it in some tattle sheet? Like any common person?"

"I am here now, Grandmamma," she said patiently. "What is it you wish to know? I can tell you what happened last night, but I fear the stories in the gossip sheets are mostly correct. Though I believe *The Daily Whisper* says that I shrieked with terror, and that is an absurd exaggeration. I may have gasped, but that is the extent of it."

"What is the world coming to when duchesses are assaulted in public? Though I vow I've never approved of Vauxhall. It is simply an excuse for lechers and roués to lure young ladies into the dark walk. The ham is passable, I suppose."

"I'm sure I don't know," Perdita said, laughing inwardly at the dowager's commonality with Blakemore over the ham. "I suppose the young man was out of his mind with drink. At least that's what we surmised. But as you can see I am quite well, and the gossips made more out of it than it was. As they often do."

"What about Blakemore?" the dowager asked, her eyes sharp. "It made mention that he was your escort in *The Daily Whisper*."

"He has escorted me as a favor to Ormond," Perdita said calmly. She did not wish to raise the dowager's hopes about a match there. "Now, if that is all, I really must—"

"Not yet, young lady," the dowager snapped. "I also heard that it was Lord Archer Lisle who came to your rescue when the drunk fellow poured blood all over you."

"Lord Archer was there," Perdita agreed. She dared not say more, else she'd reveal the true nature of her relationship with him. Or past relationship, she reflected, after that morning's conversation. A pang of sadness swept over her.

The dowager, however, seemed not to notice. "What was Ormond's personal secretary doing at Vauxhall?" she demanded.

"He is at liberty to attend whatever entertainments he pleases," Perdita said. "He is hardly a slave to be confined to the house at all times."

"No, but what was he doing by your side?" the other woman said sharply. "You are worth far more than a mere younger son."

"We simply met upon the path and chatted, Your Grace." Perdita was becoming annoyed with the dowager's inquisition. Archer had escorted Mrs. Fitzroy at any rate, so it was hardly worth mentioning. "He happened to be there when the drunk man accosted me, and assisted me. That is all.

"Now, really," she continued, trying not to show her pique, "I came to assure you that I am unharmed after the incident last evening. I really do have things to do and should be on my way."

She rose, and leaned in to kiss the dowager's paper-thin cheek. "I am sorry if the news frightened you," she told her. The dowager was crotchety, but she did truly care about Perdita. At least she thought so. There had been no one she loved better than Gervase. Perdita tried to remember this when the old woman became too difficult. It was hardly her fault that her grandson had been a monster.

"I shouldn't mind it too much," the dowager said as Perdita rose from kissing her. "If you married again, I mean."

Ahh, so she had been paying attention. "I certainly appreciate having your permission," Perdita said, "but what brought this on?"

"Well, you were escorted by Blakemore last evening," the dowager said diffidently. "His family has been here since before the Conquest. Quite respectable."

"There is no talk of a match between us just now," Perdita said. "But I will keep your approval in mind."

"So long as it's not some younger son without a penny to his name," the dowager said firmly, which of course made Perdita wish to announce her betrothal to Archer immediately despite the way they'd left things that morning. "The Ormond name demands more."

"I shall keep that in mind, Grandmamma," Perdita said before she slipped from the room.

She was retrieving her hat and coat from the butler, when Simmons, the dowager's longtime maid, appeared as if from thin air. Perdita had never really warmed to the woman, who seemed to take her position as the dowager's personal servant as some kind of license to lord her power over everyone.

"Your Grace," she said firmly—Simmons was always firm. "I hope this visit means that the dowager can count on more visits from you in the future. I realize that when the new duchess ordered my mistress to leave Ormond House, it might have caused some embarrassment on your part, the new duchess being your sister and all, but I would not have thought a little thing like sibling loyalty would keep you from spending time with Her Grace."

Perdita blinked. But it would appear that the dowager's maid was serious. It hadn't been a desire to stay in Isabella's good graces that had kept her away from more frequent visits to the dowager's new home, but disgust at that lady's attitude toward Isabella. Especially when Isabella had done nothing but follow her godmother's orders when she traveled to Yorkshire to convince Trevor to come to London and take up his duties as the new Ormond. It was hardly Isabella's fault that they'd fallen in love. And if anything, Perdita had thought the dowager would be pleased not only to have the duke taking up his duties at last, but also to have him happily married and starting his nursery. The dowager, however, had not been pleased, and in fact it had been her anger over what she considered Isabella's treachery that led directly to the old woman's apoplexy. Though it was true that she'd not been the same since Gervase's death.

Perdita said none of this, however, as she watched the tightly wound woman before her stare daggers at her. "Simmons," she said calmly. "What a delight it is to see you again. I hope you've been keeping well."

But the maid shrugged off the inquiry as if it were a mere sprinkling of rain. Instead she said, "How I am is not the point, Your Grace," she said, her thin lips pinched together. "It is your grandmother I worry about. She has been put out of her home, and as such she has been separated from her belongings and friends and retainers—in short, everything that she holds dear. And you haven't even seen fit to visit her in over a fortnight."

"I would hardly say that being moved into one of the largest houses in Holland Park," Perdita began, "along with what furnishings she needed to create a new home for herself, as well as being able to take whichever servants she chose to accompany her, is a hardship, Simmons." She pursed her own lips. "Indeed, after Grandmamma's behavior toward the new duchess, who is, yes, my sister, she received much better than she deserved. I realize it was difficult for her to be thwarted like that after years of being in control of things at Ormond House, but that hardly excuses how she treated Isabella, and indeed her grandson Trevor. She sent Isabella to Yorkshire with the express wish that she use her feminine wiles to lure him to London. Those wiles worked, but not in the way that Grandmother wished. A disappointment, true, but hardly deserving of the dressing-down she gave them."

Simmons looked as if she would like to argue, then let out a heavy sigh. "You are right to say that my mistress is difficult to deal with, Your Grace." She rubbed her eyes. "I beg your pardon. It's just that I've seen how strongly the dowager feels about her nephew's death. Indeed, how much we all feel. It was wrong of me to speak out of turn and I hope you will forgive me rather than worry her needlessly."

Seeing that the other woman was sincere, Perdita relented. "Of course, Simmons." The maid must have been under a great deal of pressure of late. And it could not be easy to wait upon someone with as many demands as the dowager. "I hope you will let me know if you need additional help in the dowager's household. I would be more than happy to hire a few more servants for you all."

The smile Simmons gave her transformed the older woman's face and for a moment she seemed quite pretty. "I thank you for that, Your Grace, but we can manage. You are better to me than I deserve and I shan't forget it."

Once the maid had gone, Perdita stood for a moment reflecting that that was one of the oddest conversations she'd ever had with a servant. Then with a shrug, she turned to the butler who'd been watching their exchange with no little curiosity.

"If you'll pardon me, Your Grace," Jennings said, "Simmons has not been quite right these last few weeks. I think the mistress's illness has worried her. Though that does not excuse the way she went on with you just now. She can be quite forthright, our Simmons. I hope you won't refine upon it too much. After all, your grandmother doesn't always agree with her."

Thanking the man, Perdita hurried away from the house and toward her waiting carriage. It would seem that even her grandmother's maid held her responsible in some way for the dowager's reduced circumstances. It was too bad that the dowager herself was unable to reflect upon herself and her own misdeeds, which was what was needed if she were to ever acknowledge her own culpability in the situation between herself and Trevor and Isabella. It was too bad, but hardly something that Perdita could control.

She'd done what she set out to do, which was to answer the older woman's summons without revealing too much about what had happened at Vauxhall the night before. If only her pursuer could be so easily appeased.

"Are all your plans in motion, then?" Lord Coniston asked Archer as he slid into the seat across from his friend in a quiet corner of Brook's Club.

Archer ran a hand over his face, and leaned back in his chair. "It would appear so," he told his friend, signaling to a waiter that he would have a brandy, which is what Coniston also drank. "I appreciate your agreeing to go along with me on this."

"When one's wife insists upon one's participation in a matter, one does it," Con said with a shrug. "The fact that Ormond and his lady have also agreed to it gave added incentive, of course. I suspect Isabella will keep us from being prosecuted should the lady cry foul."

"One hopes," Archer said, taking his drink from the waiter. "If I didn't think this was the only way to ensure her safety, I wouldn't be doing it. Whoever it is that wishes to harm Perdita has proven himself to be more violent when it comes to her, and has been more aggressive much earlier in his campaign. I do not mean for her to be here when he chooses to put her life in jeopardy. God knows what he's planning that could top what he tried with the other two."

At the mention of the attempts on Isabella's and Georgina's lives, Con's jaw tightened. It had been only a few short weeks since a woman Georgie had considered a friend had attempted to throw her from the tower of Bath Abbey. And as both men knew, it hadn't been one woman alone who had set the plan in motion. There was a single person responsible for the attacks, and Archer did not intend to give the fellow a chance to bring Perdita to the brink of death.

"I cannot blame you," Con said, his normally genial gaze serious. "But I cannot help but wonder under what guise you mean to offer your protection. After all, you are unrelated to the lady. And there is the small matter of your employment, unless, that is, Ormond has allowed you to take care of his sister-in-law under the duties of your current position as his private secretary?"

"Hardly," Archer said with a frown. "Though he has agreed with the plan to spirit her away from London. Isabella is quite worried about her sister's safety and I think Trevor will do whatever it takes to ease her mind."

"Then how will you manage it?" Con asked, his gaze still serious. "I know what he said in the carriage the other evening about writing his own correspondence but that is surely a temporary solution."

"I've resigned my position," Archer admitted, taking another drink of his brandy.

"What?" The earl's eyes were wide with disbelief. "What will your father say?"

"Likely that I've lost my mind." Archer shrugged. "But I've been thinking I should make my own way for some time now. And there's no longer a reason for me to remain in Ormond's employ really. I sent him my letter of resignation."

"And Perdita?" Con asked. "What does she think of all this?"

"I haven't told her," Archer said baldly. "It's not relevant. Besides, it's not as if she's asked how I can just leave London, especially given that she has no idea that I am leaving London by kidnapping her."

"You're a stronger man than I am," Con said with a low whistle. "If I were kidnapping a woman as strong-willed as Perdita, whom I just happened to be in love with, I'd be scared out of my senses."

At a glare from Archer, he paused. "Well, you know what I mean," he finished, flushing. "It's not as if you're completely indifferent to her. Or she to you, for that matter."

"It does not matter, Con," the other man said firmly. "She's made it more than clear that she won't have me." She'd made that clear enough that morning at breakfast, he reflected sourly. "Taking her from London against her will now will simply cause her to dislike me more."

"That's easy for you to say now," the earl retorted, "but if one word of this little journey of yours becomes known, the papers will have the two of you married off before the cat can lick her ear."

"Then we'll simply have to make sure the papers don't get wind of it," Archer said with a raised brow. "And if for some reason word does get out, then I am prepared to do the right thing."

Con rubbed the back of his neck uncomfortably. "Are you sure this is the way you wish to win her, old man?"

Archer didn't pretend to misunderstand him. "Look," he said, his gaze direct, "if removing her from town means she's safe and out of danger, then I am willing to risk a marriage by compromise to make it happen."

"And if your plan to get her out of London also removes her from the company of other men who might be interested in her?" Con asked with a sly grin.

Not even bothering to pretend discomfort, Archer grinned back. "I'm not a saint, Con."

"Then you'd better hope that Perdita is," his friend replied, "because when she finds out you're kidnapping her she's going to have your head on a spit."

But Archer simply shrugged. "She's a redhead," he said calmly. "It comes with the territory."

Fourteen

I've had a note from Georgie," Isabella said to Perdita the next morning. "She wants us to come over at once. She says she has something to tell us both."

Swallowing the toast she'd just bitten into, Perdita looked up at her sister. "You don't think she's enceinte, do you?" Even knowing that her friend longed for a child, she could not help but feel a pang of envy. If both her sister and her friend were to give birth around the same time, she'd be left out of their conversations about motherhood. Still, her better angel prodded her into excitement for her friend.

"I'm not sure what other kind of announcement she could mean," Isabella said with a smile. "It is a bit soon since the wedding, but not quite so soon as my own announcement." Perdita's sister had become pregnant almost as soon as she and Trevor wed. It was one of the reasons Perdita could not understand the dowager's continued persecution of her sister.

They called for the carriage shortly thereafter and arrived at the Coniston town house in Berkeley Square some time later. To Perdita's surprise they were greeted at the door not by the butler, but by the Countess of Coniston herself.

"I vow I could not contain myself," Georgie said in an excited tone as she ushered her friends inside and led them to her private parlor.

Once they were seated with the requisite tea tray between them, and had chatted for a few moments about the weather, and how Isabella was feeling, Perdita felt compelled to ask, "Well, what is this news that you're fair bursting to tell us?" Really, if Georgie were so excited, why hadn't she told them at once?

To Perdita's surprise, Georgie first looked into her friend's teacup before saying, "I am sorry for waiting so long, dearest, but I had to be sure you drank it all."

She was making no sense, Perdita thought foggily. A visual image of a gypsy who'd once read her tea leaves flashed in her mind. But she found herself unable to speak the words that would ask if Georgie had taken up the practice. Instead, she felt her eyelids growing impossibly heavy, and to her mortification, the hand holding her cup fell limp.

"I'm sorry it had to be this way, darling," she heard her sister say as she brushed a hand over her hair. "But you were so stubborn, you see. And we really do wish to keep you safe."

But before Perdita could puzzle out the meaning of Isabella's words, she was fast asleep.

"I hope you know what you're doing, old man," Trevor said as he stood at the door of the unmarked carriage behind the Coniston town house. The others had come out, too, but left Trevor to make their good-byes. "She's going to be dashed angry when she wakes up."

"But she'll be safe," Archer said without hesitation as he handed the bag Isabella had packed for Perdita to the coachman. "And hopefully the laudanum will last long enough for us to get a good ways away from town."

Turning to the other man, he held out his hand, which Trevor shook, then pulled him into a hug. "Thank you for setting Isabella's mind at ease. She's been terrified for her sister these last days."

"I am happy to do so," Archer said to the other man, "but make no mistake. I am doing this for my own reasons."

He expected Ormond to cut up rough with him, but Trevor just smiled. "I know. I hope that works out for you the way you wish it to."

"It can't hurt to have her away from town and other potential suitors for a bit," Archer conceded. "I just hope she doesn't refuse to ever speak to me again when she discovers what I've done."

"Can't offer you any help with that," Trevor said. "But I do recommend ensuring that she gets a hot bath at every opportunity. For some reason that never fails to put Isabella in a better mood." Brightening, he added with a wink, "And if I'm lucky, she lets me have one, too."

Archer was certain the duke wasn't referring to having the tub all to himself, either. With a grin and a wave at the two couples seeing them off, he climbed into the carriage and gave the signal to the coachman that they should set off.

As the coach rumbled through the streets of London,

Archer looked at Perdita, sleeping soundly in the seat across from him. Though she showed no signs of stirring, the angle at which her neck sat looked uncomfortable. Moving to the other seat beside her, Archer slipped an arm behind her and cradled her head on his shoulder. With a snuffling sigh, she settled into his body.

Content now that she was in his arms, Archer fell into sleep, as well.

Perdita came awake with the slowing of the carriage. She knew she was in a carriage before she opened her eyes, and for a moment she thought she was snuggled against Gervase. But that was wrong for several reasons. The first being that she'd never ridden in such a cozy embrace with her late husband. He'd not been one for carriage riding and had chosen to ride his horse alongside the carriage the few times they'd traveled together. Second, the strong arm that held her didn't feel like Gervase. Her husband had been a larger man than this one, his build bulkier. This man, while strong, felt slimmer, more compact.

It was Archer. But why were they in a carriage? she wondered. Thinking back, she realized she could remember nothing after arriving at Georgina's house that morning. She'd been drinking her tea, and then . . . nothing. The loss of memory alarmed her but not as much as the fact that she was in a carriage, and clearly on a long enough ride that both she and Archer had felt comfortable enough to fall asleep.

She'd just have to awaken him and ask. But first, she'd need to get some space for herself. Unfortunately, she couldn't pull away because his arm was locked around her like a vise.

"Archer," she hissed. When he didn't move, she said again, this time more loudly, "Archer!"

"What?" he asked without opening his eyes, though his arm loosened a bit. "Are we there yet?"

Wrenching herself away from him, she gave him a light punch in the arm. "Let me go, you blackguard!" she demanded. "And just where are we bound? I have no recollection of agreeing to go somewhere with you today." As the possibilities ran through her mind, she became more and more uneasy. Especially when she recalled the discussion in the carriage on the way home from Vauxhall.

Archer's blue eyes, rimmed with gold lashes that were really too decadent to belong to a man, flew open. To her annoyance, he yawned, then stretched before he answered her. "Your Grace," he said at last. "Are we slowing down? I suspect we're about to change horses."

"Yes, we are slowing down," Perdita said, putting her fists on her hips. "Now, tell me how I ended up in this carriage with you without having any recollection of it?"

His brows, slightly darker than his hair, drew together, then as if remembering something important, his eyes went wide. Trying to hide his response, he shrugged. "I'm not sure I follow you."

"Stop lying, you scoundrel," she said, allowing her frustration to show. "I know we are not simply on a turn about the park. We wouldn't have both fallen asleep if that were the case."

"Then why don't you tell me what you think is going on," he said, his blue eyes untroubled.

"I think that you've expressly gone against my wishes and taken me from London against my will," she said flatly. "And I'm not positive that my sister and Georgina didn't also have something to do with it."

Yawning, he covered his mouth before saying, "Then it would appear that you've guessed correctly." Taking a look out the carriage window, he said, "We're changing horses here, and I'll escort you inside if you wish to refresh yourself and have a bite to eat before we continue on."

At his words she realized that she would very much like to relieve her bladder. Her stomach, on the other hand, rebelled at the idea of food. But she said aloud, "I will go inside, thank you. But don't think that this is the end of this discussion."

He nodded, and when the carriage rocked to a stop, he pulled on his hat and stepped out, offering her a hand down once he reached the ground. Inside the inn, Perdita made use of the small room the innkeeper's wife had shown her to.

She was considering the merits of shouting to the taproom that she was being held against her will, but when she opened the door to go back downstairs, Archer was waiting outside for her. As if reading her thoughts, he returned her steady gaze with one of his own.

Annoyed, she gave him her arm and they proceeded to the private dining room he'd procured for them. To her surprise, she was able to eat some of the excellent rabbit stew and felt better. When tea was brought for her, however, she refused, realizing that something must have been put in her cup at Georgie's house.

Once they were back in the carriage, and Archer was seated across from her again, Perdita said, "I cannot believe my sister allowed you to drug me so that you could take me away from London against my will."

"Then you underestimate how concerned your sister is for your safety," he said unrepentantly. "In fact, I think you underestimate how worried we all are about your safety. Or you simply don't care. As long as you are able to make all the decisions you don't give a fig how the rest of us feel about things."

"That's not true," she said hotly. "I care."

"Then show it by not trying to escape before we reach our intended destination."

"How can I make a rational decision when I don't know where we're bound?" she asked petulantly. It was really too much of him to make her feel like the villain when he was the kidnapper.

"Oh, I don't think it really matters," he said firmly. "So long as you are not a sitting duck in London, you are safe."

"If Isabella felt strongly enough to drug me," she conceded after a moment of silence, "then I suppose I can agree not to cause her more worry by running away from you."

Archer nodded, then to her great annoyance, settled back and fell into a deep sleep.

Coward, she thought, looking out the window. But after a long enough time had passed and she found herself growing sleepy again, she moved over to the empty space beside him and rested her head against his shoulder.

Fifteen

Perdita was still annoyed about the kidnapping when the carriage came to a stop again and Archer got out to confer with the driver.

It was full dark out now, and though she'd tried to sleep for the past couple of hours, she'd been unable to do so. She still couldn't believe Archer had gone so far as to kidnap her against her will. For her own safety. She was sick to death of men who thought they knew what was best for her. Was she not even allowed to decide whether or not she would run away from her own attacker?

Fairness forced her to admit that in other things Archer was more than willing to let her have her own way. He was hardly the sort of man Gervase had been. Indeed, quite the opposite. He listened to, and even welcomed, her opinion in most cases. He was a generous lover, even curbing what she knew were his own inclinations at times to make sure that she felt safe with him. And though they'd not made any promises to one another, she knew without asking that he had been faithful to her since they'd begun their liaison.

It was only in this one thing—her wish to remain at Ormond House despite the increasing threat against her—that he had overruled her.

She had a good mind to escape at the earliest opportunity. Just to spite him. Though her innate sense of honesty forced her to admit that she might—just might—have been a bit foolish not to accept his argument that she should leave before something more dangerous than having pig's blood thrown on her happened. So far, the measures the anonymous villain had taken against her had been mere mental torture. But she knew from both her sister's and Georgina's experiences with him that sooner or later he would make an attempt on her life. Or his surrogate would. And it was to prevent this from happening that Archer had kidnapped her.

She supposed it was sweet in a thoroughly annoying sort of way.

Even so, when the carriage door opened to reveal a travel-worn Archer, she did not greet him with open arms. He might have her best interests at heart, but it was her decision to make. Not his.

"We've arrived at the Happy Hen," he said, offering her his hand. "We'll stop here for the night and should reach our destination in the morning."

Taking his hand, Perdita let him hand her down. And because it was an unknown establishment, she took his arm as they entered the inn.

"Mr. and Mrs. Lyle," the innkeeper gushed as they stepped inside, "welcome! Welcome!"

Perdita looked around to see who this Lyle couple was that the innkeeper thought more important than a duchess. Then she realized he was speaking to them. Lyle. Clever.

"We should like to have a private supper served in our rooms," Archer said to the little man. "It's been a long journey. My wife would also like a bath if that is possible."

"Of course," the man said, leading them up the stairs to the door of their room. "I'll see that your supper is brought up immediately."

Perdita stepped into the chamber while Archer tipped the man. To her surprise it was only a bedroom with an attached dressing room. Lavish, yes. But with a single large bed against the wall.

She heard Archer shut the door with a firm click behind her and immediately felt butterflies in her stomach.

He must have seen her looking at the bed, for he said, "It was the only room left. There is a local hunt ball going on at the moment. We were lucky to get this one. It's actually much nicer than I expected it would be."

"But there is only the one bed," Perdita protested, turning to face him.

Archer's brows rose. "It's not as if we haven't shared a bed before," he said mildly.

"But I'm angry with you," she said tightly. "I'm certainly in no mood for . . . for that." She indicated the bed rather than using any of the other words or phrases that might describe the wonderful things that had happened between them in a bed before. She wasn't willing to say them lest she reveal how her body was clamoring for them. Despite her mind's decision not to let any of them happen again for a long time. Or until she was no longer punishing him.

"Well," he said with a little heat, "I'm too tired for that at the present time anyway, so I plan to use that bed for the purpose for which it was made." Turning his back to her he walked into the dressing room and began washing his face and hands. "That's sleeping in case you didn't know," he called to her.

"Fine," she said, loosening the strings of her bonnet and flinging it onto a side table.

A knock on the door indicated that their food had arrived and they didn't speak again until after they'd both consumed some of the delicious stew and still-warm bread.

"You could have asked for a bath, as well," Perdita said, putting her fork down at last. She'd been much hungrier than she'd supposed. And the food had put her in a more pleasant mood.

"Too much work," he said, taking another piece of bread. "I'll make do with the basin. I know how you enjoy your bath so I arranged for it."

"Why are you being so nice?" she asked, frustrated at his consideration while she was trying as hard as she could to maintain her grudge against him. "It doesn't change the fact that you took me from London against my will."

He laughed. "I'm not trying to turn you up sweet, Perdita. I know you're upset with me. And if the situation were reversed I might be just as angry. But I did what I thought best."

Any further discussion was forestalled by the arrival

of two footmen carrying a copper tub and a pair of maids with cans of hot water.

Once the tub was filled, Perdita stepped into the dressing room, where it had been set up, and closed the adjoining door behind her.

As soon as she lowered herself into the lavender-scented water, every ache in her carriage-rattled body felt soothed. She let out a sigh of relaxation and leaned back.

She wasn't sure how long she'd soaked, but when she stepped out of the dressing room, she saw that Archer was fast asleep beneath the covers on one side of the bed.

She allowed herself the luxury of watching him in stillness. In slumber the lines that fanned out from his eyes and that bracketed his mouth were almost nonexistent. Asleep he looked younger, happier, less worried. He'd been worried about her of late, she thought ruefully. Perhaps she wasn't being fair to make him pay for his removal of her from London. After all, he truly did have her best interest at heart. Which was a far cry from any of the times Gervase had made decisions for her.

Removing her dressing gown, she slipped between the cool sheets, and despite her earlier vows to herself not to do so, she curled up against him. In his sleep, he turned and put his arm around her. Closing her eyes, Perdita allowed sleep to overtake her.

Archer awoke to the sound of Perdita whimpering. He knew that before he even opened his eyes.

"I won't do it again, Your Grace," she said in a tone meant to pacify. "I promise. I promise. Just please don't hit me again."

But he knew that in her nightmare as well as in real life, her pleas had fallen on deaf ears. She jolted as if she'd been struck and cried out. "No, no, please no!" she wailed.

He touched her on the shoulder and was sickened when she jerked away from him. "Perdita, wake up. Open your eyes. You're dreaming. Perdita!"

It took a few moments of cajoling, but Perdita finally opened her eyes. They were blank, as if she were still in the dream, but after a couple of moments, she blinked and said, "Archer? Is it really you?" She reached out and touched his face before throwing herself into his arms. Shuddering sobs wrenched her whole body.

"Easy, love," he crooned. "You're safe. I have you. It was only a dream. I won't let anything like that happen to you again."

It took several minutes of his reassurances and holding her as she wept before she finally laid her head on his shoulder and stopped. "It was that first beating," she whispered against his skin. "It's always that one I dream of. I think because I felt the most betrayed by it. Up until then he'd been everything I'd ever dreamed a loving husband could be. But that day I saw behind the mask to the monster beneath."

"What happened?" he asked, though he wanted to hear about her husband laying his hands on her about as much as he wanted to have a tooth drawn. If it made her feel better to talk about it, though, he'd do it.

"It was his b-birthday," she stammered. "I'd gone to a great deal of trouble planning the perfect birthday dinner for him. But instead of coming home for dinner he was out late carousing with friends. When he came to my bed, I refused him. It was the first time I'd ever done so. But I was so angry that he'd neglected me. At that point, you see, I was rather spoiled by him. But instead of begging my forgiveness as he would have done before, he backhanded me. And when I protested, he hit me again. So hard I fell out of bed."

Archer stroked her back, but what he truly wished was to go back in time and teach the late duke how wrong he'd been to touch Perdita with anything other than a gentle hand. As he'd done so many times before, he chastised himself for not figuring out what was going on long before he had. If he'd known, Gervase's career as an abuser would have been much shorter.

"How did he respond?" he asked, wanting to know but dreading her response.

"He laughed," Perdita said with a shake of her head. "He thought it was the height of amusement that he'd knocked me out of the bed with his fist. When I tried to leave the room, he chided me for being so missish and made me get back into the bed with him. As if he'd only been funning. He apologized for hitting me, but explained that he couldn't allow me to talk to him—a duke—like that. It was as if that excused everything. What's really awful about that night is that I believed him when he exclaimed over my bruises and dressed every wound himself. When he made gentle love to me. I was such a fool."

"You were a new bride," Archer said, trying not to think about Gervase touching Perdita at all. "You had no notion of what marriage was like. For all you knew that was how it worked."

She sighed against him. "It was what marriage was like between my parents," she said forlornly. "I'd just thought Gervase was different. He wooed me so tenderly that I thought I'd escaped the sort of marriages my mother and sister had been forced to endure. I thought for sure I had. Until that night. And even then I thought he was different than Papa because of how quickly he'd apologized. The more fool I."

"Not a fool," Archer said hotly. "A woman who wanted her marriage to work."

"Thank you," she said quietly. "For listening. For comforting me." She paused, but Archer could sense something else coming, so he didn't even try to speak. "For kidnapping me."

He leaned back to look at her face, seeking proof that she meant what she said. "You really mean it," he said, surprised.

She nodded, her silky hair brushing against his arm where he held her. "I was being foolish to remain in London for as long as I did. Every indication is that the man who threatens me wants this time to be the one where he succeeds in killing one of us. And I think it's clear that he holds me the most responsible for Gervase's death. If I have to remain out of town for months or years, so be it. As long as I have you, I don't much care where I live."

Humbled by her apology, Archer kissed the top of her head. "I'm sorry I went against your wishes, darling. But know this. I will only ever do so when I think your own choice endangers your life. I won't ever do it on a whim. Or to punish you."

"I know you won't," she said, once more snuggling up against him.

Pressed up against one another, they fell back asleep.

Sixteen

The next day's travel was much more pleasant, and Perdita found Archer to be an easy traveling companion. Not too talkative, but not completely silent, either. They talked about books, and mutual acquaintances, and Archer entertained her with some rather unflattering impressions of many members of the ton whom they both found silly or insufferable. He was never cruel, though.

She had supposed they would stop for a brief luncheon, but Archer said that they were almost at their destination. She had supposed to travel much farther that day.

"Will you please tell me where we are bound?" she asked for what felt like the millionth time. "This mysteriousness doesn't suit you at all."

He gave a short bark of laughter. "Flattery will get you nowhere, Your Grace. You'll discover soon enough. And to be honest I'd put our destination off for another hour if it were possible."

That brought her up short. Why on earth would he take her somewhere that he didn't wish to go?

When the carriage passed through an ornate gate with a coat of arms she'd seen somewhere before, she felt one particular suspicion winnowing its way to the front of her mind. "That gatehouse is lovely," she said, hoping to spark some telling conversation.

"I've always thought so," Archer said with a tight smile. "When we were boys my brothers and I used to sneak out of the main house and come here to winkle biscuits from Mrs. Rushton, the gatekeeper's wife. I'm not sure who lives there now. The Rushtons are long dead."

"This is your father's estate," she said, all the little clues falling into place. "Why on earth would you bring me here?"

Immediately she began brushing out her gown which was travel worn and dusty from the road.

"You needn't go to trouble with your appearance," Archer said with wry amusement. "You look lovely as ever. Besides, my parents have traveled before. They understand you might be a bit dusty."

"But these are your parents, Archer," she said, running a hand over her hair, which she'd dressed herself. She wished for the hundredth time that he'd let her bring her maid. "They'll already think I'm your mistress, seeing as how we traveled in a closed carriage from London." She hated thinking that they might think less of her because of it. She'd known she'd meet them one day. Archer had been her friend for years, and of course when they came to town he would introduce them.

Or would he? She wasn't so sure now.

"So what if they do?" he said with one brow raised. "To be honest, I think they'll fall dead on seeing me with a lady at all. Much less one of your stature and beauty."

"This isn't funny," she said, exasperated by his refusal to take her concerns seriously. "I am mortified."

"Because you'll be seen with me?" he asked, his mouth tight.

"No, you fool," she said, losing her temper. "Because they'll think I'm some conniving harpy who's using you to gain an introduction to them."

"Oh, so now I'm the innocent young lad blinded by love into bringing a social climber into his parents' superior sphere?"

Perdita sighed. If he was going to be this way, they might as well just stop talking. "That's not the way I meant it."

"Then how did you mean it? And might I remind you that you are a duchess? I hardly think you need their social support."

She sighed. That was true at least.

"But why here?" she asked again, never having been answered the first time. "This will surely make things difficult for you with them."

His eyes grew serious, even stern. "Because this is the one place I could think of where I felt I could keep you safe."

A few minutes later, Archer stepped out, opting to hand Perdita down rather than let the footman do it. At the door, Fawkes, the butler at Lisle Hall since he was a child, beamed. "Lord Archer, what a pleasant surprise, if I may be so forward."

"You may indeed, Fawkes," he responded. He'd always held the old man in affection. Especially since he'd helped him and his brothers out of some of their worst scrapes. "May I present Perdita, the widowed Duchess of Ormond? She's going to be staying with us for several days."

As he'd predicted, Perdita had emerged from the carriage looking as beautiful as she always did. And of course charming Fawkes to the core. "It is my pleasure, Mr. Fawkes," she said, giving him her sunniest smile. "I hope you will tell me some tales about Lord Archer in his boyhood, for I just know he must have been positively incorrigible."

The older man bowed, and Archer thought he saw his ears redden. "It will be my pleasure, Your Grace," he said. "Though in all fairness, his lordship was perhaps not the most incorrigible of them. That was likely Lord Frederick."

"I thank you for the vote of confidence, Fawkes," Archer said with a grin. Frederick had been a rascal. "Might you tell me where my parents are at present?"

"They are waiting for you in the blue drawing room, my lord," the butler said with a smile. "They saw the carriage and guessed that it might be you."

Archer shook his head at their almost intuitive ability to know when one of their children was in trouble. It had been this way ever since they were small.

"Thank you," he said to the man. "I'd like the dowager to be put in the rose room, if that's available. And we are both starving so if cook won't be too put out we should like a bit of luncheon in our rooms in, oh, around an hour?"

The arrangements made, he took Perdita's arm and led her up the wide main staircase.

"I like Fawkes," Perdita whispered as they went. "He seems fond of you."

"I am fond of him," Archer said softly. "He made what might have been an awful boyhood a bearable one."

He realized that was the first thing he'd said to her about what it had been like growing up at Lisle Hall. Ah, well. She'd find out soon enough.

Outside the blue drawing room he turned to her and kissed her briefly on the mouth. "Courage," he said with a lopsided grin. Taking her arm, they entered the room.

His father, he noticed to some surprise, looked much older than he had the last time Archer had seen him. His mother, however, looked the same as ever.

"You might have sent word that you were coming, Archer," the duke said with a frown. "We might have been entertaining."

Both his parents had risen at their entrance, and his mother in particular was giving Perdita speculative looks. "Introduce us to your friend, Archer," she said, stepping forward to give him a brief hug.

"Mama, Papa," he said, feeling suddenly nervous, "may I present Perdita, the widowed Duchess of Ormond?"

He watched with some amusement as his mother's eyes widened and his father's narrowed. Predictable.

He turned to Perdita, who was looking rather nervous herself. For some reason that gave him courage. "Your Grace, these are my parents, the Duke and Duchess of Pemberton."

There was a long pause while they all stared at one another. At a total loss for words. Then, his mother, ever the peacemaker, stepped forward and offered Perdita her hand. "My dear, we are of course pleased to meet any friend of Archer's. And I cannot tell you how sorry we are for your loss."

"Thank you, Your Grace," Perdita said, and Archer was pleased to see her looking a bit more relaxed. "It was some time ago."

"But one never gets over a thing like that, does one?" his mother persisted. Archer was somewhat relieved when his father stepped forward and bowed over Perdita's hand. "Welcome to our home, Your Grace. I hope that you will be comfortable here." Though the look he flashed at Archer indicated that might depend on what his son had to tell him about her reasons for being there.

"Why don't I show you up to your chambers, Your Grace," his mother said, slipping an arm over Perdita's shoulders and leading her from the room.

Archer felt suddenly bereft at the loss of her presence. But at least here she would be safe, he reminded himself.

His father had some of the best guards in the county thanks to an incident where his mother had been accosted in her own garden by a man from town who suffered from a diseased mind. If the gardener hadn't come upon the man shouting at her, she might easily have been assaulted. Since then, the duke had seen to it that the house and the first few acres of the park were guarded round the clock. It was perhaps overkill, but Archer was glad of it now that he was trying to keep Perdita safe.

With the ladies gone, the duke walked over to a sideboard and poured them both a glass of brandy. "I am surprised to see you here, Archer," the duke said, his back still turned to him. "I thought you had forgotten how to find the estate."

"I find that my position with the duke takes up much of my time," Archer said, though he didn't bother adding that of late he'd spent more time watching over Perdita than he did dealing with the duke's correspondence. "I hope it's not an imposition."

"Of course not," his father said, turning from the sideboard with their drinks. He indicated with his head that they should take seats before the fire. At least it wasn't the study, Archer reflected. That had been the site of all his boyhood scolds. The drawing room was at least neutral territory.

"Though I must admit," the duke continued, "I was surprised to see you with the duchess. Wasn't she the sixth duke's wife? The one who is involved in so much gossip these days?"

"I see your contacts in town are informative, as always," Archer said, taking the seat opposite his father. "Though it is true, there has been some talk."

"I believe someone accused her of killing her husband?" The duke's expression didn't change.

Archer wished he could know what he was thinking. He might be better able to form his argument that way. But it was impossible to tell the direction of his thoughts. As usual. "Yes, there has. But it isn't true."

"You were there?" the duke asked. "I don't recall you saying anything about it in your letters."

"No, I wasn't there. But I was privy to the story just after it happened." He told his father about what had actually happened to Gervase, his treatment of Perdita, how she and Isabella and Georgina had been targeted by someone who blamed them for the Duke of Ormond's death.

His father shook his head in disbelief when Archer was finished. "That is certainly a complicated tale. Though I had heard something to that effect about the young duke and his dealings with women. There was talk that he'd beaten a whore to death not long after he left university. It was hushed up, of course, because he was a duke, but you know how rumors go. Especially among the older peers. We do like a good gossip, I am ashamed to say."

Archer, who hadn't heard that about the prostitute, blanched. Had Gervase lost his control in the same way with Perdita? It was not to be borne.

His father, to his credit, said, "I admit now that I am sorry I encouraged you to take that position with young Ormond. He was not the kind of man in whose employ I wished you to be."

At an earlier time in his life, Archer would have given his right arm to hear those words from his father's mouth. But he was surprised to realize that perhaps because recounting the tale to Perdita had lanced the old wound, he no longer held a grudge against his father over the matter. "I am grateful to hear you say it, Papa, but I have reconciled myself to the matter. I would, however, like to discuss purchasing a small property some time before we leave."

The duke's eyes narrowed shrewdly. It wasn't for nothing that he'd raised five boys. "You're in love with her, I take it?"

Archer simply nodded. "It is a complicated situation. She is, as one might expect, reluctant to marry again so soon after gaining her freedom from her husband. But I would like to ensure I have some means of taking care of her if we are to wed. I have invested the money that my aunt left me and it has done quite well."

"That seems sensible," the duke said. "I will be more than happy to discuss the matter with you." His brow furrowed. "You are not in the least bit like the late duke, however. If the duchess can't see that then perhaps she's not the wife you're looking for."

"I appreciate the vote of confidence," Archer said, surprised at how warm his father's approval made him feel. "However, I do understand her reasoning. She was in love with him at first, you see, so she doesn't trust her own judgment. And means to marry someone she doesn't love."

"It's a damnable coil, son," the duke said wryly. "I don't mind telling you that I have my doubts about your pursuing someone who is so muddled about what she really wants. Marriage is difficult enough without having your wife distrust you simply because she trusts you."

When put that way it was rather more complicated than Archer had thought. Even so, he still meant to convince her of his suitability. "I'll deal with it, Father. For now, what I wish from you is quite simple. I want to keep her here for a bit until I can figure out who is threatening her."

"Of course, that will be fine," the duke said with a nod. "You know how your mother loves having guests. Though you may not have come at the most . . . amenable time considering you wish to marry the young duchess."

A knot of dread formed in Archer's stomach. "What is it?"

"Well, it's nothing too awful," the duke said with a half grin. "It's just that your brothers are here."

Archer's mouth fell open. "All of them?" he asked in a bewildered tone. "How on earth did that happen? And why wasn't I invited?"

"Oh, give over," the duke said. "There were no invitations. Rhys is here because he makes his home here, of course. Benedick has the living so he's always underfoot. You knew that, too. Frederick was a surprise, I must say. He appeared out of the blue one afternoon saying he'd grown tired of Paris and needed a bit of rustication. Your mama thinks he had his heart broken by some Continental harpy, but I don't think he's got a heart to break. Then Cam is here, of course, because he's in search of another rock for his collection or some such nonsense. He spends most of his days down at the beachhead, though."

Archer heaved a great sigh. He had thought they'd be here alone with his parents. Not the most entertaining of situations, but far, far better than being here with all of his brothers underfoot. Trying to figure out why they were here. What was going on among them. Thinking it would be a great deal of fun to seduce Perdita away from him.

Dammit.

His father gave him a look of commiseration. "I daresay it won't be as bad as all that," he said. "And at the very least they can serve as additional watchdogs for your Perdita. It will take a determined troublemaker to infiltrate six Lisle men in protective mode."

"I suppose," Archer said with another sigh.

"Come on, son," the duke said, rising from his chair. "Go upstairs and change out of your travel filth and have something to eat. You know your mama demands we all be in attendance for tea at three sharp."

Morosely, Archer followed his father up the stairs to his bedchamber.

Perdita looked avidly around her as she followed the Duchess of Pemberton up the stairs to her bedchamber. Everything was a possible clue to the inner workings of Archer's mind. Perhaps this painting had been one that he'd liked as a child. Perhaps that rug had cushioned his fall when he'd tripped chasing one of his brothers. It was impossible not to see this house as the one in which he'd grown up. And despite herself, she was fascinated by it.

Not the least of her interest was centered upon the woman at her side. Though Archer seemed to have taken most of his looks from his father, who had the same blond hair—though the duke's was graying at the temples—and build, it was his mother whose fine features he'd inherited. From the straight line of his nose to his high cheekbones, Archer looked like his mother. Though on Archer the features were masculine, on his mother they were ethereally lovely.

"I'm so pleased that Archer brought you to visit us," the duchess said as they passed what looked to be a music room. "I don't think he's ever brought a lady to visit before."

That wasn't all too surprising, Perdita supposed, since Archer didn't spend a great deal of time pursuing women. At least not that she could recall. Since he'd been at Ormond House he'd been fairly focused on his position. She didn't recall his name being linked with any ladies.

"I am grateful to you and His Grace for having me," Perdita said aloud. "We arrived here without notice, so I do understand that I am perhaps throwing your household into a bit of a crisis."

"Oh, not at all," the older lady said, stopping before a doorway, and opening the door to reveal a prettily decorated room with rose silk on the walls and lovely rose-patterned bed hangings. "Here we are."

"What a lovely bedchamber," Perdita said, stepping in, appreciating the plush Aubusson carpets beneath her feet. "I know I'll be quite comfortable here."

"There is a dressing room with a lovely large bathtub through that door. If you wish to have a bath, just ring the bell. Is your maid with you?"

"I'm afraid not," Perdita said, cringing at what she must be thinking. "We left rather in a hurry."

If she was curious, the duchess didn't show it. "Then I will have the housekeeper assign one of the parlormaids to look after you."

"Thank you so much, Your Grace," Perdita said sincerely. She was truly appreciative that rather than throwing her out, Archer's parents had greeted her with open arms. "I don't know what I'd have done if you and your husband hadn't been so welcoming."

The duchess squeezed her hand. "I know that if Archer thinks you are worth knowing, then you must be. He has always been an excellent judge of character.

I think that comes of being the youngest. He often had to guess what his brothers were going to get up to before they even started planning it."

Perdita laughed. "That makes sense. I should like to have met his brothers, too."

"Oh, then you shall have your wish, my dear, because they are all of them staying here just now."

Perdita tried to hide her surprise. She'd gotten the impression that Archer chose to bring her here because of its relative seclusion and safety. Still, she couldn't be sorry that she'd be able to meet the men whom he was closest to in the world.

"Now, my dear," the duchess said. "I will leave you to refresh yourself and to have a bit of luncheon. We will have tea in the drawing room at three. I do hope you'll join us."

Perdita shut the door behind her and went to the bellpull to ring for a bath. If she were going to meet his brothers she'd prefer to make a good impression.

Seventeen

Some hours later, Archer entered the drawing room to see that Frederick and Rhys were already there, talking in hushed tones before the fireplace. The way they broke apart when he called out a greeting let him know they were talking about him.

His mother was seated before the table where the tea would be placed in a few minutes. "Darling," she said on seeing him, "come sit by me and tell me about your pretty Perdita."

"Yes, Archie," Frederick said, batting his eyelashes, "tell us all about your Perdita. Is she really as pretty as all that, for I cannot quite believe that Baby Archie was able to land a beauty."

"Don't be an ass, Fred," Rhys said with his usual bossiness. "Archer is a Lisle, after all, and we never settle."

"Boys, you are being rude to your brother," the duchess said to her elder sons. "Don't make me call your father."

Behind his mother's back Frederick made a rude gesture to Archer, who merely raised a brow at him.

"What do you wish to know, Mama?" he said, taking a seat beside her on the settee and kissing her cheek. As the baby of the family he'd often served as the butt of his brothers' jokes, but there were benefits, as well. One was the close relationship he shared with his mother. While some ladies of the ton only saw their children infrequently and rarely visited the nursery, the Duchess of Pemberton had been very much a presence in her sons' lives. While she did hire nannies and nurses and later tutors, she made it a priority to spend at least a few hours a day up in the nursery with them. And she wasn't the sort to hand them back to the nanny as soon as things got difficult. As a result, all of her sons held her in great affection. That they were also close to their father made them a bit of an anomaly within the upper ten thousand.

"Well," she said, as she pulled a thread through her needlepoint screen. "I should very much like to know what your intentions are," she said, "though I don't suppose you'll want to tell me that."

Archer bit back a sigh of relief. The last thing he wished to speak of while his brothers were present was his intentions.

"But I will settle," his mother continued, "for hearing how you know one another and what sort of person she is."

Before he could speak, Cam, Ben, his father, and Perdita entered the room. Archer rose to go to Perdita, who looked relieved to see him. He hadn't considered that she might feel a bit at sea in his parents' home. He'd just assumed that because she was used to aristocratic homes she'd manage well enough. But this was no regular country visit.

"Are you well?" he asked in a low voice as he led her to the settee. "Did you find everything to your liking?"

"Of course," she said with a sweet smile that reminded him that after days of traveling together he'd missed her these past few hours. Which was ridiculous, but true nonetheless. "Your mama was very welcoming toward me. And your father and brothers were perfectly friendly."

Once he'd seen her situated he turned to greet Ben and Cam, who gave him hearty pounds on the back. "Didn't think we'd see you back in this neck of the woods again, little brother," Benedick said with a grin. "And here you've come, and not only that but with a lovely lady on your arm. Well done."

"That's what we meant to say," Frederick said from an armchair beside the settee. "Well done."

"Gentlemen, please," the duchess said in a scolding tone. "You are making our guest uncomfortable."

But as Archer had suspected, Perdita could more than hold her own. "I beg you will not reprimand them, Your Grace," she said, accepting a cup of tea from her hostess. "For I am quite familiar with this sort of thing, having several male cousins and indeed a brother-in-law of my own."

"You are very sweet to excuse them, my dear," the duchess said, "but my sons know very well that they are being rude."

"Sorry, Mama. Your Grace," Ben said with a slight bow. When Frederick said nothing, the duchess glared at him until he turned red. "Very well, Mama. I apologize, Your Grace. Though honestly, Mama, you are very rough on a fellow's amour propre."

"Frederick," the duke said with a sigh, "will you never be suitable for polite company?"

"I assure you, sir, I am quite suitable for some polite company," his son replied, biting into a macaroon. "Just not here."

Changing the subject, Archer said, "What brings you to England, Fred? I thought you would never return from the Continent."

"It began to pall," his brother said with a shrug. "And I thought a bit of country air might do me some good."

Rhys scowled at Frederick, but didn't say anything to refute his brother's story. Instead he crossed his booted feet and leaned back in his chair. "Archer, why don't you tell us what it is that made you flee London with the notorious dowager Duchess of Ormond? For the life of me, I cannot think of a reason that does not place you in a scandalous position."

Archer's back stiffened and he put his teacup down. "I should watch my words if I were you, Rhys," he said in a deadly calm voice. "For you are insulting the lady."

"Indeed, Rhys," the duke said with a scowl that mirrored his firstborn's. "I have accepted the widowed duchess as a guest in our home, therefore you can have nothing to say on the matter."

"I think it very much is my business when our family's reputation is at stake, Father," the marquess said, rising from his chair. "This lady has been accused of murdering her husband. As well as carrying on an affair with Archer. Is it really appropriate for him to bring his mistress to stay for an extended visit?"

Archer stood, and the entire room went still. "Watch

yourself, Rhys. I am not above calling you out for your slurs."

"Oh, I beg you, please," Perdita said, standing, as well. "Do not fight on my account. I will simply remove to the nearest inn."

Turning to the duke and the duchess, she said, "I apologize for bringing strife into your household. I thank you for your hospitality."

"You will do no such thing," the duke said. "Rhys, Archer, I will see you both in my study." When neither man broke the stare that connected them, the duke added, "Now." He left the room, and after a moment, so too did Archer and Rhys.

Perdita had never been so horrified in her entire life. Not only had her presence caused a fight between Archer and his brother, but he'd threatened to call the other man out on her behalf. This was the second time in a week that he'd defended her honor. And honestly, she wasn't quite so sure she was worth it.

When their brothers and father left the room, the remaining Lisles, along with the duchess, put themselves to great pains to make her feel better.

"Rhys always has been a stiff-rumped beast . . . er, fellow," Frederick said with a genuinely apologetic smile. "I'm sorry for my teasing earlier. It's a great failing of mine. Also, I think it goes for all of us that we're all madly jealous of Archie at the moment. Who knew he had it in him?"

"Not I," Ben said dryly. "Though I always knew he could be persuasive with the ladies. Recall the Kimball twins."

All brothers sighed at the name.

"Your Grace," Cam said, his eyes the same color blue as Archer's though with his mother's dark hair, "the Kimball twins are the daughters of a local squire, and when we were in our teens—I believe at that point Rhys and Ben were off at university—they were the prettiest girls in the county. As their parents were friendly with ours, they were frequent visitors here. And we all harbored, hm, let us say, feelings for them."

"I didn't know about that," their mother said with surprise. "I thought you hated them."

"That is the way young men show their affection, Mama," Benedick said with a grin. "Did you not know? That and pulling at their hair."

"They did have lovely hair, didn't they?" Frederick asked in a dreamy voice. "And wonderful, large—"

"Eyes," Cam said with a glare at his brother. Who only laughed and gave Perdita a saucy wink. "In any event, we were all besotted with the twins and we wanted desperately for them to put at least two of us out of our misery. At the time, Archer was twelve, I think?"

"Yes," Frederick said with a grin. "His voice had just changed and he liked to go around reciting poetry in his new deeper voice. It was like a new toy."

"Hah," Cam laughed. "I remember that! It's why we got him to do it."

"Do what?" Perdita asked, intrigued despite herself. The idea of Archer at twelve, just coming into his deep voice—which was one of his best features—was so endearing. She'd bet he had floppy blond curls and an angelic face. How could the Kimball twins resist?

"We had just read *Romeo and Juliet* and Fred had the idea to have him recite Romeo's speech from the balcony scene under their bedchamber window one summer night."

"You didn't?" their mother gasped, horrified. "Why didn't the Kimballs tell us about this? Oh, you boys! I had no idea you were getting up to something like this!"

"Of course we went along because Archer was far too young for them. They were fourteen and as I said before, they had very large—"

"Eyes," Cam said again. "At any rate, we went there, and had Archer recite the words while Fred and I stood in the moonlight, gazing up at their windows with calf's eyes, and when they called down and told us to wait for them, we thought we'd won at Ascot."

"When they finally came out, we were waiting for them in the garden. Archer had tagged along because he thought it was his right as our orator." Frederick made an annoyed face. "Leave it to him to talk his way into things. He was always doing that. He should have been a barrister."

"So what happened?" Perdita prodded.

"We thought they'd take one look at us, fall in love, and kiss us senseless." Cam shook his head at the memory. "Instead they took one look at us, and asked where the one who'd recited the lines was. Archer stepped forward and they both walked up to him and each one kissed him on the cheek."

Perdita couldn't help but laugh. It served them right for using his gift for themselves.

"That's not all," Frederick said with a grin. "They told us that we should be ashamed of ourselves for taking advantage of our sweet brother. Then they flounced off. Never to speak to us again."

Cam ran a finger under his neck cloth. "Not quite."

Frederick's eyes widened, "What?"

But Perdita had guessed. "You kissed one of them later, didn't you?"

Looking guilty, Cam nodded. "Not for about a year or so, but yes. I think it was Amy." His brow furrowed. "Or was it Amanda?"

"You never could tell them apart, could you?" Frederick asked with disgust. "Amy was the one with the mole on her right cheek. Amanda had it on the left."

"I thought it was the other way round," Cam said with a frown.

While the two debated the issue, Perdita was brought back to reality as she remembered Archer, Rhys, and their father leaving the room in a cloud of anger. As if sensing her worry, the duchess patted her hand. "Don't worry, my dear," she said in a low voice. "I doubt their father will let them shoot each other. He dislikes violence. And besides that, by questioning your presence here, Rhys has questioned his father's decision, which my Harry will not stand for."

Perdita hoped she was right. Because if she were the cause of a rift between Archer and his family she'd never forgive herself.

Archer barely managed to rein in his temper as he followed his father and Rhys to the study. This was the site of every dressing-down he'd ever received at his father's hands. And he was old enough to recognize that one of them was about to endure the same sort of scold. He just hoped it would be Rhys and not himself.

"Shut that door behind you, Archer," his father

said as they stepped inside. "I have no wish for the servants to overhear this."

After doing as he'd been directed, Archer stepped forward to stand behind one of the chairs facing his father's enormous mahogany desk. Rhys stood behind the other.

"Father, I fail to see why simply stating the facts about the lady and the rumors that follow her makes me the villain here," Rhys said before either Archer or his father could speak. "She truly is rumored, along with her sister and friend, to have murdered her husband. A duke of the realm! Even if she didn't do it, I fail to see how her presence here cannot bring down suspicion upon our own household."

Archer was ready to jump in, but his father spoke first. "Rhys, I appreciate your concern for the family name, but you forget that you are not yet the Duke of Pemberton. I am. And as long as I am, I will make the decisions about whom to welcome and whom to banish from this house. And despite your misgivings, I trust Archer in this."

The marquess let out a grunt of frustration. "Papa, he is obviously having an affair with the woman. Of course he trusts her. Men will believe anything when it comes from a beautiful piece of—"

Archer's arm shot out as he gripped his brother by the neck cloth. He didn't even realize he was doing so until he saw Rhys's face turn red with fury. "Let me say this again, my lord," he said through clenched teeth. "The lady is my guest and my friend. And I will not have you or any man speak of her in such demeaning terms. Do I make myself clear?"

Though he could see that Rhys longed to tell him

to take himself off to the nearest lake and jump in, his brother finally nodded. "Crystal," he said. Then to Archer's surprise, he continued. "I was wrong to speak of her in such terms. I apologize."

He felt some tightness within him relax as he loosened his hold on his brother's cravat and stepped back. One thing he could say about Rhys. He always admitted when he was wrong. And was never slow to apologize for it. He was still angry with him, but the apology went a long way toward soothing his ruffled feathers.

"I believe Archer has stated the case better than I could, Rhys," the duke said firmly. "I hope I won't hear you speaking that way about any other lady who is a guest in this house ever again."

"Yes, Father," Rhys said with a nod. "I apologize to you, as well."

"Apologies are very nice," the duke said, his lips pursed, "but what I think you fail to realize is that I take this family's good name very seriously. And I understand your concerns for what might be said about us for harboring the duchess. But perhaps I should let your brother explain the matter to you."

He waved a hand to the chairs, and the brothers sat. Quickly, Archer explained what had happened the day that Gervase had been killed, as well as what was going on with regard to the threats against Perdita.

When he told the story about what had happened at Vauxhall, Rhys swore. "What kind of monster thinks to do that? It's as if he is searching out her deepest fears and then enacting them upon her. The sort of man who would send a minion to throw pig's blood on a lady is not far from perpetrating violence against her person."

At his brother's capitulation, Archer breathed a sigh of relief. He'd known that as soon as he told him he'd understand why he was so worried about Perdita's safety. "I agree," he said with a nod. "Which is why I thought to bring her here."

"Because of the guards," Rhys said, grasping the situation immediately. "I think that's sound reasoning. Also, because you know Lisle Hall so well, you know every possible entrance or vulnerable spot. You can ensure that she remains in the safer parts of the house."

The hall dated back to the Normans, and like most older estates, it had been built upon, generation after generation, and thus had four wings dating from different eras. The original hall was no longer safe and had been blocked off years ago, lest the curious sons of the family should attempt to go exploring. The family stayed in the most recently constructed east wing, which offered more modern amenities than the others, though when there were a number of guests staying at the hall, they would sometimes use them to house overflow visitors.

"I agree," Archer said, grateful that his brother had changed his tone. It would have been possible to remain here while they were at daggers drawn, but it would not have been pleasant. For either him or Perdita. Not to mention his parents.

"There now," the duke said with a smile, "that wasn't so hard, was it?"

"I only needed to hear the details of it, Father," Rhys said with a shrug. "If the situation had been what I thought, I should have continued to fight you. No matter how unpleasant things might have become."

"I know, son," the duke said. "I should have expected nothing less."

"There is one other thing," Rhys said, turning his green eyes on his brother. "You still haven't explained just what is going on between you. Not that it's any of my business, but she's a damned attractive woman, and Mama has recently launched a new campaign to have me wed before the year ends."

"Touch her and you'll wish you'd never been born," Archer said with a cheerful smile.

Rhys, like all the Lisle sons, was an attractive man, with his dark gold hair, his chiseled features, and height. Archer had little doubt that Perdita would find him appealing if his brother were to woo her. But there was no way in hell he'd let that happen. Especially not when Perdita's plans for marriage involved finding someone for whom she felt nothing. Archer didn't want that for his brother. But he also didn't want that for Perdita. And he'd do his best to see to it that he was saved the necessity of stopping any sort of plans between them.

He needn't have worried, however.

"Say no more," Rhys said with a grin. "Just wanted you to tell me to my face. When's the wedding?"

Archer felt red creep into his cheeks. "It's complicated," he said shortly.

"She's a lady, son," his father said with a laugh. "Of course it's complicated."

Eighteen

$\mathcal{D}$inner that evening was a spirited affair. Nothing like the tension-filled occasion tea had been.

Perdita could see from the duke's and duchess's demeanor that they were genuinely fond of their sons, though at times exasperated by them. To her relief, the duchess had seated her between Archer and Benedick, though Frederick did his level best to flirt outrageously with her throughout the entire meal.

When the meal was ended, Perdita expected that she and the duchess would retire to the drawing room for tea, but to her surprise, the men followed as well. "Since when we are without guests 'the ladies' consists of me alone," the duchess told her as they sat near the tea tray, "I have never much cared for the practice of the gentlemen separating from the ladies after dinner."

"Mama is an original, Your Grace," Archer said from his position propping up the mantel. "As you can see, she makes the most of her title by setting her own rules."

"If one cannot make one's own rules when one is a

duchess, my dear," the duchess said with some asperity, "then when, pray, may one?"

"She has a point," Rhys said to his brother, handing him a glass of port.

"I suddenly wonder," Perdita said with a slight frown, "if I have been making the most of being a duchess. I think I should have been taking lessons from you, Your Grace."

"You should take advantage while you can," Frederick said, in a flash of white teeth. "If you marry this fellow you'll be doomed to becoming a plain missus. Though you can retain your title, I suppose."

Perdita felt a flush rise in her cheeks. She dared not look at Archer who was likely sending a look shot through with daggers at his brother.

"I'm not . . ." she began. "That is to say, we haven't . . ." She struggled to find just the right words to announce that she had no intention of marrying their brother and son.

Rescue came from an unlikely source, however. "There, there, my dear," the duke said, patting her on the hand. "There's no need to explain things. It's none of our affair."

Rhys looked as if he'd like to overrule his father, but said nothing. Archer, when she dared look at him once the conversation had moved on to other topics, gave her a rueful smile. She wasn't sure if the apology was for his brother, his father, or himself for not having explained the situation to them. Regardless she was glad he'd not taken offense at her demurral. She had hoped that they wouldn't need to say anything to his family, but that had been naïve she now realized. Family always found a way to winkle information.

Especially when it came to the romantic relationships of their relations.

Sometime later, she was brushing out her hair at the dressing table, the maid the duchess had assigned to her having just left, when she heard a scratching noise coming from the direction of the fireplace. She shouldn't have thought the Lisles the sort to stand for mice in their walls, but supposed that the mice had no way of distinguishing between a prince or a pauper.

When she saw a figure standing in the candlelight behind her, however, she gave a muffled scream as a male hand covered her mouth.

"Easy," Archer said in a low voice. "It's me."

Turning to look, she saw that it was indeed Archer and immediately slapped his arm. "You beast!" she hissed. "Are you mad? I thought you were the note-writer!"

At once he looked contrite. "I'm sorry, love," he said, pulling her close. "I didn't think. I only knew that I wished to see you and took the most expedient, and least conspicuous, means to get here."

She pulled back slightly, grateful for the strength of his body against hers even as she calmed after the fright he gave her. "How did you get in here? I didn't hear the door."

He grinned. "That's because I didn't use the door. I used that." He pointed to a secret door, slightly ajar next to the fireplace. The mice, she thought ruefully.

"A secret passageway," she said. "Like the one at Ormond House." She shook her head at her own foolishness. "I should have guessed."

"We had an ancestor with church leanings during the reign of Henry VIII." Archer shrugged. "He put in the passageways so that visiting priests could find a quick way out should the king's men arrive unexpectedly." He pulled her to him again and stroked her hair. "I am sorry, though. I'd forgotten that that woman used the passages at Ormond House to torment Isabella."

"I should have been alert to it," Perdita said. "I am in a new house and should have been on the lookout for anything that might be used to begin the game again with me here."

"You shouldn't have to live your life waiting for the next bad thing to happen, Perdita," he said, kissing her. "And I brought you here because that is precisely what I wished to happen. That you would forget about that coward. I knew if there was one place in England where you'd be safe it would be here."

She looked up into his eyes, took his face in her hands and stroked her thumbs over his cheeks. "You are such a dear man," she said with a sad smile. "I wish that I could give as much to you as you've given to me."

He leaned in and kissed her again. This time, more passionately. When they were both breathless, he pulled back and gave her a crooked smile. "You have. Don't ever doubt it."

"But I haven't—" she began to say, but he put a finger over her lips.

"Hush," he said. "Let us not discuss it now. I know how you feel. There is no need for apologies. I know."

But she wasn't sure he did. She was almost positive that she was very much in danger of falling in love with him. Or worse, that she already had. And knowing that, she felt doubly as unhappy about her need to marry elsewhere. She tried to tell herself that she was only worried about it because that was what her heart—her traitorous heart, which fell in love at the drop of a hat—wished her to feel. But she could not for the life of her think that Archer was hiding his real, cruel self behind a façade. It was impossible.

Even so, she let him silence her, and when he kissed her again, this time with a carnality that could mean only one thing, she let him lead her into an embrace that became more and more sensual by the minute.

When she pulled away to lead him to the bed, however, he shook his head and led her by the hand to stand before him, with their backs to the fire.

"What are you doing, you odd man?" she demanded, trying to turn in his arms.

"Not yet," Archer said, slipping his hands down to grip her by the hips. "Look there." He pointed with his head toward the wall before them. Perdita looked up to see that they were opposite a tall pier glass.

She looked at their reflection. His tall form, his arms, in bright white shirtsleeves, his dark hands gripping her through the lawn of her night rail. She watched appreciatively as his hair glinted gold in the firelight. She, herself, looked like a different woman altogether. Her hair cascaded in soft red-gold waves down over her shoulders. And with her eyes wide and her lips parted, she looked like a veritable wanton.

"Look at us together," Archer said in a low, sensual voice. "Look at how well we fit." As he spoke, he stroked his right hand up the curve of her hip, over the dip of her waist, and then up and over to take her breast—just visible through the fabric of her gown. "Watch me touch you, Perdita," he whispered against her ear as he stroked his thumb over the tip of her dark nipple. It was as if she were looking at someone else. Some other man. Some other woman.

Immediately, she felt a jolt of warmth between her legs.

"Look at how your body responds to me," he said, stroking a finger over her other breast as it hardened, as if he'd ordered it to do so on cue. "I'll bet even now, your sweet crevice is readying itself for me. Is it, Perdita?"

Unable to form the words, she nodded, and saw the woman in the mirror nod, too. Behind her, she felt the stiffness of his own response pressing against her bottom. Unable to resist, she moved against him, and was pleased to hear him hiss in a breath.

"Naughty girl," he said, stilling her movements with his hands. "You know just how to tease me, don't you? I think that deserves a reward." With a sharp tug, he began lifting her gown, gathering it in one hand, while he caressed her through it with the other. Once it had bared her legs and the triangle of red-gold at their juncture, he pulled her back against him again. She was tempted to move, but anticipating what was to come, she remained still for his hand, which she watched slide across her belly and down.

When he touched the center of her, Perdita all but purred. "Easy, now," he said, his voice just a shade on the shaky side. "I'll give you what you want." He stroked a finger through the hot wetness at the heart of her. "There, is that it?" He stroked over and then into her and Perdita closed her eyes. "No," he said in a firm voice, "don't close your eyes. I want you to see us. See what I'm doing to you." When she opened them, he kissed her ear and said, "This is us, Perdita. You with me. Archer. This is what we are together." As he spoke, he stroked over her with his thumb while stroking into her with first one, then two fingers.

Unable to hold back, she began to move against his hand, faster and faster until she felt the earth shatter around her, and felt Archer mutter a curse and lower her to the carpet beneath them. Now, on her back, she opened her eyes to see him grip the neck of her night rail and tear it in one strong movement right down the middle.

"So much for that," she said with a half-smile.

His face was dead serious, however. "I'll buy you another," he said, pulling off his shirt then shucking off his breeches and smalls in one quick move. Almost as quickly as he'd left her, she felt him return, only this time, skin to skin. And without preamble, he thrust into her.

Perdita had thought she was finished for the night, but as he stroked into her body, it spasmed, inch by inch around him. When he was fully seated within her, they both sighed with completion.

Archer pressed a swift kiss to her mouth. "This is going to be rather quick, I'm afraid." With that, he pulled both of her knees up to her chest, and went even deeper before pulling back out and setting a steady pace of strokes. As he moved in, Perdita thrust her hips up and as he pulled back away, she tightened her inner muscles around him. "God, that's good," he muttered as they moved together, faster and faster until they reached a point where Perdita could no longer stop herself from crying out. As the crisis overtook her she heard Archer give a hoarse shout as he pulled out of her and spilled himself onto her belly.

He flung himself onto his back beside her as they both tried to catch their breath.

Once they'd come back to themselves, he used her ripped night rail to remove the traces of his release from her stomach. When he came back from disposing of the thing, she had removed to the bed, the covers open as she waited for him to climb in. "Why did you do that?" she asked as he slid in beside her and pulled her back to spoon in front of him.

She felt him exhale onto her neck. "It's another method of preventing conception," he explained. "Though there is a name they call those who practice it."

Oh, dear, she thought. Probably something lewd or awful because those who practiced it were guilty of fornication. "What is it?" she asked, hating for him to say, though her curiosity was great.

"Parents," he said wryly. "I am rather angry with myself for forgetting the French letter, again. But I find myself having to have you, and it becomes impossible to think of anything else but being inside you."

Perdita turned in his arms. "I am sorry," she said, kissing him softly.

"No," Archer said almost angrily. "This is not any failing of yours. It's mine. I should be taking precautions. I wish to marry you, but not because you have to."

She tucked her head into the crook of his neck. "I shouldn't think it is something we need worry about," she said softly. "After all, I was married to Gervase for some years and we never had a child."

"I like to think that was because God knows better than to give men like Gervase progeny," Archer said darkly. "Though I know that's a bit of wishful thinking on my part."

"I don't think the problem was his," Perdita said not daring to look at him. "There was one time, when I did conceive, but not too long after I discovered it, he became angry about something. I can't recall what it was. Just that he was rather more violent than he had been before and . . ."

She felt him tense against her. She hated this. Having to reveal how and in which ways her late husband had made her life a living torment. When would she and Archer be able to just be happy together? Except, a little voice warned her, she would never be able to just be happy with Archer. Not if she went through with her plan to marry elsewhere.

"He made you lose the child, didn't he?" Archer asked tightly. "I swear to you, Perdita, if it were possible to bring a man out of hell and kill him again, I would do it."

"I lost the child, yes," she said flatly. "And something else went wrong. The physician said that it was possible I'd never conceive again. And of course, I never did, so he must have been correct."

She felt Archer kiss her eyelids and then her mouth. It wasn't a kiss of passion or lust, but one of comfort. "I'm sorry," he said. "It does you no good for me to express anger against him all the time, does it?"

"Not really," she said with a sigh. "But I do like knowing how protective you are about me. It makes me feel safe."

He laughed shortly. "For all the good it's done you.

First I worked in the same house with you for years without even realizing that he was beating you, and now I've let this unnamed person threaten you and in general terrorize you. If I were a much better protector, you'd be dead."

"Hush," she said sharply. "Do not speak about yourself in that way. You are a darling man and you've worked yourself silly trying to see to it that whoever it is that's threatening me is kept away. I call that a hero. And I don't wish to hear one more time about how you didn't know about Gervase. That was by his own design. He'd been cruel like that his entire life. He'd fooled everyone around him, except those he brutalized. Why should you have been any different?"

"Are you quite finished?" he asked, the surprise still there on his beautiful face.

"Yes," she said meekly.

"Thank you for the defense," he said with a wry smile. "I should quite like to hire you if I'm ever in the dock for murder."

"I just feel . . . passionate about it, I suppose," she said, laying her head down on his chest.

"Noted, my dear," he said, kissing the top of her head. "Duly noted."

Nineteen

Archer was awakened some time later by the sound of something very like pebbles hitting the window. When the noise sounded again, he eased away from Perdita, but she woke up anyway—as was the case with most women he'd known. Ladies seemed predisposed to light sleeping.

"What is it?" she asked, rubbing at her eyes and yawning. "Is something amiss?"

"I'm going to go find out," he said, pulling on his breeches and stepping over to the window. "It looks as if there is a lit torch out there."

The bedchamber faced the carefully designed wilderness of the gardens beyond the house, which included a folly resembling a Greek temple and an ornamental lake. Archer could remember house parties from when he was a boy, when it seemed like the whole of the estate was bathed in firelight. And for a moment, he felt the odd sensation of déjà vu, as if he'd been here looking out this same window before.

Once the window was open, however, he saw that he'd only been partially right about the light.

On the lawn below, two figures stood, one a young man, holding a torch.

He felt Perdita slip up beside him, into the circle of his arm. "Who is it?" she asked, watching the scene below. She shivered. Whether from the cold or from the eerie tableau Archer couldn't tell. "One of your brothers?"

"It's hard to tell," he said, squinting. "Though the stature doesn't look right. We're all rather tall."

"I know," she said playfully. "I've noticed."

"I don't understand what this fellow is doing," Archer said, his attention on the man below. There was something about him. Something familiar.

"Duchess Perdita," the young man called, the torchlight reflecting on his face as if it were made of papier mâché like the puppets in a show Archer had seen as a boy. "Duchess Perdita, I have a message for you!"

At the mention of her name, Perdita stiffened, and Archer felt the hairs on the back of his neck stand at attention. The only messages she'd received of late had been of ill portent, and Archer suddenly wanted to shield her eyes from the sight below.

Before he could do anything, though, they watched horrified as the young man—whom he'd just realized was young Peter Gibbs, the simple-minded young lad who lived in the village with his grandmother— cried out, "See what you've made me do now!"

Then he touched the torch to the figure beside him.

"No!" Archer shouted, staring helplessly for a moment before his muscles could react. "Stay here," he told Perdita, who nevertheless followed him as he raced out of her bedchamber and past his yawning brothers who stood in various stages of undress in the hallway.

In other circumstances, Archer might have been embarrassed to be caught coming out of Perdita's room in his parents' house, but all he could think was that he had to get outside. Whether to catch the man behind the display or to save the figure engulfed in flames, he couldn't have said.

Finally, he reached doors leading from the ground floor hall into the garden beyond and raced through them.

But it was too late. He realized that as soon as he saw the form beside Peter dancing within the flames. Smelled the unmistakable stench of burning flesh.

"Did I do good, Lord Archer?" Peter asked, his eyes illuminated in the firelight. "I did just as mister said I should. Did I do good?"

Archer was at a loss for words, and was grateful when his father stepped forward, wearing breeches and a hastily donned shirt. "Aye, Peter. There's a good lad. Come with me to the kitchens and we'll see if cook has any biscuits for you."

With the unknowing Peter off in search of a treat, Archer stared sightlessly at the flames. When Rhys and Frederick came forward and doused the flames with buckets of water from the fountain, he came to himself. "I should have thought of that," he said woodenly.

"I rather think you were too shocked," his mother said, draping a blanket over his shoulders. "Come, my dear, let's go into the house and get you a strong drink."

Wordlessly he followed her into the drawing room, where Perdita had lit the lamps and rung for tea. She was, he noticed, fully dressed in a morning gown, a shawl thrown over her shoulders. Putting two spoons of sugar into a cup she'd just poured, she handed it to him. "Drink this," was all she said before giving up the pouring responsibility to his mother and sitting beside him. Her arm snaked around his back, with little regard for the way his brothers watched them.

"Who was it?" he asked, once he'd finished the hot drink. "I wasn't able to recognize him through the flames," he said, grateful that Perdita was seated beside him. Because he had little doubt that whoever had killed the man out there fully intended to do the same to her.

"Young Peter said he didn't know the fellow," the duke said, handing him a brandy. At Archer's look, he shrugged. "The ladies think tea is the cure for all ills, but I think brandy does far better."

Silently agreeing with his father, Archer downed the glass in one gulp and set the glass down on the side table.

"If Peter doesn't know," Rhys said from his customary place before the fireplace, "then he's not from around here. Peter knows nearly everyone in the county on sight. He's a special talent for recognizing faces."

"Is it possible that he was already . . . that is to say," Perdita stammered. "Could he have been deceased before the fire was set?"

Archer thought back to the scene he'd looked at from her bedchamber window. His eye had been drawn to the torch and Peter, but in the aftermath of the drama, he didn't recall seeing the staked figure moving. At all.

"I do think it's possible," he said, squeezing her hand. "I was half asleep when I looked out at them, but now I'm quite sure the fellow was slumped over. So, if he wasn't dead, he was at the very least unconscious."

"That's a relief," his mother said with a hand to her chest.

"How was it you were able to see all that, Archie?" Frederick asked slyly, injecting himself into the silence. "Your bedchamber is on the other side of the wing. I think it overlooks the kitchen garden, doesn't it."

"Frederick," Archer said silkily, "kindly keep your speculation to yourself."

"Why don't we discuss this tomorrow," the duke said smoothly. "Once we've all had a sound night of sleep."

Archer was about to agree when Perdita stood. "I won't get a chance to say it in the morning," she said briskly. "But I thank you for your hospitality. I will be leaving as soon as I am able in the morning."

"What?" the duchess asked, coming forward and taking Perdita's hands into hers. "What's this? I thought you were meant to remain with us for a good while."

"That was before whatever darkness it is that follows me made itself seen on your lawn," Perdita said tightly. Archer stood, but didn't go to her as he longed to. They were already compromised. He knew that as soon as he'd seen his brothers in the hallway beyond her bedchamber. But he could hardly make that argument before the family at large. "You didn't hear . . . Peter, was it?" At the duchess's nod, she continued. "You didn't hear Peter's words. They were meant for me. He said my name. He said he had a message for me. There is no doubt in my mind that the man who is stalking me would harm one of you if he thought it would affect me."

"He might just as easily decide to harm you," Archer said softly, stepping forward to take her hands from his mother's. "Indeed he already has. Perdita, that message may have been meant for you, but if you think running is going to rid you of this, then you're wrong."

"That's not what you said when you kidnapped me and brought me here," she said, tears running down her cheeks. "You said that there was no way he could possibly get to me here at Lisle Hall. But not only did he find me, he killed a man to let me know that leaving London was exactly the wrong thing for me to do."

"I brought you here to protect you," he said, thrusting a hand through his sleep-mussed hair. "I thought you'd be safe. How the hell was I to know this bastard can get past armed guards? Or that he'd follow us?"

"Archer, there are ladies present," his father said sharply.

"I beg pardon for my language," he said, his frustration nearly choking him, "but, Perdita, you must see that this was simply out of my control."

"Yes," she said, brushing the tears from her cheeks, "it is beyond your control. As are many things. It's time for you to realize, Archer, that you aren't God. You can't decide who lives and who dies. Who abuses and who is abused. You are a man, and as such, you are mortal. And I would die if something happened to you because of this bastard as you call him!" She took his hand and brought it to press against her breast bone. "I would die, do you hear me? And the only way . . . the only way I know to protect you is to leave. And so I must."

With that, she ran from the room, her red-gold curls streaming behind her.

He started to go after her, but was stopped by the staying hand of his father. "I think, son, this is one of those times to give a lady some time alone."

Mutely, he went back to the settee he and Perdita had vacated and lowered his head into his hands. This was all his bloody fault. He should have found out who was threatening her in London and killed the man. What had possibly made him think that coming to Devon could protect her?

"If it's any consolation," he heard Benedick say as he sat down beside him, "I'd have done the same thing. Brought her to Lisle Hall, that is. It is, in most cases, quite easy to police, what with one side of the park giving way to the sea."

"Thanks for that," Archer said with a hearty sigh. "I'll be sure to put it on my tombstone."

"Don't be overly dramatic," Frederick said scornfully. "That's my role in this family."

Archer looked up to see that his parents had left the room, and promptly made a rude gesture at his brother.

"There's the old Archie we know and love," Frederick said with a grin. "I thought you'd become some sort of mollycoddled man-child what with the lady and you being in her bedchamber and all."

He very much would have liked to make the rude

gesture again, but the reminder that they'd seen him leaving Perdita's room took any anger he felt toward his brother and directed it straight at himself.

What kind of cocksure idiot spent the night in his ladylove's bedchamber under his parents' roof?

As if reading his thoughts, Benedick said softly from beside him, "You're going to have to marry her, you know."

He knew. But given the way she'd just left the room, he thought it was rather unlikely that she'd consent to have him at her side for a few minutes, let alone a lifetime.

"We all saw," Rhys said, for once saying it kindly rather than in that condescending tone that all his brothers loathed. "And I'm not at all convinced that Mama and Papa didn't."

"Oh, they saw," Cam, who'd been silent throughout the entire exchange, said wryly. "I know because I saw them both come from the same bedchamber. Which means they were together. Tonight."

All four of his brothers groaned. "Why?" Frederick cried. "Why do you do it?"

Cam shrugged. "I dunno, I suppose I think it's good to see they still care enough about one another to . . ." He paused. "Okay, I see what you mean now. Why do I do it?"

"Is there such thing as lye soap for one's mind?" Rhys asked plaintively.

"Not that I'm aware of," Archer said, with a shudder. Leave it to his brothers to give him something else to think about in the midst of a crisis. At the memory of the crisis, he felt his smile die away.

"I can talk to her if you like," Ben said. "I'm a vicar. I do things like that now."

"Says the man who gets an eyeful of Rosie Dale's bosom just like the rest of us every time he goes to the village pub," Rhys said with a snort. He'd always made it a point to puncture Benedick's pretensions to religiosity.

"Her bosom is one of the Lord's great wonders, Rhys," his brother said with a shrug. "I'd not wish to be unmindful of it."

"I don't think so," Archer said, getting back to Ben's offer. "I'm not sure it would make a difference. She's damned stubborn when she wants to be."

"Ah, a failing of the entire female sex, I fear," Frederick said, handing Archer another glass of brandy.

"What's this for?" he asked.

"Since we can't help you by speaking to your beloved, we're going to do the next most logical thing," his brother said with a grin.

"What's that?"

"We're going to get you roaring drunk, of course," answered Cam, carrying the decanter over and placing it where the tea tray had been.

But there was something Archer needed to do first. "I'll be back," he told his brothers as he strode from the room.

When she stepped back into her bedchamber, Perdita felt as if weeks had passed instead of merely an hour. And in the space of that time a man had lost his life. And she'd destroyed her relationship with Archer. Perhaps irreparably.

Quickly, she undressed and searched out a night rail, her mind flinching at the way her other had been removed. Even now she could feel Archer's hands on her body. His sex moving within her. It might very well have been the last time she'd feel his touch. The thought left her with a tight knot in her stomach.

As she crossed to the bed, she saw his cravat, which he'd removed in some haste, carelessly laid over the chair beside the bed. Picking it up, she brought the starched linen to her face, inhaling the mingled scents of sandalwood and clean male sweat. It was a fragrance that would always remind her of him, she realized, her eyes filling with tears.

Why could she not simply forget about her fear of trusting again and just let herself be with him? It would have been an easy enough prospect for anyone but her, she thought. Anyone who hadn't learned to mistrust her own instincts through the repeated abasement by a man whose affection for her had been a mask almost from the moment they met. It felt wrong, utterly so, to punish Archer, whom she was beginning to suspect did care deeply for her, for another man's mistakes. But Perdita had no way of knowing if her instincts about him were right, or simply unreliable as they had been with her husband.

Curled up on her side, she left the lamp burning as she went back over everything that had happened that night. From the moment he came through the passageway door, to the awful moment when she realized that her stalker had murdered a man before her very eyes. Tears welled as she thought about him. Who was he? Did he have a wife and children who were even now missing him at home? Or was he, like the others that the stalker had killed during his campaigns against Isabella and Georgina, compatriots who had crossed him, or worse, investigators who had gotten too close to the truth?

The very idea that someone had lost his life because of her made her ill.

A knock at the corridor door of her room brought her from her reflections. Dashing the tears from her eyes and hiding the cravat beneath the counterpane, she pulled on her dressing gown and went to the door, opening it slightly. To her surprise, she saw the duchess, also in night dress, bearing a steaming cup of what looked to be warm milk.

"I hope you don't mind, my dear," she said, her eyes so sympathetic that Perdita wanted to throw herself into the older woman's arms and weep. "Whenever one of the boys had a fright when they were young, I always found that a cup of warm milk spiced with cinnamon could put them to rights soon enough."

Perdita's mother had died years ago, and since then she'd had only Isabella and the dowager to step into the maternal role. And while she loved them both— though the dowager could be extraordinarily difficult at times—neither of them had ever filled the hole left by her mother's absence. That the duchess might have sensed this both alarmed and relieved her.

Opening the door wider, she welcomed Archer's mother in, trying not to think of what they'd done right there before the mirror earlier that night. Indicating that they should be seated in the chairs facing the fire, Perdita took the cup from her and inhaled the sweet and spicy aroma of it. "I haven't had warm milk since I was a child, I think," she said, taking an appreciative sip.

"I hope it does you some good, dear," the duchess said, watching her with a speculative look. "I must admit to you, I suppose, that the milk was a ruse, though I do hope it helps."

So much for motherly instincts, Perdita thought wryly. "I hope you feel welcome enough to speak to me whenever you wish," she said cautiously. Given her outburst in the drawing room, she had an idea that the topic the duchess broached would not be a comfortable one.

"Even if it is a two o'clock in the morning?" the duchess asked with a rueful smile. "You are sweet to indulge an old woman, Perdita. And I hope you will do so for a bit longer. You see, I came because I wish to know what your intentions are regarding my son."

Perdita had been expecting an uncomfortable discussion, but she hadn't imagined getting this question. "I'm sorry, Your Grace," she said with a frown. "I'm not sure how you mean the question."

"I should think it's a fairly easy thing to understand," the duchess said, a hint of steel underlying her pacifying voice. "I wish to know whether your intentions toward my son are honorable."

Yes, Perdita thought. That's what she thought she meant. But the very idea was absurd. Aloud she said, "I think that's something that is between Lord Archer and myself."

"Ah, but you see, when you spoke about leaving my son for his own safety," Archer's mother said, "I thought that might mean that you care for him. Quite a bit. But if that were true, then you'd already be betrothed to him because I know my son and he's head over ears for you."

"It's . . . complicated," Perdita said carefully. How did you explain to a mother that you cared desperately for her son, but didn't trust your own judgment and feared he'd become a soulless abuser once you wed him? You didn't.

"I can understand complicated things," the duchess said easily. And for a moment, Perdita thought about just unbuttoning her thoughts about the whole business to her. But that would entail speaking of just how close she and Archer were, not only emotionally but physically.

Instead, she said, "I wish I could explain the thing to you, Your Grace, but this is a matter between Archer and me. And I have a sneaking suspicion he would not like to know I'd spoken to his mother about how I felt before I spoke to him."

To her surprise the duchess gave a hearty laugh. "Well played, my dear. A very diplomatic way of telling me to mind my own business."

Perdita felt herself flush. "That isn't quite what I intended, Your Grace, I merely wished to say—"

"No, no," the duchess said, waving away Perdita's explanation. "I don't mind. You aren't the first young person under this roof to tell me to see to my own affairs. But I am a mother, and we aren't known for our lack of interest in the affairs of our children. Even once they are grown. Though I suppose that's rare for mothers in the beau monde."

"Rather," Perdita said in agreement. "I think it's quite rare to find a mother in the ton who knows much more than her child's birthdate and names, to be honest."

"Unfortunately, I fear you are correct," the duchess said. "Though Lisle and I make it up to London rarely these days, I never found the other matrons to be overly maternal. I should certainly not have considered the dowager Duchess of Ormond to be so."

Wondering what this conversational turn would lead to, Perdita nodded.

"I seem to recall she had the raising of a grandson." The duchess's eyes were intent. "Gervase, I believe was his Christian name. The sixth duke. Was that your husband, Perdita?"

Feeling as if a layer of protection had been peeled away from her, Perdita nodded again.

"The thing is," Archer's mother continued, "I heard nasty things about the grandson when he grew up. That he drank to excess, and that he'd married a pretty wife whom he did not treat with the respect due a lady. Or any woman for that matter." She leaned forward and took the cup of milk from Perdita's hands, which she'd only just realized were shaking. "The thing is, Perdita, you may not know this about me, but the Duke of Lisle was not my first husband."

"W-was he not?" Perdita asked, curiosity cutting through her anxiety.

"No, he wasn't," the duchess said, chafing Perdita's hands between her own. "My first husband was a mere mister. A young man of wealth whom I met during my very first season. While he wasn't of noble birth, however, he was used to having everything he wanted, which included me. Of course I was young and silly and I thought myself in love with his lovely dark curls.

I thought him to be the very embodiment of the Byronic ideal. Even his petulance seemed to point to his exquisitely sensitive manners. But you know the rest of the story, don't you, my dear?"

Perdita felt her heartbeat slow, her own nerves settling, as she concentrated on the duchess rather than herself. She had a difficult time imagining the confident woman before her as a naïve and trusting young wife. Having her own will bent to match that of a mercurial husband whose every whim was catered to by those around him. But she could not. "I don't see how it is possible," she said softly. "You're so strong. So self-assured."

"That came of years of working at it," the duchess said, her expression kind, sympathetic. "We were only married a year before he was killed in a riding accident. It took me nearly two years before I could go out in company. Not because of any visible scars, but the ones inside. The ones he left on my spirit. My soul."

The duchess smiled. "I believe you and I are the only two ladies in the county who know what it is to feel relief instead of grief upon the death of a spouse."

She did understand, Perdita realized. How awful she'd felt, how guilty, as she stood over Gervase's grave. She was supposed to be in mourning but she could think of nothing but her freedom. "Did he hit you?" she asked quietly.

The other woman nodded. "Nearly every day that we were together. He went from being mysterious and handsome to brutal and ugly within the space of a week. And I don't need to tell you more. You know. You've suffered it." She squeezed Perdita's hands. "But I came back to myself. And you have, too."

"But how?" Perdita asked, tears springing to her eyes. "How can I possibly trust myself again?"

"A very wise man once told me that the fault wasn't mine in trusting, but in my husband's for thinking he could stamp out the spirit of such a strong woman." Now the duchess's eyes glittered with tears. "That man was the Duke of Pemberton, who pursued me after I'd given him every sort of rebuff possible. He wouldn't take no for an answer. And when I finally relented and said I'd allow him to become my friend? Well, that was the beginning of the end." She smiled at Perdita, who felt the stirrings of hope within her. "I love all my sons, but Archer is my baby. And I think he's grown into a fine man. His father's son. And if I thought he bore any resemblance at all to my first husband, I'd be the first woman to tell you so, Perdita."

Thinking about Archer and how gentle he'd been with her those first days after Gervase died, when she'd been almost unable to even speak to a man, let alone let him touch her, she knew that the duchess was right. She'd need to think about it a bit more, but there was no doubting his mother's story. No woman would admit to having been in such a demoralized position without having experienced it. Even if that woman wished to see her son's love requited.

"Now," the duchess said, rising, "it's quite late, and if I know my sons they are probably all getting roaring drunk. I suggest that you and I get some sleep so that we can lord our sobriety over them in the morning."

"Your Grace," Perdita said as she followed the duchess to the door. "Thank you. I . . . It helped to hear what you had to say. I know that happiness after such awfulness is possible, for both my sister and a dear friend have found love with men who treat them as if they are precious things. But to know that someone of your strength and disposition could learn to trust her own instincts again? Well, I don't need to tell you how much it has affected me."

"I only wish it might help you make up your mind," the duchess said, kissing her on the cheek. "And whether you decide that you will accept my son's love or not, I will respect your wishes. Because I know that anyone who has been through what you have deserves the courtesy of having her wishes respected."

Twenty

The Duke of Pemberton was talking to Alfred Miller, the man who oversaw all the guards on the estate, when Archer found him. They were standing near where the dead man had been staked. The body had been removed from the thick wooden pole and laid out on the ground, a sheet covering what was left of it.

"Archer," his father said as he approached them. "You remember Alfred, do you not?"

When he nodded, the duke continued. "We were discussing possible identities for the dead man."

In the flickering torchlight, Archer could see that his father was looking older than he had just yesterday. It hadn't occurred to him when he decided to bring Perdita here that the person threatening her might actually succeed in bringing his campaign of terror to Lisle Hall. He hadn't thought the man would know where they were bound when they left London. Clearly he'd been overconfident in his ability to protect her.

"I'd like to speak to Peter," he said to his father. "Will you come with me? I believe he trusts you and will respond more readily if you are with me."

The duke simply nodded and they went back into the house through the kitchen door. The cook, Mrs. Winfield, was just placing a plate of biscuits before Peter. They both scrambled to their feet at the sight of the duke and Archer.

"Sit down, sit down," the duke said as Peter tugged his forelock. "Enjoy your biscuits, my boy." To the cook he said, "I think we'd both appreciate a cup of tea, Mrs. Winfield, if you please."

The round little woman nodded and went to put the kettle on while Archer and the duke sat down at the well-worn kitchen table.

"Peter," the duke said firmly, "Archer and I would like to ask you some questions about what went on here tonight."

Exchanging a look with his father, Archer said to the young man, who was happily munching away, "What can you tell me about the man who asked you to light the fire tonight, Peter?"

Clearly mindful of being in the presence of the duke, Peter brushed the crumbs from his mouth before speaking. "He said it was a surprise. For the pretty lady, Duchess Perdita."

"What did the man look like?" Archer queried. "Was he tall like me? Or short like Mrs. Winfield."

Peter's eyes brightened. "Short," he said. "I'm tall. Like you, Lord Archer."

"What else can you tell me about him?" Archer continued. "Where did you meet him? Out in town?"

"In the street," the boy said with a vigorous nod. "I carried the box from the inn and Mrs. Wilson gave me a farthing. Then I saw the man."

Mrs. Wilson was the local seamstress.

"What color was the man's hair, Peter?" Archer leaned forward as if proximity could make the young man remember.

"Brown." Peter grinned. "And he had mustachios." He said the word again as if liking the feel of it on his tongue. "Mustachios."

Archer gave his father a questioning look, but the duke gave a brief shake of the head. The boy's description was ringing no bells, it would seem.

"Why didn't anyone else in the village do it this year?" Peter asked, as if confused. "Gram always lets me have a Guy, but not tonight." He gave a little chuckle. "I thought he was real tonight, but the man said it was just a . . . a very good Guy. I never saw one like that before. Are all the Guys in London like that, Lord Archer?"

Good God, Archer thought. The villain had convinced the boy the figure he burned was a Guy Fawkes effigy. It was an easy enough way to overcome the young man's reluctance to burn an actual person. And he was trusting enough to believe—even a stranger.

"Not quite like that, no," he told Peter. Realizing they'd gotten all the information they could from the boy, he rose. "Thank you very much, Peter, for helping us. If you see the man again, you must come tell us at once."

"Was he a bad man, Lord Archer?" He looked troubled. "Gram told me not to sneak out at night, but the man said he would give me a pound if I helped. And Gram needs money."

"He is a bad man, Peter. But you did nothing wrong." Archer grasped the boy by the shoulder. "He was wrong to ask you to sneak out. But you did it for the right reason."

"Very much so," the duke echoed.

The two men left the kitchen just as Peter's grandmother was arriving to take him home.

"I'm that sorry," the old woman said to them. "I shall have to lock the boy in his room from now on."

"There's no need for that, Mrs. Gibbs," the duke assured her. "I think Peter has learned his lesson."

Archer reflected that he had certainly learned his. No longer would he underestimate the scoundrel who'd orchestrated tonight's incident.

"Let's go to the library," the duke said, breaking into Archer's thoughts. "I've asked Miller to come in as soon as he's able."

They found the guard waiting for them in the duke's inner sanctum. Once they were seated, Archer asked the third man, "What have you come up with? Is anyone local missing?"

Miller shook his head. "None that we know of. And your father being the local magistrate, he'd know. Far as I can reckon this fellow's likely just a vagrant or some unlucky traveler he encountered and decided to use for tonight's display."

Archer ran a hand over the back of his neck. "Something just doesn't seem right about that," he said after a moment. "The stalker has always used surrogates to do his work for him, so Peter's role isn't a surprise, but the people he's actually harmed have been those who got in his way somehow. Apprentices who either turned on him or got too curious about him. What they haven't been is complete strangers."

His father nodded. "You know more about the man than we do," he said. "Can you think of anyone who might fit that description? I know you said that Perdita was accosted in London. A few times. Could it have been any of them?"

"He might want to have a look at the things we found near the body," Miller said, removing a leather pouch from his enormous coat pocket and handing it to Archer. "They don't mean anything to us, but they might to you."

Unfolding the leather, he saw a jeweled stickpin and a fine lawn handkerchief embroidered with a coat of arms he didn't recognize. But it was the signet ring that gave him pause. He remembered that ring on a hand he'd seen quite recently.

"I know who it is," he said grimly. "But it muddies the waters a bit."

"Why?" his father asked. "Who is it?"

"I think it's a friend of the late Duke of Ormond's, Lord Vyse." Quickly, he explained about the altercation that had happened at the Elphinstone rout. And Vyse's accusations against Perdita. "What I don't understand," he continued, "is why he would kill Vyse of all people. He'd have needed to transport him here against his will. Why go to that trouble?"

"It's a fair question," his father responded. "It's no small thing to carry a man cross-country when he's not willing to go."

"The other thing that doesn't make sense," he said, "is that Vyse is on the stalker's side. He thinks Perdita had a hand in killing Ormond, too. So why would he wish him dead?"

"Perhaps Vyse was working with the stalker?" Miller suggested, his gray brows furrowed in thought. "You said that he only kills those who get in his way or his compatriots. So if Vyse wasn't getting in his way, perhaps he was helping him. And followed you and the dowager from London in order to make some further attempt to frighten her."

Archer hadn't thought of Vyse as someone who played well with others, but anything was possible. Especially when it came to the stalker. He'd been adept enough at convincing others to do his bidding in the past. "If that's the case, then Perdita has never been safe. Even while we were traveling." The very idea frustrated him beyond bearing. Was there nowhere that this monster couldn't find her?

Perhaps sensing that the father and son needed to be alone, Miller excused himself to see to it that the perimeter of the house and immediate grounds were under watch by his men.

Once he was gone, the duke said, "There's nothing else you could have done, Archer. Every step you've taken is exactly what I would have done myself." He steepled his fingers before him, thinking. "The only thing you've done that I would not have recommended was taking the lady into your bed."

"Papa," Archer protested. "I'm not a green lad with his first woman. I have no need for you to explain the fine points of behavior toward the female sex. I know what I owe her."

The older man's brow arched, in a manner that looked familiar to his son. "Then why haven't you done it?" he asked quietly. "I'd have expected something like this from Frederick. Or even Rhys in one of his more high-handed moments, but you are the one I thought I needn't worry about."

"And you needn't worry about me now," he assured his father. "I mean to marry her as soon as I convince her to have me."

"What can be her objection?" To Archer's amusement, he looked affronted that Perdita hadn't leaped at the chance to become Mrs. Archer Lisle. "You are a fine prospect. Especially now."

"What do you mean, now?" Archer asked. If he'd suddenly been given a peerage or inherited a fortune, he'd like to know it.

"Well, I was waiting until the last bit of the paperwork was finalized," his father said, drawing on his spectacles as he shuffled through the papers on his desk. "Ah, here it is." He handed a piece of parchment across the desk.

"What's this?" Archer asked, even as he noted that it was a deed. With his name on it.

"It's the Waltham estate," his father said with a rather pleased expression on his countenance. "I've had it made over to you."

"Yes," Archer said, still dumbfounded. "But why? I thought you meant to settle this on Rhys when he married."

"As it happens," the duke said mildly, "Rhys has decided that he does not wish to marry yet. And for all that your Perdita seems resistant to the idea, you are."

"But you've only just learned of my attachment to her in the past couple of days," Archer argued. "Have you been studying fortune-telling at the gypsy encampment?"

"Not at all," the duke said, leaning back, folding his hands across his middle. "But I've known from what you weren't saying in your letters that you had some kind of attraction for the lady. Your position is as the private secretary to the Duke of Ormond, but your talk was of little other than the young dowager."

Archer fought the sudden desire to duck his head. Apparently he'd been more transparent in his missives home than he'd thought. "I'm not sure I know what to say, Papa. I'd planned to use the money that Aunt left me to purchase a small farm, but this is more than I could possibly have afforded on my own."

"I expect it is," the duke said. "There's a rather good living at Waltham. And I've got a good man as estate agent there, so you won't need to rush there and take over the running of it before you're ready."

Standing, Archer offered his hand to his father, which he took then covered with his other hand. "All I want for you, Archer. All I want for all my sons, is for you to find the one woman who will give you the same kind of happiness your mother has given me."

"I think I have," he said. "And once we get this madman who threatens her in shackles, I shall convince her that she wants me as much as I want her."

"Then you'd better stop her leaving in the morning." The duke's face turned serious. "For the sake of your heart, and her safety."

Archer's jaw clenched in determination. "That's exactly what I intend to do."

But first, he had to go back and see what his brothers were getting up to.

Twenty-one

The next morning, Archer felt as if a small man were hammering on the inside of his skull. His mouth was dry and if the response of the footman who was acting as his valet to seeing him was any indication, he looked like death. Fortunately, Jem had been talking with Frederick's valet that morning while he mixed a morning-after remedy for his master, so he'd been able to nip down to the kitchen and have Samson mix up another one for Archer.

So, by the time he walked into the breakfast room—having tracked Perdita there—the smell of food didn't make him want to put a bullet in his brain like it had on previous occasions the morning after overindulging.

Perdita was seated at the table in conversation with his mother, who was telling her about some system for organizing the linen closet or whatnot. Archer didn't particularly care what they were talking about so long as they were doing so and Perdita was still there. She was so beautiful, despite the late night they'd all had. And he was reminded of how glorious she'd been when they'd stood together in the pier glass, before the horror that had occurred on the lawn.

Reminded of the reason he'd wanted her to stay, he was suddenly glad for more reasons than his foolish heart that she was still here at Lisle Hall.

"I'm grateful to find you haven't left," he said as he took the seat next to her. "Were you not able to get a lift into the village?"

She looked a little sheepish. "I've decided," she said, letting her gaze meet his for just the barest moment before she lowered her lashes, "to remain here for the time being. You were right to say that it is safer here. I was so overset by what happened last night that I was thinking only of the most expedient way to keep you out of danger."

Wishing that he could kiss her, or at least take her hand in his, Archer had to make do with dipping his head so that he could meet her downcast eyes. "I'm glad you stayed. And I hope that you won't spend time worrying about my safety. I am well able to take care of myself. And if you are concerned for me, think of how out of my mind with worry I would be if you went back to London without me.

"Speaking of London," he continued, accepting the cup of tea from a hovering footman, "if you really wish to return, I will take you back. I don't think that you will be as safe there as you are here, but if you wish it we can leave as soon as I can arrange it."

But Perdita shook her head. "No," she said, glancing at his mother who was making no secret of her interest in their conversation. "I had a long think last night, and after some discussion about it with your mother, I decided to stay."

Archer was at once suspicious. "What did you say to her, Mama?" It wasn't so much that he wanted to know how she'd persuaded Perdita, it was more that he wanted to know what she'd said about him. Because his mother had been known to reveal embarrassing secrets in her quest to get what she thought her sons deserved.

"I don't think that's any of your business, Archer," she said with asperity. "It was private between Perdita and myself."

"Count on it," said Frederick as he carried a plate heaped with food to the table and took the seat beside Archer. "It is something incriminating. Remember what she told Louisa Claremont on the day of the village fair."

"Oh, really?" Their mother groaned. "Must you bring up Louisa Claremont at every turn, Frederick? She is married with four children now. And has become a dead bore besides."

"She was not a dead bore when I was fourteen, Mama," Frederick said with as much dignity as a thirty-one-year-old man can muster while discussing an injury done to him by a parent some twelve years previous. "When I was fourteen she was as close to a Greek goddess as I'd seen, and when you called me 'Freddykins' in front of her, she looked at me as if I were four and wearing short breeches."

Archer whispered to Perdita, "This is a sore subject with Frederick, as you can see."

"I should think so," she whispered back, "'Freddykins' is an awful nickname."

"Freddykins," their father said from where he was filling his own plate at the sideboard, "stop castigating your mother. It's been twelve years and, as has been noted, Louisa Claremont is many years happily wed. If a match were going to be made between you then it would have happened by now."

"It wasn't a life match I was hoping for," Frederick said under his breath.

Perhaps deciding that a change in subject was needed, he said to Archer, "Any news on your dead man from last night?"

Brought back to earth by the reminder of last night, Archer winced. He'd need to tell Perdita about the man's identity, but he didn't think she'd want an audience for it.

But beside him, she frowned. "What is it?" she asked. "What have you learned? Is it someone I know?"

When he hesitated, she said, "Archer, you're frightening me. Who is it?"

Deciding that he'd better tell her before she worried any more, he said, "It was Lord Vyse, I'm afraid."

Perdita gasped. "But why?"

Before Archer could answer, Frederick interrupted. "Vyse? You mean he was the man on fire last night? But I just saw him at the tavern only a few nights ago."

Archer turned to him. "You did?" he demanded. "Why didn't you tell me that before?"

"How the dev . . . er, deuce, was I to know he'd go getting himself burned to death in view of Lisle Hall?" Frederick defended himself. "Last I saw of the man he was beating me at darts and pinching the barmaid's ar . . . er, cheek."

"It's not as if he could know that Vyse accused me of murder in London," Perdita said rationally. "For all Lord Frederick knew he was just a friend from London staying in the neighborhood."

"But wouldn't we have heard if a nobleman was staying in the neighborhood?" Archer asked his mother. "Whoever he was visiting would surely have sent word if only to blow their own trumpet at getting such a prestigious guest."

"I'm hardly going to be impressed by a mere lordling, Archer," his mother responded with a shrug. "I am married to a duke, you know."

"He wasn't staying with anyone," Frederick said. "He told me he was in town looking to buy a horse from some fellow on the other side of the village. A man named Cartwright. I had never heard of him, but this is the first time I've been home in a year or so, so I thought it was just some newcomer."

"No," the duke said, his expression serious, "there's no one named Cartwright in the neighborhood. Not that I've heard of. On either this or the other side of the village. It sounds like your Lord Vyse was telling tales."

"So we know he wasn't brought here against his will," Archer said, stroking his chin. "And if that's the case, then he very well might have come here at the stalker's behest."

"But why?" Perdita asked. "Was he working with the man who is threatening me?"

"Either that," Archer said, "or he was here on his own."

"The question is," the duke said thoughtfully, "how can you find out what Vyse was up to? Could it be that his things are still at the inn?"

"It's worth a look," Archer said. He turned to Perdita. "Would you care for a trip to the village?"

"I'll go get my hat," she said, hurrying out of the breakfast room.

Despite the drama of the night before, Perdita enjoyed the walk with Archer into the village of Little Lisle. The fresh air was invigorating, reminding her just how much she enjoyed the country.

As they went, they chatted about any number of things that were completely unrelated to threats against her. For the first time in a long while, Perdita began to think she could have a life without being constantly under the cloud of her previous marriage and the fear of how he'd really died coming to light.

"What did my mother say to you last night?" Archer asked after a while. "And don't gammon me with something about your safety because you were dead serious about leaving when you stormed out of the drawing room. And it was over my safety, not yours."

She thought about what the duchess had told her, and how it might make him feel to know his mother was meddling in his affairs. But when it came down to it, she would give anything to have a mother who was so obviously interested in her life as Archer's was with his. "I will tell you," she said, "but you must promise me that you won't tell her that I told. We came to a meeting of the minds last night, and I don't wish to endanger that."

"All right," Archer said without hesitation. "I won't tell her."

"Well," she said, "the first thing she asked was what my intentions were toward you."

"I'm going to kill her," Archer said, shaking his head in disgust. He stopped in the middle of the path.

"I hadn't thought I was the sort of man who could stoop to matricide, but sometimes it's just necessary for the good of humanity, and—"

"Don't be so dramatic," she said, gripping him by the shoulders. "It's not how you think."

"How can it be anything other than what you just said?" he demanded. "My mother, as if I were a gentle young debutante being pursued by a fortune-hunter, asked you what your intentions are. I don't see how there's any way I can salvage my manhood from that. When all this time, I thought I was the one debauching you!"

"You were!" she said hotly. "Of course you were!"

"Well," he sniffed, "I hadn't realized you thought about it in those terms."

"Do not split hairs, Archer," Perdita said, getting annoyed. "We have debauched each other. And it has been wonderful. Your mother simply guessed that you might harbor feelings for me, so she wished to know if I meant to marry you."

"Which is none of her business," he said, turning to stare off into the trees. "I cannot believe her!"

"I told her it was none of her affair," Perdita said, walking up and placing her hand on his back, feeling the strength of his muscles beneath her hand.

"You did?" he asked, turning toward her.

"Of course I did," she said. "I'm not a green girl. And I've lived with the dowager for all these years. I know how to tell a duchess to get out of my business."

"I'll bet you do," Archer said, pulling her into the circle of his arms. "So what did you tell her?"

"That I was still figuring things out," she replied. "Which is the truth."

"It is," he said, kissing the end of her nose. "I hope you'll figure them out soon."

She sighed. "I know," she said. "Me, too."

He took her hand in his and tugged her along, "Come on, I've something to show you."

Curious, she followed him as the woodland path emerged into wide open fields on the left and the English Channel on the right. They were on the South Downs, she realized.

"We are still on my father's land here," Archer said as he stood beside her staring out at the choppy surf before pointing out a well-worn path leading to a set of stairs cut into the chalk cliff. "I want to show you something."

Perdita allowed him to lead her down the steps to the beach below, appreciating the moment. The feel of the sea breeze against her skin and the sight of Archer looking perfectly at home in the out of doors, his dark blond hair ruffled from the wind. Finally they reached the rocky beach below and she was shocked to see a blanket spread upon the ground, a picnic feast arranged there, complete with a bottle of wine and two crystal glasses.

She could not help uttering a small gasp at the perfection of it. It was a veritable romantic dream and she wasn't quite sure she believed it could be true after the horror of last night.

"When did you arrange this?" she asked him, noting that he seemed to be waiting to read her response.

"This morning," he said, his eyes intent upon her.

"I wanted you to have a new, happy memory to re-place the one from last night."

Turning, she kissed him tenderly and felt the safety of his strong arms as he pulled her to him. "You are the sweetest man," she said, laying her head against his shoulder. "I don't know what I did to deserve you but I know how incredibly fortunate I am."

"I could argue with you," he said with a half-smile, "but I'd rather not waste time arguing."

She allowed him to lead her to the blanket where they lowered themselves to sit and exclaimed over the delectables that had been laid out for them by the Lisle Hall staff.

"I told the cook to choose what to send and it would appear that she thought you deserved the best," he said with a grin, pouring the wine. "She likes you, I think, because you complimented the dinner last evening."

Taking a sip of wine, Perdita chided, "Do not try to cozen me, Lord Archer Lisle, for I am quite aware of the effect you have on females. I have little doubt everyone from the housekeeper to the lowliest kitchen maid is besotted with you."

To her delight, he actually blushed. "I haven't done anything to woo them," he said quickly. "I treat them just like I treat everyone else."

"Yes," she said with a smile, "with fairness and courtesy. You'd be amazed at how far that will go to earn a servant's loyalty."

"I suppose," he said, biting into an herb tart. "But you're not exactly loathed by the staff here or at Or-mond House."

She conceded the point, and brushed the crumbs of her own tart from her hands. Looking at Archer, who seemed more carefree than she'd ever seen him, she said, "It wasn't all bad, you know."

At his puzzled look, she took his hand, felt the strength of it in comparison to her own. "Last night," she continued, stroking her thumb over the back of his hand. "In fact, I quite enjoyed myself before the interruption."

Understanding dawned in his eyes, which then darkened with remembered passion. "I'm glad to hear it," he said with a grin. But then his gaze turned serious. "I've been continually impressed with your ability to take pleasure in the moment. Even when things seem to be devolving into chaos around you."

"It is a skill I acquired during my marriage," she said wryly. "Though I had hoped it would be unnecessary once he died. But it would seem that fate had other plans for me."

"Not fate," Archer said firmly, "but a madman. A madman I mean to stop before he can give you another moment of fear."

His handsome face was determined and Perdita longed to beg him to be careful. But she knew it would do little good. Men like Archer stayed the course until what they saw as their duty was done. And if it meant putting himself in danger, he would do it. It was the way he was made.

She leaned in and kissed him. "I do appreciate you," she said quietly. "So much."

If he wished for her to say something more, make a declaration of love, he didn't say so. Instead he busied himself with helping her pack up the remnants of their picnic into the hamper and then pulled her to her feet.

"A stroll along the beach, I think," he said, "before we allow reality to intrude upon our idyll."

Perdita did not argue, and when after meandering along the water for a while hand in hand, they turned back, she wordlessly allowed Archer to lead her to a small corridor created naturally by the rocks. Spreading the blanket on the ground within, they went into each other's arms with a passion born of last night's distress, and a need to affirm life in the face of another's loss of it.

She stroked her hands over his chest while Archer shrugged out of his coat, tossing it to the ground beside them. Eagerly, she surrendered to his kiss, even as she unbuttoned his waistcoat and pulled his shirt from his breeches. Archer pulled away for a moment to unwind his neck cloth and Perdita almost screamed with the frustration of it. She wanted him against her, skin to skin, now. But soon, he'd divested himself of his shirt as well and set to undoing the tiny row of buttons down her back.

Finally, Archer in stocking feet and breeches and Perdita in only her shift, they came back together. His kiss was surprisingly tender, and Perdita felt tears well in her eyes even as she moved her mouth against his, welcoming the gentle thrust of his tongue against hers. She allowed her hands to roam over the chiseled perfection of his chest as Archer's hands embarked upon an exploration of their own, stroking over the peaks of her breasts, making her gasp.

"Archer," she whispered, as his mouth roamed

down over her chin and stroked a path down to where he'd pulled down the front of her chemise to reveal the hardened point of her breast. When he took the nipple in his hot mouth, she nearly cried out from the wonder of it. Restlessly, she threaded her hands though his hair, holding him to her as he sucked. "Dear God," she exhaled.

"Easy," he said, pulling back and moving to expose her other breast. At the same time, he used his other hand to slip beneath the fabric of her petticoats to stroke up past her knee, to her thigh, and then to hover over the aching center of her.

Giving herself up to him, Perdita opened to him, while at the same time releasing his hair to stroke down the front of his chest and downward. She was diverted, however, by the simultaneous stroke of his hand over her wetness and the feel of his teeth scraping over her nipple. "Oh, yes, please," she murmured, "there."

In response, he gave a tug on her breast and stroked a finger inside her, rhythmically stroking inside her as her hips began to move of their own accord. It took only a brief caress upon the bud of pleasure there for her to lose herself altogether, and with a sharp cry she shattered.

It took her only a moment to recover herself, and at the feel of Archer unbuttoning the fall of his breeches, she reached down to take him in hand, guiding him into her, and at the first thrust they both gasped. Perdita closed her eyes at the delicious fullness of him within her. And gave an experimental squeeze of the muscles there, drawing a wonderfully filthy curse from Archer.

"This won't last long, I'm afraid." His voice was deep, husky with desire, and the timbre of it sent a ripple of answering lust down Perdita's spine. And then there was no more time for talk as he kissed her, then pulled almost all the way out of her before stroking slowly back in. He set up a steady rhythm that soon had them both gasping and it wasn't long before they were moving back and forth in as ancient a dance as that of the sea behind them.

When she began to lose herself again, when the pulse of orgasm overtook her, Perdita clung to him, her legs and arms trying to hold him still within her even as he began to move faster and faster. Finally, just as her own release subsided, he gave a hoarse shout and thrust once more inside her, holding still as pleasure overtook him.

Despite her protests, Archer reversed their positions as soon as he came back to himself. "What was I thinking to take you on the rocks like that. Your back must be bruised."

"You'll hear no complaint from me," she said, moving off him to set her chemise back to rights before picking up her discarded gown and pulling it over her head. "I don't know that I've ever felt as . . . invigorated as I did just now. There is something about making love in the open air."

Having discreetly adjusted his breeches, Archer pulled his own shirt back on before tying his cravat into a loose knot. "I am glad to hear it, Duchess," he said with a grin. "For there are a few more spots along the coast where I'd like to . . . invigorate you."

Relieved to see his eyes twinkling again after the darkness of the past few days, Perdita grinned. She'd been afraid her unhappy life would leach all the mirth from him. And that would have left her inconsolable.

Allowing Archer to button up her gown, she twisted her hair back up into some semblance of neatness, and soon they were presentable, if not as tidy as they'd been a few minutes earlier.

"Thank goodness for the sea wind," she said as they made their way up the stairs and toward the path again. "I think it can be blamed for all kinds of sartorial sins today."

"Indeed." Archer grinned as they walked hand in hand away from the sea and toward the path leading into the little wood on the far side of the village. "Though I don't know if it could have covered up for your misbuttoned gown. I'm glad I caught it before we made it to the village, or your reputation would be in tatters."

"It's already in tatters," she said without any real distress over the matter. After so many years of living under Gervase's thumb, she was prepared to endure much in exchange for Archer's company. "Do not forget that your entire family caught you emerging from my bedchamber last night."

"I have not forgotten," he said with a shake of his head as they moved into the cool shade of the wood. "And on that same subject—" he began, but broke off at a loud blast. "Get down," he said, pushing her to the forest floor, then dropping down to cover her with his body. As they lay there, Perdita could hear the sound of footsteps thrashing through the underbrush going in the opposite direction. Finally it died out, and the only noise was the whisper of the wind in the trees.

Finally, when there had been no sound for some minutes, Archer stood and helped her to her feet.

"What was that?" Perdita asked, knowing even before she asked.

"A gunshot," Archer said angrily. "Someone took a shot at you."

Twenty-two

$\mathcal{P}$erdita began to tremble, and Archer pulled her into his arms. His own heart beat much faster than normal still, so he knew that she had to be feeling the aftereffects of fear, as well.

"I'm sorry," she said against his shoulder, where she'd tucked her head as if she could hide from the world outside the cocoon of their bodies. "I shall be back to my usual self in just a moment. It's just that—"

"Do not apologize to me again for reacting in the manner of a rational human being in the face of terrible fear, Perdita," Archer said, unable to keep the anger from his tone. "You were just shot at, for pity's sake. I think a bit of fright is allowed."

"I didn't mean—" she began before Archer cut her off. "I know," he said firmly. "I know you were simply being polite. It's what one does when the world is falling apart around them. But you don't need to pretend such things with me. I know good and well that this monster frightens you. And if you weren't frightened I should think you were completely mad yourself."

"I hate this," she said fiercely, her spine stiffening

with frustration. "I hate constantly being afraid that he's going to hurt me, or you or someone I care about. I want him caught."

"I know you do, my dear," Archer said, kissing the top of her head. "And I will do whatever I can to make sure that he's caught. Sooner rather than later. I am hoping we'll find something in the village that might help us in this regard."

Pulling back from him, Perdita brushed off her skirts and said, "Then let us go there at once. For I can't wait another minute to find out who this person is so that we can get on with our lives."

They made it to the village without further incident, though both Perdita and Archer were vigilant about keeping watch for the shooter.

As they stepped into the Pig and Whistle, a well-dressed gentleman looked to be on his way out. When he saw Perdita, he stopped.

"You!" he said, pointing rudely at her. "It's all your fault. You weren't content to murder only your husband, but you had to see Vyse murdered, as well."

"I think you'd better consider your words more carefully, my good man," Archer said, placing a hand on the other man's chest to keep him away from Perdita. "The duchess had nothing to do with Lord Vyse's death. Nor did she have anything to do with her late husband's demise."

Before Perdita's accuser could continue, she spoke up. "Indeed, Lord Loftin, Lord Archer is correct. Though whoever killed Vyse did so in an effort to torment me over Ormond's death, make no mistake, I had nothing to do with it."

Like Lord Vyse, Lord Loftin, a viscount, had been

a crony of her late husband's. And, she recalled, he had a country house in the area. He hadn't been quite as wild as the rest of them, but his association with them had certainly been enough to give him a reputation for deep play and womanizing. His eyes narrowed as Perdita spoke. "You can make up whatever sort of stories you like, Your Grace." He spat out the courtesy as if the very words tasted foul. "Vyse was a friend of mine. When the local magistrate discovers who was responsible for his death, I have little doubt that whoever set the blaze will be found to have a connection to you. Everything you touch, it seems, turns to ruin." He turned to Archer. "I'd watch out, Lord Archer, lest you discover that you're next on her list."

"I thank you for your concern," Archer said coldly, "but I believe I can get along quite well without it."

"Suit yourself," Loftin said, pushing past them and out the door into the street beyond.

Her heart pounding from the confrontation, Perdita was grateful for Archer's arm as he led her to a tidy woman carrying a pile of linens.

"Lord Archer, as I live and breathe," the little woman said with a wide smile. "I had heard you were home." She set her burden down on a chair and stepped forward. "And you must be the young widow staying at Lisle Hall. Just as pretty as I've heard, too."

Quickly, Archer introduced Perdita to her. "This is Mrs. Jane, Your Grace. And don't tell Cook up at the hall this, but she makes the best biscuits in three counties."

The older woman blushed. "Go on with you, you young flirt." Then, turning serious, she said, "I am that sorry about what happened up at the hall. Whatever is the world coming to? That young man that died, Lord Vyse. Poor fellow. Can't be an easy thing. I hope your father discovers who killed him as soon as he can. I don't know how we'll be able to sleep at night knowing there's such a villain lurking about Little Lisle."

As she went on, Perdita felt more and more guilty about having brought such perversity into their village. There was no doubt in her mind that had she not come here, none of this would have happened. As if he sensed her thoughts, Archer squeezed her hand where it rested on his arm.

"I thank you, Mrs. Jane," he said aloud, "as I'm sure my parents would if they were here to do so. And we're here about that same matter. I was hoping you could help."

The innkeeper's eyes widened. "I'm sure I don't know how I could help, but you know I'm willing to do whatever it is you need, Lord Archer."

"We were wondering," he said carefully, "if Lord Vyse's things had been removed yet from his rooms here. My father is hoping that he might be able to glean some information about why Lord Vyse was here, or even who he met with. It would be a great help, Mrs. Jane."

But Perdita could tell from the woman's expression that her response would be bad news. "I'm that sorry, Lord Archer, but I'm afraid that friend of his, Lord Loftin, gathered them all up this morning just as soon as he arrived."

"That's all right," Perdita said, trying not to sound disappointed. "We can just wait for Lord Loftin to return from wherever it was he was going."

But again, Mrs. Jane shook her head. "He just left to go back to London. I thought he'd have said something when you spoke to him on your way in."

"I'm afraid not," Archer said before Perdita could reply. "Thank you for your help, Mrs. Jane. I'm sorry to have troubled you in the middle of your work."

They said their good-byes and were headed for the door to leave when Mrs. Jane came hurrying up behind them. "I've just remembered something, Lord Archer," she said breathlessly. "When Lord Vyse came here he asked me to store one of his cases here for him. I thought it was odd, but we do occasionally get guests who like to leave some things in the storeroom because they don't trust the maids and footmen not to steal them."

Leading them to a door off the main hallway, she retrieved the large ring of keys from a chatelaine hanging at her waist. Finding the right key, she turned it in the lock and stepped into the darkness, finding a candle holder just inside the door by touch. When she'd lit it, Perdita and Archer could see into the chamber, and it was clear that others besides Lord Vyse had asked to store things here. Or that Mrs. Jane used it for storage herself. Stepping forward, she pointed to a small leather case sitting on top of a wooden crate. "There it is," she said. "It's a bit heavy, so I'll just let you lift it, my lord."

"Is there somewhere that we can be private as we look through it, Mrs. Jane?" Perdita asked once Archer had picked it up. "If Lord Vyse thought it was worth locking away in this room, then whatever is in there must be important. And perhaps valuable."

The innkeeper agreed and showed them to a private dining room. When she'd gone, Archer set the case upon the table and began to check the locks. But to their surprise, it wasn't locked.

"Curious," Perdita said. "I should have thought he'd want to lock it if he thought it was important enough to keep hidden in the storage chamber."

"Who knows," Archer said, opening the case wide so that they could both look inside. The first thing he pulled out was a diary, which he handed to Perdita.

It was a very well made piece, she thought as she noted his name tooled into the leather of the cover. Opening it, she saw that it was a personal diary, though instead of his thoughts and feelings, the pages were covered with notations of what appeared to be wins and losses. At cards, at horses, at anything that could possibly be wagered over. Only near the end did he begin to write about his life. And then it seemed to be limited to his dealings with someone he called D:

D. is convinced that the duchess is responsible for O.'s death. But there is no way that we can prove it. We will remind her of it at every turn. Surely this will drive her to admit her crime.

Then:

D. chastised me for the public row with the duchess. Says it calls attention to our campaign and garners sympathy for her. But it felt good. I regret nothing.

And:

Vauxhall attack was perfection. The look on her face when Tewkes tossed the pig's blood on her was priceless. I thought D. might give the game away, but I should have known better. Made of sterner stuff than I thought.

Dated just four days earlier:

I am beginning to think D. is wrong that the attacks will make P. capitulate. D. also seems to be becoming a bit unhinged about the whole thing. I wonder how much longer this can last.

Finally, on the night he was killed, Vyse wrote:

Asking the innkeeper to lock this case in the storage room so that D. doesn't find it. I am convinced now that there is more madness to this plan than sense. The questioning of my motives again and again, along with the tirades about P.'s sins is more than a little unsettling. I will leave for London in the morning whether D. likes it or not.

"Archer, look here," she said, her hands shaking as she showed him the passages she'd been reading. "I can think of only one person whose initial is D. and that's Dunthorp. But why on earth would he wish to frighten me? I wasn't even aware that he knew Ormond. Gervase certainly never mentioned him."

He flipped through the book. "It could explain why he was there for so many of your incidents. Though I wonder at Vyse's not ever naming him here.

If he suspected Dunthorp of running mad, why not say his name in case someone looked through his belongings later?"

"It is odd," Perdita said. "Though he said that he feared D. would find his journal, so perhaps he chose not to name him outright as a means to appease him just in case he did find it."

"Look at these," Archer said, handing her a stack of letters tied with a bow. "The correspondent is never named. Just signs them as 'your dear boy.'"

Taking them from him, Perdita opened the first one and her eyes widened. "This is Gervase's handwriting," she said. "How on earth did Vyse get hold of them? And to what end?"

"That throws a different light on them," Archer said. "I'd just assumed they were Vyse's. But you're right. The writing doesn't match that in the journal."

One by one, she opened the letters, reading her husband's sometimes sweet, sometimes crude words of affection for a woman she didn't know. "I'd assumed he kept a mistress," she said, shaking her head as she realized just how long this affair had lasted, "but it never occurred to me that it was the same one for the entirety of the marriage."

"Perhaps he met her before you. And she was unsuitable so he married you instead." Archer rubbed her upper arm, a gesture of comfort that she appreciated. "It is odd that Vyse would have these, though. I wonder if perhaps he and Dunthorp had plans to use them in their campaign against you somehow."

"It's possible, I suppose," she said, a shiver of unease running down her spine. "I just cannot quite believe that Dunthorp was collaborating with Vyse of all people. That night at the Elphinstone rout they behaved as if they'd never met one another."

"I have little doubt that they are both quite capable of lying when they see fit," Archer said, tucking the journal and the letters back into the case, along with a three-volume novel and a packet of tooth powder. "Let's get back to the hall. I need to tell Father about what we've found. I'm not sure the journal is enough for him to have Dunthorp arrested, but it will definitely help the investigation."

"What if the shooter comes again?" she asked, as he hoisted the leather case onto his hip.

"We're going to ask Dr. Franks if he'll give us a lift back to the hall," he assured her. "I'm not taking the chance of traveling across country with you again until Dunthorp or whoever else it could be that shot at you is apprehended."

"I just never would have guessed it of him," Perdita said as they left the inn. "All the while he was pretending to woo me, he was planning to terrify me. I had thought I was becoming a better judge of character, but this just proves how wrong I could be."

"This has nothing to do with your ability to judge character," Archer said fiercely, "and everything to do with Dunthorp's skill as an actor. You cannot hold yourself to blame for believing him. I cannot stand to think that these scoundrels have made you lose your trust in people."

"I'm afraid that's just something I shall have to work out on my own," she replied, wondering who else might be deceiving her. She didn't think Archer would do such a thing, but now she had to question her trust of everyone. Including Archer, no matter how much it hurt her to think it.

When they arrived back at Lisle Hall, Archer's mother was pacing back and forth in the entrance hall. Upon seeing them, she threw up her hands in relief. "Thank goodness you're here," she said, "for you'll never guess who is sitting in our drawing room!"

"No," Archer said, "we won't, so you may as well tell us who it is so that we can help."

"The dowager Duchess of Ormond," she said in a hiss. "Do you know how terrifying that woman is?"

"Grandmamma?" Perdita asked, puzzled. "What on earth is she doing here?"

"How did she learn your location?" Archer asked, answering her question with a question. "I made great pains to hide our leaving London at all, let alone the destination. For all she knows you're still abed with measles at Coniston's town house."

"I wouldn't put it past her to threaten Con and Georgie with social ruin," Perdita said, shaking her head in exasperation. "She knows how worried Georgie is about her own middle-class origins reflecting poorly on Con."

"I'm afraid I cannot say that would be implausible for the dowager," Archer's mother said with a frown.

"I suppose we'd best go face her," Archer said. "Mama, how long has she been here?"

"Not very long. I've called for tea. I only came out here to pretend to see if there was a problem in the kitchens."

"Give us a few moments alone with her," he said,

taking Perdita's hand and leading her upstairs. Opening the door, they went in to face the wrath of the dowager.

"Well," she said from her position in the room's most comfortable chair beside the fire. "I thought you'd eloped to Gretna upon learning I was here."

Perdita pulled away from Archer and went to kiss the old woman's cheek. "Grandmamma, what a delight to see you here."

At that, the old woman cackled. "Perdita, you might fool this young Lothario with taradiddles like that, but you won't fool me. Even the saints in heaven would have difficulty delighting in the presence of the old woman who chased them down during their elopement!"

"It's not an elopement," Perdita protested, taking a seat on the settee opposite the dowager. "We left town because it was becoming dangerous for me. Especially after what happened at Vauxhall."

She resisted the urge to take Archer's hand again when he seated himself beside her. That would certainly not do anything to bolster her argument against their elopement.

"It was, indeed, Your Grace," Archer said. "In fact, I was greatly afraid that something more permanent would happen to the widowed duchess if she were to remain in London."

The dowager turned her gimlet gaze on Archer. "Yes, Lord Archer. I believe you've spent a great deal of time these past weeks worrying over Perdita's safety, haven't you. I cannot help but wonder if that concern has something to do with the size of her widow's portion."

˙ "Think what you like, Your Grace," Archer returned blandly, "the lady knows what my motives are."

"Oh, I very much doubt that, sir," she retorted. "I've seen how you've been trying to turn her head away from that simpleton Dunthorp. I daresay you are blessed with more brains than he has, but the fellow is a viscount. What are you but a younger son?"

"Grandmamma, please!" Perdita said, aghast. "You have no right to speak to Lord Archer that way."

"I'll say whatever I please in the quest to see that you don't marry a fortune-hunter, Perdita," the dowager said, banging her cane on the floor for emphasis.

"If it will make you feel better, Your Grace," Archer said dryly, "I am not in need of a fortune, as it happens."

Both ladies looked at him as if he'd sprouted corn from his ears.

"But, I thought . . ." Perdita began.

"I've had you investigated, young man," the dowager said with a frown. "You haven't a penny to your name until your great-aunt Alice kicks off. And she's as healthy as a horse. I should know, because we were at school together."

"Well, being at school together is not the same as being in close contact, Your Grace," Archer said with conviction. "I regret to inform you that she died some time ago and I invested the inheritance she left me and made quite a tidy sum from those investments."

Before the dowager could interject, he continued, "What's more, my father made the deed of one of his small estates some twenty miles away from here over to me just last night. It is one of his lesser properties that he meant to settle on my eldest brother, but as he chose not to take it, I shall be its master instead."

"Last night?" Perdita asked, still shocked about his father's gift of the estate, her eyes wide. "After . . . ?"

Archer nodded, and put his hand over hers. "He guessed where things were going, and thought you'd be more inclined to look favorably upon my suit if I had something to bring to the marriage besides my good looks and winsome charm."

"But what about a title, sir?" the dowager demanded. "Even that bag of hair, Dunthorp, has a title."

"Oh, Grandmamma," Perdita said, smiling radiantly, "I don't need a title."

Before the older lady was able to respond, the butler appeared at the door and announced, "The Viscount Dunthorp," in stentorian tones.

If Perdita and the dowager had been shocked by Archer's announcement that he was now a man of property, all three of them gaped to see Lord Dunthorp step into the chamber.

His eyes scanned the room until they landed on Perdita. Then like a loved one sighting a traveler after a long trip, he beamed and hurried toward her, going so far as to kneel down before her and take her hands in his. She recoiled at his touch, remembering the notations in Vyse's journal. If they were right, D. was Dunthorp and he'd not only been threatening her for months, he'd also killed Vyse last night and shot at her this afternoon.

Seeing her dismay, Archer gave his head a slight negative shake. Whatever her feelings for Dunthorp, Archer wished for her to let him talk. Bracing herself, she forced herself to relax.

"My dear duchess," Dunthorp said breathlessly, "I cannot tell you how relieved I am to find you safe. I was given to believe you were harmed, or worse!"

He paid not the slightest bit of attention to Archer or the dowager who both looked at him askance, albeit for different reasons.

"Hello, Dunthorp," Archer said tersely. "I am surprised to see you here. I had supposed our direction was unknown to our London friends. Unless," he continued, casting a glance at Perdita, "the widowed duchess informed you of where we'd gone, as well."

"Certainly not!" Dunthorp said, his brow descending in anger. "It would be highly improper for the widowed duchess to correspond with me."

"It's interesting you should say so," Archer said. "For I thought you considered yourselves all but betrothed."

"It's the first I've heard of it," the dowager said. "And I have no doubt that Perdita would inform me should she take such a step."

"Well," Dunthorp conceded, "I might have overstated things in an effort to make you see my point. But it's just a formality between us." He looked at Perdita, and she schooled her features not to show her disgust. "My dear duchess, you mustn't leave town without informing me again. I was terrified that the lunatic who attacked you in the park and at Vauxhall finally managed to harm you seriously."

"Yes, well," Perdita said, hoping she sounded more friendly than she felt, "that is why we left. To avoid more attacks."

"Only," Archer said conversationally, "we found

that the fellow followed her here into south Sussex. You wouldn't happen to know how he found us out, would you, Dunthorp?"

Not taking his eyes from Perdita, the other man said, "Of course not. I only learned it because I happened to follow the dowager's coach thinking she knew your true location. It was fortunate that I had a bag packed and waiting in my coach."

"Wasn't it?" Archer said grimly. "I say, Dunthorp, are you acquainted with Lord Vyse?"

Shifting on his knees—it was clearly not the most comfortable position for the fellow—he said with a frown, "Of course, but I don't like him. Keeps bad company, that one." Patting Perdita on the hand, he said, "No offense to your departed husband, my dear. I know Vyse was his friend."

"Indeed," Perdita said, her lips pursed. "He was. In fact, I'm sorry to say that an accident has befallen Lord Vyse and he is dead. What do you say to that, Lord Dunthorp?"

If he was trying to distance himself from the dead man, he was doing a very good job, Perdita thought. Dunthorp shrugged at the news of the other man's death. "I am sorry to hear it, of course, but as I said we were little more than acquaintances. What has his death to do with me?"

For the second time since they'd come into the drawing room, the conversation was interrupted by an arrival. The butler didn't announce this person, who stood just inside the door, her dull gown perfectly pressed. Her hair coiled tightly against her head.

"Simmons," the dowager said when the servant

cleared her throat. "Whatever are you doing here? I thought you were on holiday visiting your ailing mother."

"I'm afraid not, Your Grace," the ladies' maid said, her plain face alit with some emotion Perdita couldn't name.

Heedless of proper behavior, she walked toward them, one hand hidden in her skirts as she came. "I am sorry to do this here, Your Grace," she continued, "but I'm afraid it isn't to be helped. You see, I've spent a very long time trying to make this one atone for what she did."

Perdita felt the hair on the back of her neck rise as the woman looked at her.

"You see, Duchess Perdita," she said coldly, "I know what you did last season."

Twenty-three

$\mathcal{A}$t the drab woman's words, Archer's body went on alert. A glance at Perdita revealed that she was on guard, as well. "What did you say?" she asked the eerily calm Simmons.

"Oh, let us not play games now, Your Grace," Simmons said with a slow smile. "We are old foes by now, are we not?"

"Tell us what you mean by this, ma'am," Archer said, hoping to draw the woman's attention away from Perdita. Though she was in no position to run given that Dunthorp was clinging to her gown like a limpet, he thought angrily. Would the man do nothing but drag her down?

"Oh, Lord Archer," Simmons said, her eyes not leaving Perdita. "You needn't play coy with me. I know you've been party to all of my missives at this point. It's hardly possible for you to ignore them given how *close* you and the young duchess have become of late."

He was more than aware of the meaning she imbued in that one word, "close." Though how she'd known about him and Perdita when she lived in an entirely different house was baffling. Unless of course she had spies in Ormond House; which was not impossible given that she'd made her home there for many years and likely knew all the servants as well as anyone.

"You see, even before this one killed my young master I could see how your eyes followed her." Simmons grinned as if she were sharing a great joke. Archer wondered if she was mad or just evil. Whatever the case, she'd been able to dissemble in a way he'd never seen anyone do so skillfully. "There was no shame in it until she took you to her bed, of course."

A gasp—he thought from Dunthorp—shattered the utter silence in the rest of the room.

"And when I heard your father offer you the estate nearby, Lord Archer, I knew I had to act quickly. I tried to rid myself of the young dowager when you were passing through the woods earlier. But, unfortunately, my aim from a distance isn't so good." The maid smiled malevolently. "I don't think I'll have that same issue in this setting, do you?"

Simmons walked forward and stood beside where Dunthorp hovered over Perdita. Like the brave specimen he was, the marquess scrambled away to the other side of the room almost as soon as the maid reached them. It was hardly surprising, Archer reflected, but he still despised the other man for his cowardice. When he thought about the fact that Perdita had considered marrying that buffoon, he felt ill.

A movement by the maid distracted him from thinking about Dunthorp, however. Almost like a master stroking a favorite spaniel, Simmons reached out and ran a hand over Perdita's hair. "You were such a prctty girl. I thought when you wed the young master that you'd be happy ever after. But it wasn't long after the celebrations had ended that I realized you weren't nearly what he needed. Did you really think that shrinking from him was what he needed? When he was crying out for your strength?"

There was something about the way she said the words, her voice gently chiding, that put the hair on the back of Archer's neck up. Clearly she had a different opinion of the late Duke of Ormond than nearly everyone else of the fellow's acquaintance. He wondered if she'd been Gervase's lover. She was quite a bit older, but he supposed she was comely enough for a man of his appetites. Archer wondered if she'd always had a tendency toward madness or if it was her involvement with Ormond that pushed her over the edge. His behavior had certainly caused Perdita her own share of torment. But the difference between Perdita and Simmons was that Perdita had an inherent goodness about her that was missing in the other woman.

"I wonder if you know what it is like to fight back against a man who weighs stones more than you do, Simmons?" Perdita demanded of the other woman, her face white with fear and anger. "I can assure you that Gervase managed to show me just how little my strength, as you call it, could compete with his own."

Though she was clearly overset by the situation, Archer was pleased to see that Perdita wasn't allowing the other woman to cow her. He'd always admired her, but seeing her now, standing firm in the face of this woman who dared take her to task for her very natural response to the brute she'd married,

Archer could not help but feel a thrum of pride that she was his. For this situation had only made it clear to him that no matter how she protested, he would convince her that they belonged together. He was surer of that than he was of anything else in the world. If only they could get out of this situation alive.

"Not like that, you ninny," the maid said with disgust, her face twisting into an expression of distaste. "You weren't supposed to fight back. It was his right to punish you. You were supposed to accept the pain. It's the pain that matters, you see. It's what makes you feel alive! It is the bond that ties you together forever. But you were too weak. You shrieked at his first strike. Like a coward."

Archer felt his stomach turn. He'd known Gervase to be a monster, but he hadn't realized that pain and domination had been part of his repertoire of brutality. He should have guessed it, though. The outsized appetites, the demands he'd made on Perdita—it was all beginning to make sense now. There was even, Archer knew, a particular brothel in town that catered to men with such tastes. But he'd never heard a whisper about his former employer frequenting it. Perhaps Gervase had been discreet about one thing after all.

Now as he listened to Simmons, he knew that his suspicion that they'd been lovers was right. But despite the woman's words, he didn't think she was mad. Angry? Yes. Though she might not have admitted it yet, she was most angry that Gervase had married Perdita and not her. Jealousy was there in every word she uttered to the other woman. Vindictive? Absolutely. But though there was the hint of fury in her eyes as she looked at Perdita with hate, there didn't seem to be madness. Besides, no madwoman could have orchestrated the campaigns against Isabella, Georgina, and Perdita. They had been planned down to the last detail.

Oh, no, Simmons was quite sane.

Just evil.

"Of course I cried out," Perdita said to the other woman, her back ramrod straight, "he struck me in the face. With his fist. I shouldn't wonder if even the likes of you would cry out at such abuse, Simmons."

"Never," Simmons said coldly. "I took every blow he gave like the gift it was. Every stroke of the lash meant we were growing that much closer. Each time I felt the leather it was as if the pain were binding us closer together."

She laughed, and it was an ugly sound. "And you may well speak of me as if I am some ugly thing beneath your notice but Gervase never did. He thought I was beautiful. Far more beautiful than you with your simpering looks and missish ways. You disgusted him with your weakness. I was the true lady."

But the dowager could not possibly let that pass without protest. "Tcha, Simmons," she chided, pounding the floor with her walking stick for emphasis. "You are no more a lady than my best spaniel Toby. Your father was a butcher, woman. There are no ladies born above a shop."

To Archer's surprise, instead of responding angrily to her mistress, Simmons's expression softened. "I do regret having to lie to you, Your Grace," she said, her brow furrowed with real distress. "But there was no other way for me to get close to my dear Gervase. So I had to apply for the position with you. In all our time together his one regret was not telling you the truth of things. He was so fond of you, you see. So very fond."

"You have lied to me about quite a lot, I think," the dowager said sharply, her eyes narrow with annoyance, "about any number of things." Archer suspected that she was more disappointed at having trusted the other woman than she was letting on. "And of course Gervase was fond of me. He was my grandson. But I don't see where you think saying these things against Perdita will do you any good, for it's plain that you're as mad as a hatter."

Despite her affection for the dowager, however, Simmons was still not able to let that particular slur pass unremarked upon. "I am not mad," she said through clenched teeth. "And I will thank you to remember it. As well as the fact that I am a lady and as such I deserve your respect."

"Why must you continue with this fiction?" the dowager demanded, thumping her stick on the floor again. "How is it that you think you, of all people, can be called a lady? Hmm? Tell me that, if you please!"

The smile that broke across the maid's face was one of devilry. "Remember once this is finished that you did ask, Your Grace," she said with something akin to glee. "I am a lady because my father was a duke."

The words hung there in the air for a moment, as if the very atmosphere were affected by the woman's enmity.

"Really?" the dowager asked, having recovered herself. "And who, pray, is this duke you claim to be your father?"

But Archer had guessed, and when Simmons said

the words he nearly cried out for her to stop before they could escape her. Whatever impulse he'd felt, though, was not fast enough and the words fell into the chamber like a live round of ammunition.

"Your late husband, my dear duchess," Dolly Simmons said with an expression like the cat who licked the cream. "I wonder you have never noted the resemblance."

He'd rarely seen the dowager Duchess of Ormond speechless, but she was now. The old woman's face was white, and it was as if all the temper that had kept her upright had seeped out. She leaned forward, her shoulders drooping with the weight of Simmons's declaration of war.

"You see," Simmons continued, "before he ever met you, he married my mother. Of course his father thought it was an ineligible match, my grandfather being a butcher, and did all he could to separate them. But they were clever, and managed to see one another even after you married him and bore him sons. My mother died soon after giving birth to me, the silly bitch."

The woman's voice dripped with contempt for the mother she clearly saw as too weak to fight for her child, and Archer found it impossible to pity the creature.

"This is absurd," the dowager said, regaining some of her vigor, banging the floor with her walking stick. "My Bertie would never have left a child of his to be raised by a butcher. Even if your mother was a butcher's daughter."

Simmons gave a ghost of a smile. "He never knew," she said softly. "And by the time I knew he was long dead." For a moment Archer almost felt sorry for her, the little girl who'd lost both her parents before she could know them. But that didn't make up for the lives she'd affected with her vitriol.

"Then why didn't you come forward sooner?" Perdita asked, injecting some perspective into the maelstrom of pity Simmons was drawing around herself. "Surely it would have made more sense to simply inform the dowager of your identity rather than insinuating yourself into her household as you did. She is intimidating, but she is also fair."

Simmons's expression turned cold again. "Because, you fool," she hissed, "I was my nephew's lover! Do you really think that would have played well in Mayfair? Should I have simply asked for the dowager's blessing? Waved away my concerns by rationalizing that the aristocracy are all interrelated anyway? I think not."

The whole room fell silent as the words sank in. Simmons—Gervase's aunt by blood—had been his lover.

It made a horrid sort of sense. It especially explained everything Simmons had done to punish Perdita, Isabella, and Georgina since Gervase's death. If she thought they'd killed him, then of course she'd wish to make them pay. In her eyes they'd murdered her lover. Her nephew.

Archer felt his skin crawl at the idea.

"Yes," Dolly Simmons said silkily. "It was hardly the sort of thing I could simply announce to the company at large. It's not done. And you must imagine what I felt when he married you, little coward," she said to Perdita. "To know that he was going to your bed night after night? Of course after a while, he came back to me. He knew that I could give him what he needed."

"Stop saying these filthy things about my grandson," the dowager shouted. "He would never have done what you say he did with you had he known." She pounded on the floor again. "He. Would. Not."

But Simmons laughed. "Dear Duchess, do you really think I could keep a secret like that for long? Oh, I'll admit at first he was taken aback, but he got over it after a bit. He was a man, you see, and his appetites were large."

Perhaps thinking to distract her, Perdita asked, "So you orchestrated the campaign against Isabella, Georgina, and myself? I must admit that I find myself quite impressed with your skills."

Simmons preened. "Indeed I did," she said proudly. "I learned quite a bit at the side of the dowager for all those years. She is quite good at manipulating and scheming, is she not? I simply used what she taught me to manage my surrogates." Frowning, she continued, "I had no idea how fulfilling it would be to do things myself, however, as I did with you, Perdita. I hired people in London of course—my grandfather, the butcher, left me an inheritance that helped me out there—and one of the dressers at the Theatre Royale was from my old neighborhood. Really, it pays to keep up with old friendships, doesn't it? In any event, here in the country, I was able to manage on my own. I donned men's clothes to speak to that young simpleton, Peter. And I watched from the woods as he touched the flame to Vyse's body. It was most stimulating, I can assure you."

Revulsion skimmed down Archer's spine. He'd let this woman watch over Perdita after the attack in the park, he thought with horror. Only luck had stopped her from killing Perdita then and there. Luck and Simmons's desire to toy with her prey like a cat with a mouse.

Tired of listening to the woman's rant, he demanded, "What do you want from us now, Simmons? We cannot give you Gervase back. And short of killing this entire household, you cannot leave here without being prosecuted for what you've done."

"Oh, I do not wish to kill you all," Simmons said, removing her hand from where it had thus far rested inside the folds of her skirts. To Archer's horror, he saw that she held a pistol there. Which she lifted to point right at Perdita's head. "Just her."

Twenty-four

Perdita's mind raced. Ever since Simmons—Dolly Simmons, if she recalled correctly—had entered the room, she had been on edge. There was relief in knowing who it was that had perpetrated the attacks on her sister and Georgina, and herself for that matter, but from the moment the woman began to tell her story, Perdita had been waiting for her to strike out.

That her threat against Perdita's life had come in the form of a gun that looked quite similar to the little pistol of Georgie's came as no surprise. The gun would allow her to kill Perdita from a distance, and since Georgie's gun had been among the weapons that killed Gervase, there was symbolism there as well.

"I've done enough talking, now, I think," the woman said, just as cool and calm as if they were discussing the weather. "It's time for you to meet the fate that you wrote for yourself the day you murdered the man I loved."

Perdita braced herself for the bullet, thinking of Archer and closing her eyes. At the sound of the gunshot, she flinched, only to realize that she'd not been hit. She opened her eyes to see Simmons flat on the floor, her arms stretched out at her sides, her face to the thick carpet.

"Are you all right?" Archer demanded, jumping up from the floor where he must have leaped to push Simmons down. "My God," he said, holding her so tightly she almost lost her breath. "If she'd succeeded in killing you I'm not sure how I'd have gone on."

"I am fine," she said, surprised to feel that he was shaking against her. "Archer," she whispered, pulling back to look him in the eye. "I am well. I am safe." Perdita felt tears in her eyes as she kissed him.

He kissed her back, neither of them mindful of the room behind them which was quickly filling up with Archer's family thanks to the sound of the gunshot.

At the sound of several coughs they pulled apart, though Perdita remained in the circle of Archer's arm. "What?" he demanded.

"We thought perhaps you'd like to stop before you consummated things here on the drawing room floor," Frederick said with a grimace. "What with the dead body and all, it wouldn't be quite the thing, you know."

"Dead body?" Perdita asked, frowning. "I thought she was just unconscious."

"No," Archer assured her. "She is indeed dead. I'm not sure whom, but one of my brothers shot her from the secret door."

They all watched as Simmons's body, covered in a sheet, was carried from the room by two footmen.

"That would be me," Cam said with a bow. "We heard the dowager's repeated thumps on the floor with her cane and thought that Archer and Dunthorp had come to blows—he's run off, by the way—and I was about to open the door when I heard that woman saying something about beatings. So I listened for a bit, realized who she was, and snuck into the secret passageway."

"Dunthorp has run away?" Perdita demanded. "What a coward!

"I always said the fellow was unreliable," the dowager said, her complexion white beneath the thick layers of powder. "Whatever were you thinking to entertain the man, Perdita?"

"Grandmamma," Perdita said, rushing to the old woman's side. "You must be exhausted. I'm so sorry about Simmons." Even if the maid had been a madwoman bent on killing her, Perdita knew it couldn't have been easy for the dowager to learn she'd been harboring a viper in her bosom for all these years.

"No more sorry than I am, my dear," the dowager said emphatically, shaking her head in disbelief. "When I think of how much I entrusted to that . . . that . . ." And to Perdita's astonishment the redoubtable dowager Duchess of Ormond burst into noisy tears.

Perdita indicated to Archer that he and his brothers should leave her to speak to the dowager alone. And like the males they were the Lisle men fled the scene.

"I always knew there was someone else," the dowager said once her tears had subsided. "A wife knows."

Remembering how fondly the dowager had always spoken about the late duke, Perdita felt her heart constrict. Though from the stories she'd heard—such as how he'd banished Trevor's father from the family simply for marrying someone his father disapproved of—she'd never thought the duke was someone she would particularly like, she had thought he at least held his wife in some affection.

"But I knew," the dowager continued. "I pretended ignorance, of course, because that's what we were taught to do, the gels of my generation. We did not live in our husband's pockets like you young people today."

Reflecting upon her own marriage, Perdita disagreed, but let the dowager continue uninterrupted.

"I even thought Simmons seemed familiar when she first applied for the position," the dowager continued. "Of course now I know why."

Perdita took the dowager's hand and squeezed. "There's no reason why you should have suspected her true origins, Duchess. It's not as if her origins were plainly writ upon her face. I certainly never suspected her of anything untoward."

"But . . ." The other woman shuddered. "Her own nephew! It's disgusting. When I think of her hands on me while she helped me dress and bathe . . ."

"Don't think of it," Perdita said quickly. She would do well to heed her own advice, she told herself. For she was having as hard a time as the duchess banishing from her mind all the little familiarities she'd granted Gervase's lover over the years. "I pray you, do not."

They sat in silence for a moment before the dowager said, "There is something I must tell you, Perdita. Something that is very difficult to admit."

What on earth could she be talking about? Perdita wondered before saying, "I feel sure it cannot be as shocking as what Simmons told us, Your Grace."

But she was wrong.

"I poisoned Gervase," the dowager said baldly. "That is how he died. Not the gunshot or the knife."

Perdita opened her mouth and then shut it again. "You . . . you what?"

"I poisoned him," the dowager said morosely. "I didn't know about his . . ."—she seemed to search for a word—"*relationship* with Simmons, of course. But I knew he was carrying on with other women."

Sensing that the older woman needed to get the words out, Perdita remained silent.

"And I knew about the beatings," she continued. "I . . . I overheard him hitting you just days earlier. I'd known about it for a long while, but I'd never actually witnessed anything." Her eyes were troubled. "I thought if you were a better wife he would not have to hurt you, you see. But I didn't know the extent of it. I never realized just how vicious he could be.

"Perdita, I do hope you will forgive me. For waiting so long. I could not admit it, you see. I could not admit that my precious boy could be that sort of man. A man cut from the same cloth as his grandfather, I mean."

"As his grandfather?" Perdita asked hollowly. "Do you mean to say that the old duke did to you what Gervase did to me?"

The dowager nodded. "I thought I deserved it, too. It's really why I never confronted him over the affairs. Oh, I told myself it was because weeping over a husband's indiscretions was not done, but it was actually because I feared what his response would be. Bertie could be incredibly kind, but he could also be ruthless. And I knew that if I complained about the mistresses that he would just come back to my bed." She frowned. "I could not do that again. It . . . it hurt too much. What he wanted from me."

Perdita knew what it must have taken the dowager to admit such a thing. "I do not blame you," she said kindly. "Not a bit."

"I'm just sorry it took me so long to come to your aid, my dear," the dowager said. "And equally sorry that the people of the ton blamed you for my crime. For I really did mean for it to free you. Not to make your life more difficult. And I certainly had no notion that Simmons would hold my sins against you."

"How can you have known?" Perdita asked simply. "We certainly had no notion that you poisoned Gervase. Indeed, I had thought you knew nothing of what went on between us."

"Can you ever forgive me for turning my back on you?" The dowager's face constricted with remorse. "I will never feel more disgusted with myself than I do right now."

"Of course, Your Grace." Perdita patted the old woman's hand. "I do not think it would have done you any good to confront Gervase any earlier, either. He would likely have hit you just as he hit me."

"What a mess things are," said the dowager in a sad voice. "When I think of the hopes I once had for Gervase. Of the great-grandchildren he'd bring me . . . and all the while he was *fornicating* with that woman."

Perdita shuddered. "Let's not think of her any longer," she said with a smile. "Why don't I fetch the duchess for you. I'm sure she can have one of the housemaids act as maid for you while you're here."

Looking older than her years, the dowager nodded. "I hope you will not abandon me, Perdita. For I do think of you as my granddaughter. Even if I have not shown you the affection you are due as such."

"Of course I won't, Duchess." Perdita gave her a little hug. "And I do thank you. I know what you did must have been terribly difficult for you."

Before the dowager could apologize again, she left the room, closing the door firmly behind her.

The Duchess of Pemberton was waiting outside the door along with Archer. Telling the duchess that she was wanted within the room, Perdita then allowed Archer to lead her into a small sitting room down the hall.

Shutting the door, Archer pulled Perdita into his arms. "I thought I'd lost you," he said fiercely as he held her against him. "When I think again of that woman pointing her pistol at you . . ."

"Do not think of it," Perdita said, kissing him.

They moved to sit together on a small sofa. "Was the dowager terribly upset about Simmons?" Archer asked once he'd kissed her again. "It cannot have been easy for her to hear that her maid was her husband's baseborn daughter as well as her grandson's lover."

"No, it was not easy," Perdita agreed. Quickly, she explained what the dowager had just told her.

When she was finished, Archer whistled. "Just when I thought things could get no worse."

"Will you mind very much being married to a member of such a disturbing family?" Perdita asked, her voice betraying her worry. "For if you wish to cry off, I will understand."

"Of course I do not wish to cry off," Archer replied, in a chiding tone. "It takes more than a little incest and murder to frighten me off."

Perdita couldn't help it. She giggled. And all the

tension of the day seemed to overtake them as they dissolved into helpless laughter.

"You don't mind having Benedick marry us, do you?" Archer asked once their laughter had subsided.

"I wouldn't have it any other way," Perdita said, kissing him. Then, in a soft voice, she whispered, "I love you, you know."

"I know," he whispered back. "It's about time." His face turned serious. "What about your fears about marrying again?"

"I realized while listening to Simmons that there was no way on earth that you were the same kind of man Gervase was. And besides that, when I only had what I believed was one last thought, it was of you."

He kissed her. "I'm sorry it took the threat of death to change your mind," he said wryly. "But I'll take what I can get."

"Don't think like that," she chided. "I was halfway to changing my mind before Simmons revealed herself."

"Really?" he asked, leaning his forehead against hers.

"Really," Perdita said, her heart full. "I think I've been in love with you since you kidnapped me at the very least."

"Then," Archer said with a grin, "I think it's time to kidnap you again."

"Won't your family miss us?" Perdita asked, her brows drawn together with worry. "I wouldn't wish to shock them."

"The only thing that will shock them, my dear," Archer said, kissing her, "is that it took me so long to bring you to the point."

Perdita wrinkled her nose. "I suppose I did lead you on a merry chase, didn't I?"

"Anything worth having is worth fighting for," Archer said simply.

"Especially true love," Perdita said, feeling as if she would burst with love for him.

Which was fine considering that Archer looked exactly like she felt.

"Most especially true love," he said, raising their clasped hands to kiss the back of hers. "Now, let's go spread the good news. When a man finally convinces the woman he loves to marry him, he wants an audience to share in his good fortune."

"I agree," Perdita said with a grin, "so long as we can be alone to share our good fortune with one another later."

And much, much later, that's exactly what they did.

Epilogue

Three weeks later

*A*re you really saying that the dowager poisoned her own grandson?" Georgina demanded as she sat across from Perdita and Isabella in Perdita's sitting room at Ormond House.

Much had happened since that afternoon in the Lisle drawing room. First, and most importantly, Perdita and Archer had been married by special license in the little church on the Lisle estate where Benedick did the honors. They were attended by Archer's family, Isabella and Trevor, Georgina and Con. And, not to be pushed away, the dowager, who gave Perdita away.

Now, she and Archer were back from their brief honeymoon, and just as always Perdita, Isabella, and Georgina were sharing gossip over tea.

"I cannot believe it, either," she said in response to Georgie's pronouncement. "I thought Simmons must have lied to implicate her. It never occurred to me that the dowager would have poisoned her own grandson."

"Well," Isabella said with a grin, "this certainly makes things easier for Trevor. And for me. She can hardly continue to cast aspersions upon me while she is guilty of trying to kill her other grandson. I mean, we were defending you from bodily harm or worse." She shuddered. "But the dowager was simply determined to murder."

"It does make a strong argument," Perdita agreed. "I am just relieved that we can all go on with our lives without fear of being terrorized anymore."

"Here's to freedom from persecution!" Georgie said, lifting her teacup. The others clinked their cups with hers, though Perdita said coolly, "I'm not sure I've forgiven the two of you for drugging me, you know."

"Oh, dearest," Georgie said with remorse, "please don't be like that. We were doing it for your own good."

"And," Isabella added, "you must admit that it worked out rather well for you. I mean, you'd hardly be married to Archer if we hadn't allowed him to kidnap you."

"I suppose when you put it that way," Perdita agreed grudgingly, "it's true. But I will never again be able to take tea in your company with complete trust."

"Oh, pfft," Georgie said, grinning. "There is no reason for us to have you kidnapped again. We are all married to the most wonderful men in the world."

"And we are safe," Perdita agreed. She turned to her sister. "And Isabella is about to give birth to what I suspect will be the most spoiled infant in all of Christendom by the time we are finished with her."

"Or him," Isabella put in with a smile as she placed a hand on her belly.

Not so long ago, they'd all three become friends because of their similar circumstances as the wives and widows of men who treated them with little kindness and much brutality. Now, they faced the future with hope.

It was enough to make three wicked widows look upon the coming season with something like joy.

Meanwhile, in another part of London

"I still can't believe all that's behind us," Archer said to his companions with a grin. He leaned back in his chair, stretching his legs and crossing them at the ankles. "This time six months ago, Isabella was embarking upon a journey to Yorkshire. Who knew the dowager's demands would lead to so many life changes for the rest of us?"

"Or that my cousin's lover would turn out to be so bloody good at manipulating people into doing her bidding," Trevor added, swirling the brandy in his glass. "I don't recall seeing her more than a few times while the dowager was still staying in Ormond House, but she never gave me a reason to suspect her of what happened to Isabella."

"She was there all the time," Con added, leaning forward on his elbows. "I think we tend to forget just how powerful servants can become over time. They know so much about our lives. When we have relations with our wives, when we fight, when we make up. And a servant like Simmons, who as the dowager's ladies' maid was of the highest rank in the house with the exception of the butler and the housekeeper, has the most power of all. She holds the same sway in the servants' quarters as the dowager does in the family's."

"What gets me," Trevor said, "is that she was able to infiltrate the family so easily. What's to stop some other person with a grudge against us from slipping in through the back door like that?"

"Nothing," said Archer wryly. "To some degree you have to trust that the people you hire are there because they need the work. And you must trust your own instincts."

"Well, I can tell you this much," Con said with conviction, "I won't ever make the mistake of blindly trusting a servant again. From now on it's going to be suspicion they'll get from me until they can prove they aren't hiding something."

"It's a shame, really," Archer said, finishing his brandy. "Before all this we were so innocent. We trusted our servants. We believed that women and children were off limits when it came to dark plots. We thought only strange men we didn't know beat their wives."

He shook his head and continued. "Now there is an awareness of how ugly our world can be if you only scratch the surface a bit. It's disillusioning, to be sure."

"But it also makes me appreciate the good things more," Trevor said with a smile. "The servants you do trust, time spent alone with your wife, really good friends."

"Did you hear that, Archer?" Con said with a grin. "The duke just paid us a compliment."

Trevor made a face. "Who said I was talking about you lot? As far as I can tell you've only made my life more difficult. You"—he pointed at Archer—"for leaving me in the lurch without a private secretary." Then he scowled at Con. "And you for causing Isabella so much worry by engaging yourself to Perdita then changing your preference to Georgina."

"That is annoying," Archer agreed. "Especially because you knew I was head over ears for her!"

"Stuff," Con said dismissively. "You didn't tell me about your preference for her until after we broke it off."

Turning to Trevor, he continued, "And as for you, I was engaged to Perdita for less time, I'm sure, than it took for you to kiss Isabella for the first time. And my affection for Georgina happened well before you even got to Bath, so I do not accept that our joining forces hindered you in the slightest."

Archer sighed. "I suppose we're going to have to agree to disagree."

"Pax?" Con asked, looking from one man to the other.

"Pax," Trevor agreed.

"Now," Archer said standing, "let us go search out these troublesome brides of ours. For I have the most fearful notion that they are plotting against us."

"Whenever the three are gathered," Con confirmed, "there is always a higher possibility for mischief among us."

"I rather enjoy the mischief," Trevor said with a grin. "It definitely has its benefits."

"It does, indeed," Archer agreed, thinking of just how mischievous Perdita had been that morning. "I think we'd better hurry," he continued. "I find myself very much in need of another dose."

Laughing, they left the club in search of their respective wives.

Alone in their bed that night, having just finished what Perdita considered the sweetest lovemaking since they'd become involved, the newlyweds snuggled together. "Just think," Archer whispered against her hair, "if you'd married Con, you would not have been gifted with my far superior lovemaking skills."

"You must get over your obsession with Con," she said with a sigh. "We didn't even kiss. That is how engaged we were.

"Besides," she continued, "I can't think of Con that way anymore. Not while he's married to Georgie and they're so amazingly happy. I never thought I'd see her look as carefree as she did when they danced at our wedding."

"It was rather a relief," Archer said, stroking her back, "to see all three of you ladies able to enjoy yourselves without the threat of harm or some awful disturbance ruining everything."

"It's been a long while since any of us were able to sleep soundly or enjoy more than a half hour at a time without remembering something awful, or worse, experiencing it."

"Which reminds me," Archer said disentangling himself from her and climbing out of bed. While he walked, Perdita allowed herself to appreciate her husband in all his naked glory. It was a beautiful body, not least because she trusted that he'd never use it as a weapon against her.

As she watched, Archer slipped into the dressing

room that adjoined their bedchambers. She heard the sound of a drawer opening and closing. Finally, a triumphant grin on his face, Archer came back clutching a jeweler's box.

More curious than she could admit, Perdita sat up against the headboard, and waited while he slipped back into bed beside her.

"My dearest Perdita," he said with an uncustomary serious expression, "from the moment we met I knew you were going to be important to my life. I simply didn't know how important." She felt her eyes well up at his words, especially since she'd felt the same way about him. "I saw this a few years ago—yes, I know, I was being extremely premature—but I had to buy it for you. Because to me, you share its strength, but also its fire. It is hard to break, but even then, it is still beautiful."

Archer gave her the box, and carefully, as if she were handling spun glass, she opened it. And gasped. Nestled within the folds of the black velvet that lined the box she saw the most perfectly cut ruby pendant she'd ever seen. Removing it by the chain which held it, she watched in wonder as the candlelight illuminated the fiery facets of the stone which was set simply in gold. It was the most beautiful thing she'd ever laid her eyes upon.

"How did you know?" she asked her husband, not daring to look away from the gem lest it disappear from her hand. "How did you know years ago that I could be as strong as this? As fiery."

"Call it instinct," Archer said with a shrug. "I knew from the moment we met that you were tough. I only learned how tough later. And, unfortunately, when it was too late to help you."

"Don't say that," she said, turning to look him in the eyes. "You helped me in countless ways you weren't even aware of. Just knowing you were in the house reminded me that good men did exist."

She let him hook the chain around her neck, and though she longed to see it in the glass, she chose instead to turn around and give him the most frantic kiss she'd ever initiated. "I love you so much, Lord Archer Lisle."

"And I love you, Mrs. Lisle," Archer said, kissing the tip of her nose. "Do not ever doubt it."

And Perdita knew she never would. She knew now what love was. And she would never, ever let it go.

Coming soon…

'Tis the season for a brand-new e-novella from
Manda Collins

ONCE UPON A CHRISTMAS KISS

Available in October 2014

. . . and look for the first novel in Manda Collins's
brand-new Lords of Anarchy series

A GOOD RAKE IS HARD TO FIND

Available in April 2015 from St. Martin's
Paperbacks